The Clairvoyant

The Clairvoyant

Marian Thurm

𝒵

ZOLAND BOOKS

Cambridge, Massachusetts

First edition published in 1997 by
Zoland Books, Inc.
384 Huron Avenue
Cambridge, Massachusetts 02138

FIRST EDITION

Book design by Boskydell Studio

Printed in the United States of America

04 03 02 01 00 99 98 97   8 7 6 5 4 3 2

This book is printed on acid-free paper, and its binding
materials have been chosen for strength and durability.

Library of Congress Cataloging-in-Publication Data
Thurm, Marian.
The clairvoyant : a novel / by Marian Thurm. — 1st ed.
p.   cm.
ISBN 0-944072-72-0 (alk. paper)
I. Title.
PS3570.H83C57 1997
813'.54 — dc21   96-50139   CIP

For George, with love

I WOULD LIKE TO

ACKNOWLEDGE MY GRATITUDE

TO

Frank Andrews

FOR SO GENEROUSLY

OFFERING ME A PEEK INTO

HIS WORLD;

TO

Sam Axelrod and David Umansky

FOR BRINGING ME

INTO THE COMPUTER AGE;

AND TO

Gail Hochman

FOR HER UNFAILING SUPPORT

AND ENCOURAGEMENT.

The Clairvoyant

VICTOR MACKENZIE was a few weeks past his eighth birthday when he happened to see his first ghost, the first of many, as it turned out. Lying in his bed sometime after midnight, he was awakened from the deepest sort of sleep feeling the presence of someone in his small darkened room. He recognized the ghost at once; inexplicably, he was neither astonished nor terrified at the sight of him there. The ghost was named Murray Weinbaum, and he owned the candy store where Victor stopped every afternoon after school with his friends.

In the store, Victor took his time making his selections, lingering over the cardboard boxes filled with packages of bubble gum in their pink-and-blue wrappers, the gleaming rows of Life Savers and Hershey's chocolate bars, the racks of ten-cent comic books. Murray never hurried him along, never lost patience as Victor contemplated the possibilities, his hands cupped behind him, his body swaying slightly on the heels of his black canvas basketball sneakers. On that long-ago night, the ghost hung in the air above Victor's bed like a balloon, transparent and utterly expressionless, saying nothing at all.

The air grew chilly; Victor drew the bedclothes tight about his chin and stared, still unafraid, waiting for an explanation. And then it came to him: Murray was simply there to say good-bye. *I'll miss you,* the little boy said, not aloud, but silently. The ghost must have heard him, because he nodded and smiled slightly and then seemed in an instant to turn to sparkly dust that drifted without a sound to the floor.

Falling swiftly back into a dreamless sleep, Victor arranged his mouth in a peaceful half-smile. In the morning, hurrying to get ready for school, Murray Weinbaum forgotten, Victor focused on his breakfast, a small glass bowl of Wheatena into which he dumped several teaspoons of vividly colored sugar crystals. He watched the crystals melt in the hot cereal, leaving behind streaks of red, turquoise, yellow, and green. After he'd eaten a few teaspoonfuls, and when his mother's back was turned, he set the bowl under the table and let Al, the family cat, have a go at it.

It wasn't until school was over for the day that he thought again of Murray. He and a couple of his friends stood in front of the candy store's plate-glass window and read the sign lettered in black Magic Marker on white oak tag:

CLOSED DUE TO DEATH IN THE FAMILY

Victor understood then that Murray had died during the night; what he did not understand was why the man had chosen to visit *him* just before he'd turned to brilliant dust. And he had to wait all the way to dinnertime until he could talk to his parents, who were both doctors and practiced out of a small rented house on the other side of town.

At dinner that night his mother and father listened attentively. They were older than the parents of his friends, well into their forties, and they had always treated him with exceptional kindness. In the homes of his friends, Victor had occasionally heard mothers and fathers calling their children nitwits and morons, and once he had witnessed his best friend, Wayne, being smacked over the head by his mother's high-heeled shoe. Victor's own mother called him "darling precious child" almost as frequently as she called him by name. His father gave him an hour of piano instruction one night a week and taught him how to make a skateboard from his old roller skates and how to field a baseball. And since his parents were either unwilling or unable to provide him with a brother or sister, Victor had the two of them all to himself. This seemed like a good thing whenever he thought of it, which wasn't often.

"The reason Murray's ghost revealed himself to you," his mother said, brushing away a few strands of vermicelli that were stuck to the front of Victor's polo shirt, "is that he no doubt knew you were someone who could see him. That you were capable of seeing him. That's my guess, anyway."

"Not everyone possesses the gift," his father explained. "It happens to run in the family, as a matter of fact. Your grandmother was remarkably clairvoyant, though we don't like to talk about her much because she was also a home wrecker and a drunk."

"Pardon me, but your father was no saint either, as I recall. He drove her into the arms of what's-his-name, the optometrist, and you know it, Hank."

Hank sighed. "Fine," he said. "Now that we've established what a swell family I'm descended from, let's get started on yours."

"Let's not," said Lila. "More broccoli, anyone? It's loaded with vitamins."

"So what's 'clairvoyant'?" Victor asked, waving away the broccoli that was headed his way on a large slotted spoon.

"Well," said Lila, "it's being able to perceive things that most people can't see or feel or know about."

"Most people," said Hank, "think it's a crock. So if I were you, sonny boy, I wouldn't go around blabbing to your friends all about how you saw the ghost of Murray Weinbaum hanging around your bedroom last night."

"But I did see him," Victor said. "He was in his pajamas and slippers and he had a baseball hat on. It was definitely Murray."

"I'm sure it was. Even so, it's not a great idea to talk about this with people. They might start to think you're a little nutty."

"That's right, darling precious child," said Lila. "And if you won't have the broccoli, how about another lamb chop?"

"What do I do if he comes back again?" Victor asked.

"Send him my best," said Hank.

"And be polite," Lila added. "It's always important to be polite, no matter who you're talking to."

"He might be hungry," Victor mused. "Maybe I should leave a plate of Oreos for him in my room."

Hank rolled his eyes. "Let's not get carried away with this. I'm sure we all have more important things to think about."

"I don't," said Victor.

"Don't you have any homework?"

"I have multiplication and division, and I have to write ten sentences using compound words. You know, like *bug spray* and *sleeping pills*."

"Homework," said his father. "There's a compound word for you." He lit a cigarette using a see-through lighter with a pair of miniature dice floating in it, and then he leaned across the table to light Lila's.

Victor watched the twisting plumes of smoke as they drifted up toward the ceiling and out the open window. He wondered if Murray's ghost had flown in through his bedroom window. He should have asked Murray when he had the chance, he realized. He should have asked him a lot of things, but all he had done was tell Murray that he would miss him. It was the right thing to have said, though, because it had made Murray smile. Next time he would have a list of questions to ask him; he would write them out on the little pad he used to copy down homework assignments. If Murray didn't want to answer him, he would understand. Sometimes *he* didn't feel like answering anyone's questions either. Sometimes his teacher, Mrs. Rose, who was young and very pretty and famous for wearing a green wig and green lipstick to school every St. Patrick's Day, had to ask him a question two or three times before he would answer her. "Rise and shine, Victor!" she would say sharply. "Look alive!"

Once, on a snowy day after New Year's, he saw, perfectly clearly in his mind, a large calendar like the kind they had in the classroom, one made of shiny cardboard and able to stand upright on its own. He saw the date January 18 surrounded by a bright circle of light, and he understood immediately that after that day Mrs. Rose would never see her husband again. Her husband was going away to Florida without her; Victor had no idea why. Mrs. Rose didn't come to school on the nineteenth or the twentieth. She came back the following Monday, crankier than the class had ever seen her. She said she'd had a bad cold and a fever and that she still wasn't feeling well. All day long she blew her nose and wiped at her eyes; at three o'clock, when school ended, Victor approached her at her desk, arranged catty-corner at the front of the room. "I'm sorry your husband went to Florida without you," he said. "Maybe he'll like it better there because it's warm all the time."

Mrs. Rose grabbed his arm and squeezed it urgently. "Let's hope the bastard chokes on an orange peel," she said, and let go of his arm. "And you tell all the Nosy Parkers in this wretched little town that I'm the one who kicked him out on his rear."

"So what about your homework?" Victor heard his father asking.

"I'll do it," Victor said, "even though there's no point. I'm going to be the manager of a baseball team when I grow up, so all I'll really need to know about is baseball."

"Really," said Hank, as he winked in Lila's direction. "Says who?"

"*I* do," Victor said. "I'm going to manage the Phillies for a few years and after that I guess the Dodgers." He knew this with all certainty, just as he had known Mrs. Rose's husband would desert her.

This was, as it turned out, a mistaken notion, the presumptuous claim of an eight-year-old boy who'd been crazy about baseball, Victor would say some thirty-three years later, laughing at just how wrong he had been.

1

THOUGH IT WAS a freakishly warm day just before Halloween, Victor's eleven o'clock appointment emerged from her silvery limousine with a mink coat thrown over her arm, and a pair of emerald green leather gloves on her hands. Watching from the living room window of his turn-of-the-century town house, Victor could see the woman's chauffeur leading her up the steps to the front door.

"Welcome," he said, keeping the door open with one arm and holding back his three tiny, yapping papillons with the other.

The woman frowned; her face was pale and severe-looking, her eyes narrowed in suspicion. She was in her early fifties, with a thin head of dark hair that was lacquered against her skull and pulled back so tightly in a large black velvet bow that Victor was surprised she wasn't moaning in pain. He knew in an instant that she was trouble, and he almost asked her to leave on the spot. "I'm Mrs. Luminari," she said, still frowning, "and this is my assistant, Bernard."

"See you at noon, Bernard," said Victor. "There's a café with excellent coffee around the corner, in case you're interested."

"Bernard stays with *me*," Mrs. Luminari said. "And incidentally, I'm afraid of dogs, even little ones. Can't you lock them up somewhere?"

"Bernard goes, the dogs stay here," Victor said firmly. "I'll put them behind the gate in the parlor, is that all right?"

"Bernard is like family to me," Mrs. Luminari whined.

"I'm sure he is," Victor said. "And there's a nice hot cup of espresso waiting for him around the corner."

"I just don't know."

"You'll make out OK, Doris," Bernard said. He was burly and handsome, a young guy dressed like a doorman in gray pants with black ribbons running up the sides. Victor wondered how much Mrs. Luminari paid him to be like family to her, probably a princely sum. He sensed that they were occasional lovers and was amused at the thought.

"See you later, Bernard," he said, shutting the door behind him decisively.

Mrs. Luminari and the trio of dogs followed alongside Victor as he approached the consultation room, which doubled as his dining room. He herded the dogs behind a four-foot-high gate, murmuring to them in apology.

"Oooh, I love what you've done to the room," Mrs. Luminari said. She nodded at the large gold-leaf Buddha seated on a chest between a pair of bookcases, and, across the table, at the fish tank built into the curved wall. "Are you a Buddhist?" she asked. "Do you believe in your heart of hearts that only self-purification and self-denial can liberate one from bodily pain, sorrow, and desire? Or did your decorator find that gorgeous Buddha for you?"

"I don't have a decorator," Victor said. "And I'm not a Buddhist. But there's something so serene about that statue that I just needed to have it here."

"I *do* feel a kind of serenity in the room, now that you mention it," Mrs. Luminari said and, pulling off her gloves, began to pick nervously at the deep purple polish on her thumbnail. "Do you believe self-denial will enable the soul to reach Nirvana?"

"Look," Victor said, smiling slightly, "are you here to question me about my philosophical beliefs or are you here for a reading?"

Sitting with her fur coat in her lap at Victor's table, Mrs. Luminari continued to scrape at her nail polish. "I *did* come for a reading," she told him finally, "but I have a list of subjects that I definitely don't want to hear about." She produced a scented sheet of monogrammed stationery from her coat pocket, saying, "Let's see: don't tell me about my mother, I don't want to know about my husband or my children, and if my housekeeper's going to leave me you can't tell me, and if anything's going to happen to my cat, I don't want to know about it."

"Well, that about covers it," Victor said. "We might as well end it right there."

"I'm sorry. I know you come highly recommended," said Mrs. Luminari. "My sister-in-law thinks the world of you. It's just that, now that I'm here, I don't know if I can go through with it, if I can bear hearing anything you have to tell me."

Taking her hand, Victor said gently, "What are you so afraid of?"

"I don't know, actually."

"Did you bring a blank tape with you?" he asked her.

"Was I supposed to?"

"All my clients are supposed to. That way you'll have a record of everything that's said today."

Mrs. Luminari shrugged.

"Let's have a look at your palm," Victor suggested, and reached behind him for a large magnifying glass.

"No bad news," said Mrs. Luminari. "If it's bad news I don't want to know about it."

"Sit quietly, please."

"I feel like I'm in a doctor's office," Mrs. Luminari said, and giggled.

"I see that you have two children, two sons, am I right?"

"Mark and Francis, yes."

"Please don't tell me names," Victor said. "Let me get them myself."

"Can you do that?"

"Did you have a miscarriage? I see something shadowy here, another child, the shadow of one, actually."

"You're right!" Mrs. Luminari said excitedly, and he knew that he had her — she was his. With some people, he had to hit it specifically or he lost them; mistaking a daughter for a son, seeing two boys and a girl instead of two girls and a boy, and he was done for; it was absolutely impossible to gain their trust. But now he could feel Mrs. Luminari's heart, her whole being, opening up to him. So he relaxed a little.

"You and your husband are living apart," Victor said. "They've got him somewhere upstate." He realized, his arms suddenly prickly with goose bumps, that her husband was some sort of gangster, that he'd been in prison for quite a while. "Oh Jesus," he groaned. This was what he got for letting strangers in his door.

He stirred in his seat, letting go of her hand.

"Please," she said, and offered her palm. "Tell me more."

"Well, your husband loves you," Victor said, "even though you're living apart."

Mrs. Luminari winced, closed her eyes briefly. "Yes," she said, "he does love me."

"I think that maybe sometime during the summer they're going to be moving him down south, to one of the Carolinas, and then, after that, they're going to let him go."

"This coming summer?" Mrs. Luminari shrieked, pulling her hand away. "He's getting out *this* summer?"

"It looks that way."

"Well, you're wrong, he won't even be up for parole for at least two years."

"I do sometimes make mistakes," Victor admitted. "I'm only human, after all. But usually it's a matter of mistaking a son for a daughter, an abortion for a miscarriage, that sort of thing. And sometimes I miss things, like a man was in here once and we were talking about his sister, and everything seemed fine, and then I found out a week or two later that she'd been killed in a car wreck. I don't know how I missed that, but I did. Maybe the man simply wasn't meant to know that he was going to lose her — that's the only explanation I can think of."

"I have the beginning of a headache," Mrs. Luminari announced. "And guess who gave it to me."

"How about a couple of aspirin or Tylenol?"

"Could you massage my head for me?"

"I'm afraid I don't do that sort of thing," Victor said. "I'm not a healer."

Mrs. Luminari looked at him in annoyance. "You're not? Well, hand over the goddamn aspirin, then."

"Don't use that tone on me, or I'll throw you right out of here," Victor said, amazed, a moment later, that he had spoken to a client this way. It happened, occasionally, that the wrong sort of person called for a reading; usually he was able to tell just by listening to a voice on his answering machine that it was best to turn away a potential client. But Mrs. Luminari's sister-in-law was an old and loyal customer who had sent plenty of business his way over the years, and it was she who'd made the appointment for the gangster's wife seated at his table now with her palms pressed against her temples.

Mrs. Luminari was laughing at him, he realized. "I love it when a man plays rough with me," she said.

Ignoring this, Victor said, "How's your headache?"

"On its way out," she said, "though I can't imagine why."

Victor folded his arms against the table. "Look," he said, "you came here to ask me something."

"I did not."

"Of course you did. Almost everyone who comes to see me comes because they're troubled about something, and you're no exception. It's something about Bernard, isn't it?"

"How dare you!"

"He's like family to you," Victor reminded her. "You care a great deal for him."

"He has a girlfriend." Mrs. Luminari sighed. "A hairdresser. She's done my hair for me, in fact. I went all the way to the East Village to her place of business to get a good look at her."

"And?"

"She's young, of course, a hundred years younger than me. Very attractive in a slutty sort of way, and not too smart. I took a cab there because I didn't want Bernard to know what I was doing." Her voice faltered; she looked down at the unopened pack of tarot cards across the table. "He's going to marry her, isn't he?"

"I don't know," Victor said. "Maybe the cards will tell us."

"Will they?"

"Let's find out," Victor said, and instructed her to shuffle the cards and divide them into three piles, using only her left hand. She followed his directions, then collected the three piles and mixed them together.

"I can't," she told him apologetically. "I wish I could, but I can't. If he's going to marry her, I'll die. And if he doesn't, and we keep going along like we've been, as soon as my husband gets out of the slammer he'll kill us both. Or at least he'll kill Bernard. Not personally, of course. He'll have someone else do his dirty work for him."

"Well, that's a sorry picture you've painted," Victor said. "I might be able to offer you a more positive one, if only you'd let me take a look at those cards."

"My headache's back," Mrs. Luminari said. "And I want to go home." Digging for a while in the large lizard bag in her lap, she eventually came up with her checkbook. "How much do I owe you?"

"One fifty," Victor murmured. "Look, come back when you're not feeling so negative, and we'll try this again. On the house next time."

"I'm just a big chicken," Mrs. Luminari said as she wrote out a check. "A first-class coward."

He didn't tell her that he had never been able to risk reading his own palm, that the thought was too unnerving. Like her, there were many things he would rather not know. When he read for someone else, of course, he could always soften the blow, minimize the worst of it by being selective in what he offered up aloud. But if he were to examine his own palm, it would be impossible to shield himself from the full truth.

"Don't feel too bad about it," he told Mrs. Luminari and patted her soft hand.

After she left, he leashed the dogs and took them for a leisurely walk. He needed to clear his head, to shake off the uncomfortable feeling that he had somehow failed this client. Roaming through the clean streets of this downtown neighborhood of galleries, expensive, coyly named shops, and sidewalk cafés, he looked ordinary enough, like a man who earned his living in any one of the usual ways — in his corduroy pants, denim shirt, and dark knit tie, he might have been a teacher, a shopkeeper, a photographer, a gallery owner. His hair, just long enough for a tiny ponytail, was perfectly straight, a mix of blond and gray that kept people guessing about his age. In spite of his beakish nose, he had the sort of strong, almost handsome face that women found appealing. He was long limbed and slender, except for his broad shoulders, which made it difficult for him to find clothing that fit exactly right. (If he cared enough, he supposed, he would have had his shirts custom-made.) His hands were smooth and boyish, his eyes a startling, clear blue. In one ear he wore a pair of tiny silver hoops, in the other, a single silver star.

He walked with a bit of a slouch, but for some reason it wasn't unattractive on him. Or at least none of the women he'd been with had ever mentioned it or begged him to stand up straighter. (His last girlfriend, who played the oboe with the Philharmonic and was strikingly pretty, had dumped him last summer for a cellist who sat two rows in front of her onstage at Lincoln Center. Victor had taken the news hard and hadn't been involved with anyone since.) Women seemed easily attracted to him, another gift he'd never been able to explain. He met them waiting for the subway at odd hours, at the dry cleaner's, in the vet's office when he brought in any of his three little papillons. His heart had been broken several times over the years, but he liked to think of himself as resilient, not one to sink too deeply into despair. He couldn't afford to, not in his profession. It was essential, he knew, that he let every client who came to him feel the absolute confidence with which he approached his life, and his work. And he loved this work of his, loved the privilege of opening up people's lives, each of them like a novel full of large and small dramas.

He had to admit he'd done quite well, attracting his share of movie stars and other celebrities over the years, along with the everyday people who made up most of his clientele. Usually it was women who filled his appointment book; this, he suspected, was because they were generally more sensitive than men, more receptive to the very notion of things beyond the range of ordinary perception. When they came to him, what they most often needed was information about their husbands and lovers. The men who sought him out were remarkably self-confident, usually successful people who wanted to know about their careers rather than matters of the heart. Though sometimes, if they were married and involved with a lover or two, they'd want to know if they were in danger of being discovered by their wives. *You guys are all the same,* Victor almost told them, exasperated at hearing, in one week, the same old story from a rock star, the owner of a string of restaurants, and a Broadway actor. He studied their palms and saw long lives and short marriages, guardian angels watching over them. He couldn't afford to lose his temper with any of them, so he made the effort to keep his voice amiable and soothing, though he sometimes heard himself turning a bit sharp when his readings were challenged. He wanted to be heeded, after all; for him, there was nothing more frustrating than a client who denied the accuracy of whatever information Victor had offered. "Why did you come to me if you're not going to listen?" he would say, holding back the urge to grab the shoulders of the person across the table from him and give him or her a good shake. He imagined that this was what it must be like to be the well-meaning parent of a stubborn child; you knew your instincts were absolutely on target, yet the object of your interest and concern remained unconvinced. Those were the clients it was best to let go of, to erase from memory as soon as they'd walked out the door.

And there were those he worried about, whose names he wrote down on scraps of paper so he would remember to check up on them in a day or two — the young woman who had been in and out of mental hospitals, another woman who was about to lose her job, a man who was HIV positive and terribly depressed. It was gratifying to know that for many he was like a therapist, a father, a priest, someone they could rely upon to guide them through life. Occasionally, a client might become a friend, and then Victor would find himself invited to birthday celebrations, dinner parties, weddings, christenings. For him, the great pleasure was in watching these lives unfold over time. He'd had clients return year after year for a decade or more, and there were those who disappeared after a single reading, only to turn up years later saying, "I woke up yesterday and just needed to see you." He welcomed them back, often having forgotten their names and their histories, never letting on that he hadn't remembered.

A rewarding life, all in all, one he'd never once considered trading for another. He reminded himself of this now as he stopped on the street to gaze at a pair of elderly women seated in the window of a coffee shop, each holding an open tortoiseshell compact in her hand, each outlining her mouth in scarlet lipstick, wrist movements synchronized, like a rehearsed duet. Seeing Victor observing them, the ladies smiled in his direction. Gratefully, he returned their smiles.

2

I N A LOFT in Soho, not far from Victor's town house, Katha Randall was struggling to clean the brittle crusts of multi-colored clay that had dried under her fingernails. She was a painter who hadn't been shown in a gallery in almost a decade, and so she had, over the past few years, resigned herself to organizing children's art parties at two hundred dollars a pop. Cleaning up after a dozen well-behaved seven-year-old girls who had recently departed in a trio of taxis for their homes uptown, Katha had swept all the little rinds of clay from her varnished floors, put away the folding chairs, thrown out the paper plates and half-eaten wedges of birthday cake. Scrubbing her nails, which were usually rimmed in paint, she had to admit that they never quite managed to look entirely clean, no matter what she used on them.

Parker, her lover, was an attorney who had *his* nails mani-cured every six weeks or so, whenever he had his hair cut. He urged her to do the same and couldn't understand why Katha always refused, or how she could be content to walk around, day after day, in leggings and cowboy boots and a blue denim shirt that skimmed her knees. Once he had told her gently that she was "a bit of a slob," an accusation that didn't bother

her in the least. "I'm an artist," she replied. "And if that doesn't excuse my many faults, I don't know what does." Actually, Parker had few complaints about her, though he'd found her housekeeping skills marginal at best. When she and Julia, her young daughter, had first moved into his loft a little less than a year ago, he had to take Katha in hand and explain that, in his view, pots were meant to be shining, sinks gleaming, rugs lint-free. He hated bathroom mirrors speckled with toothpaste, glasses left behind in the kitchen sink, dust-covered bookcases and television screens.

"Just remember to clean up after yourself, and we'll all get along fine," he'd said evenly.

"Got it," Katha said, and immediately decided to forget the conversation had ever taken place.

The truth, she soon discovered, was that Parker was a martinet of sorts when it came to cleaning. He fired every twice-a-week housekeeper he'd ever hired, because, he claimed, they couldn't follow his simple instructions. Katha sympathized with every one of them, even those who'd come and gone before her time. She loved Parker but sometimes feared that the strain of living in his meticulously kept household would send her to the loony bin. Every night when Parker came home, he bent down to straighten the tassels on the Persian rug under the coffee table. He checked the glass-topped table for fingerprints and smudges and also the glass doors that covered the VCR cabinet and the CD player. He went through dispensers of Windex as if they were water; Katha once joked, "Don't you think you deserve a citation from Procter and Gamble or whoever, for being their best customer worldwide?"

"Very funny," Parker said. "Hilarious."

It wasn't, she told herself, that Parker was neurotically obsessed, it was just that he was irritating in his way, in his endless desire for perfect order. But his affection for her was undeniable; he kissed her long, fluffy, pale blond hair and fingered it with great tenderness, held her hand tightly in public, embraced her as she stood unloading the dishwasher or poised in the bathroom doorway. He brought her expensive bouquets of fragrant roses and bunches of yellow and white freesia, not when the occasion called for it, but on no particular occasion at all.

Tom, Katha's ex-husband, had offered her something entirely different. He was Parker's idea of a loser, a part-time sociology professor at NYU and the New School, and part-time pothead. He'd always looked a little stoned, or at least suspect, with his salt-and-pepper hair that could not be tamed no matter what you did with it, and the T-shirts he wore over and over again, emblazoned with images of Jimi Hendrix, a bespectacled John Lennon, or the Rolling Stones' huge, garish tongue. One of his customary times to smoke pot was after dinner, when he would light up at the table as casually as if he were smoking a cigar, sometimes in full view of their daughter. If he had ever laid eyes upon Parker, who dressed in seven-hundred-dollar suits and expensive tasseled loafers, he would have dismissed him as a raging conservative, someone whose worldview would no doubt have made him cringe. (In fact, Parker's politics were middle of the road; he just happened to like Bally shoes and suits from Barneys.)

Parker and Katha had met shortly after her divorce came through, on a blind date arranged by a mutual friend who worked alongside Parker at the law firm where they were both in the tax department. Parker was red haired and stocky, pink cheeked as a child who'd been out playing in the cold. On their first date, Katha had been profoundly touched by his solicitude, the way he helped her on with her coat in the foyer of her apartment, and into and out of the taxi that took them to dinner. How attentively he'd listened to the story of her divorce, his chin resting on the bridge of his folded hands above the beautifully set table, his eyes warm with sympathy. He seemed gentlemanly in the extreme, murmuring "Pardon me" when he accidentally kicked at the tip of her shoe under the table, apologizing when their hands grazed each other's as they reached for the butter dish at the same moment.

"You can't imagine what a pig my ex-husband was," Katha had said cheerfully over dessert that night.

"Excuse me?"

"Now there are two words you won't find in his vocabulary."

Parker smiled. "You seem thrilled to be rid of him."

"I have to say it was one of the most glorious days of my life when I finally decided to file the papers."

"Divorce and marriage," Parker sang softly, sweeping a few crumbs from the tablecloth into his palm, "go together like a horse and — "

"It's awful to be so disappointed in the person you loved, believe me."

Shrugging, Parker said, "I'll take your word for it."

"You can't be serious — you've never been disappointed by someone you loved?"

"Never been in love," Parker responded as the check arrived. He took out a credit card and used it to sweep away a few more microscopic crumbs.

Katha put her hand over his. "Stop that," she said. "You did tell me you've never been in love, didn't you?"

"My standards are very high," Parker said.

"You'd never marry a pig, in other words."

"Or a heavy-duty pot smoker."

"It's possible to love someone despite his or her flaws, you know," said Katha. "It's possible to be swept away by the feel of someone's beard beneath your fingers, by the sweetness in his eyes, by the sight of the pale band of skin around his wrist when he takes off his watch just before you make love for the first time."

"All right, all right," Parker said. "I did feel that way about someone once. There was no beard, of course, but the rest sounds right."

"So what happened to her?"

"It didn't work out. She was married to my brother, which was kind of a problem."

"No kidding," Katha said.

"They moved out to San Francisco to get away from the whole business. Eventually they split up, but she wouldn't see me. It turned out she was already involved with someone else. My brother was pretty messed up for a while, but he's all right now. However, it's been almost two years, and he's still not speaking to me." Parker exhaled noisily. "I'm still waiting to be forgiven, I guess."

"What a mess," said Katha. She took a final spoonful of her white chocolate mousse, which was so sweet it made her teeth ache. "Dinner was wonderful," she said. "The lobster ravioli was spectacular."

Parker nodded. "I can't abide messes of any kind," he said. "Emotional or otherwise."

"Then it's a good thing you didn't see the inside of my bathroom before we left," Katha said, laughing. "There was a laundry explosion in there, among other things."

"Laundry explosion?" Parker said, and then he leaned across the table to kiss her. His lips were slightly sticky with mousse; Katha licked them delicately, feeling the tiniest shiver of pleasure. Blushing, her face warmed as if she had suddenly stepped out into the sun.

Her daughter thought Parker was a geek, a conclusion she'd reached after living with him for only a few weeks.

"Look how good he's been to you," Katha had pointed out. "He's bought you so many nice things for your new room."

"He's no fun," said Julia, who was eight. "He bought me Scrabble and Pictionary, but he won't ever play with me. Every time I ask him, he tells me he has work to do, but really he's just sitting there on the couch reading the newspaper."

"Not all grown-ups like to play with children," Katha said carefully. "And it's too bad for them, really, because they're missing out on a lot, but that's the way it is sometimes." She had been helping Julia clean up her room, putting away the clothing her daughter had worn the day before, straightening the piles of notebooks and papers on her desk, neatly arranging the throw pillows that were lying haphazardly on the bed. She felt Julia watching her, felt her disapproval as she moved quickly from one task to another. "What?" Katha said. "What is it?"

"Who cares if my room is a mess?" Julia asked. "You never cared before. And neither did Daddy."

"This is Parker's home," Katha explained. "If we're going to live here with him, we have to respect his rules, his way of doing things. It's as simple as that." Playfully, she threw a nightgown at her daughter, then a sweatshirt and a jeweled headband. "Put your stuff away, Lazy Jane."

"Like I care," said Julia, pushing her things over the edge of the bed and onto the floor.

"You'd better care, sweetie."

"Look, Parker's sort of nice to me, but not really. He buys me presents, but he doesn't like me that much. And he's very annoying. Whenever we sit down to have dinner he says, 'Napkins belong in laps, everyone,' but he doesn't mean everyone, he means me. And he knows I'm always going to put it in my lap, but he always has to say it anyway, before I even have a chance to do it. So," Julia said, "I think he's saying it just to make me feel bad, to make me feel like a dork, like I'm not smart enough to figure out for myself what I'm supposed to do."

Katha was nearly overcome by the sound of her daughter's earnest little voice. "What do you mean, he doesn't like you that much?" she asked. "Of course he likes you."

Julia gave her an exasperated look. "I'm not stupid, Mom. Did you know there are even teachers in my school who don't like kids? They have mean faces on mostly, and you can just tell what they're thinking about. All they're thinking is that kids are a big pain in the neck."

"And that's what Parker's thinking?"

"He's a geek, OK? Daddy smoked drugs, but he's not a geek. He likes me a lot, OK?"

"You miss him," Katha said. She sat down on the bed and stroked Julia's tiny wrist, ornamented with a homemade bracelet, a single ceramic bead on a silky length of rope.

"Do you?" Julia asked.

"Not really," said Katha, then hesitated. "I don't know if you can understand this, but believe me when I say he wasn't a very good husband."

"That's your opinion!" Julia said angrily, and wrenched her arm away. (*Opinion* had recently become one of her favorite words; when Katha criticized the string of idiotic sitcoms her daughter loved to watch before dinner, Julia always responded, "That's *your* opinion. How come all my friends think they're good and you're the only one who thinks they're garbage?")

"You're right," said Katha. "It *is* my opinion. But since I'm the one who was married to him for ten years, it's my opinion that counts."

"I don't see why we had to trade him away for Parker, that's all. Just because Daddy smoked drugs doesn't mean I have to like Parker better than him. And anyway, why should I like someone who doesn't really like me?"

"He *does* like you," Katha said. "And when he gets to know you a little better, he'll like you even more."

"Could you please get out of my room?" Julia said stiffly. "Like now, OK?"

Sliding off the bed, Katha kissed the tip of her daughter's ear. "Who do you think loves you more than anything in this world?"

"Duh," said Julia. Then, "If you love me that much, why are you forcing me to live here with the geek?"

"He's not a geek, sweetie."

"That's your opinion," said Julia, and she smiled halfheartedly as Katha left the room.

After Julia had gone to sleep, Katha made a cup of Red Zinger for Parker and brought it to the corner of the couch where he'd settled for the night. His headphones were plugged into the CD player, and he was watching a basketball game on television with the sound off. It was clearly the wrong time to talk to him, but she couldn't wait for the right time, she decided, so she slipped the headphones down around his neck, saying, "Guess what. Julia's more perceptive than you give her credit for."

"Excuse me?" said Parker. From the headphones, Beethoven's *Pathétique* could be heard faintly.

"She thinks you have very little affection for children in general and for her in particular."

"Well, she's the only child I know, really," said Parker. "I'm new at this game. She's going to have to be patient with me while I learn the ropes."

"She's a wonderful little person," Katha said, her voice suddenly trembly. "And she deserves better than what you've given her."

"Yesss!" Parker cheered, as Patrick Ewing scored on a fadeaway jumper from the baseline. "Oh, yesss!"

"Like you give a flying fuck," said Katha.

"What? Wait, look at this instant replay."

"I can't live here with you if you can't find time in your busy schedule for a game of Scrabble now and then."

"Scrabble?" said Parker. "What are you talking about?"

"She was insulted because you wouldn't play with her."

"Oh, that," Parker said. "Tell her I don't play board games. If I didn't when I was a kid, I'm certainly not going to now. It's nothing personal, believe me. Make sure you tell her that."

"Tell her yourself," said Katha.

"Fine." Clamping the headphones back on, Parker turned away from her.

"Fine." Katha stared at a shamelessly sentimental commercial for, she guessed, a dishwasher. A husband and wife were shown over the years together, surrounded by a loving family. Their hair turned silver, their loving family grew to include grandchildren, and a state-of-the-art dishwasher was ever a part of their lives. Switching on the sound, Katha listened as the lush and heartfelt music accompanying the commercial filled the room, and she was startled to find herself moved to tears. How privileged these people were to have spent a lifetime together. How did anyone hang on to anyone else for so long? The people on the screen were actors, of course, but there were real people out there who had somehow managed to reach anniversaries of a half century and beyond. She had already wasted a decade with Tom, who had been weak and selfish and irresponsible but also wonderfully mellow, and loving, from time to time, in his way. Her mistake, she knew, had been in assuming that he would eventually straighten himself out, that he would wise up to the indisputable fact that the sixties had come and gone, that his hair was graying, that he had a wife and a child who needed him sober. Sometimes, she remembered, it had seemed that her anger and disappointment were boundless; once, when she'd learned in a phone call from a fellow second-grade parent that Tom had been stoned as he arrived to pick Julia up at school, she turned on him with such fierceness that she actually clawed his face. "I could kill you for this!" she shrieked at him in the doorway of their kitchen, already horrified at the welts she'd raised across his cheekbones.

Backing away from her, Tom said calmly, "I'm sick of people, I don't care about dying, I'm fed up with the whole fucking world."

It was the matter-of-fact way he'd spoken that frightened her most, that and the realization that they'd come to the end of the line, that they'd traveled together as far as she was willing to go.

He would have stayed married to her forever, he told her when, soon afterward, she broke the news that she'd filed for divorce. "We could have spent our — what do you call them? — golden years together," he said. "Picture us as two little old people struggling down the street together on a blazing summer afternoon in our buttoned-up cardigan sweaters, leaning on matching his and hers walkers. Cottage cheese for lunch and dinner every day, dentures soaking side by side on the bathroom counter every night. And when I fall on an icy street one winter and break my hip and it's all over for me, you'd die the following spring of a broken heart."

"Lovely," said Katha.

"It could have been," Tom told her. "I have no doubt that it could have been."

She'd helped him find a studio apartment in a brownstone in Brooklyn but did not tell him how relieved she was now that they were living in separate boroughs. When he came over once a month to visit with Julia, Katha offered him a hug of sorts, just so she could sniff his clothes to see if he'd been smoking anything. He never once showed up stoned, though he looked as he always had, like someone who might have been growing magic mushrooms in his backyard or basement.

He and Parker had finally met for the first time one Friday night after Parker had arrived home from work. Katha watched anxiously as they gave each other the once-over, Tom unshaven and dressed in torn, bleached-out jeans and a down vest, Parker in his Versace suit, extending a manicured hand to grip Tom's icy, reddened one. It was midwinter; looking down at Tom's bare white feet in their rubber thongs, Parker whistled softly. "Don't you own a pair of shoes?" he said at last. "Could I lend you a pair?"

"Sure I have shoes," said Tom. "I save them for special occasions, that's all."

"What kind of occasions might those be?"

Tom flashed him a brilliant smile. "More formal ones than this," he said. "Got a problem with that?"

"No problem at all," said Parker.

"That's cool," Tom said. "Well, nice meeting you, man."

"You bet."

Taking Julia's hand and leading her to the doorway, Tom had turned back for one last look at Parker in his beautiful suit, a Rolex gleaming at his wrist. "I've got a fashion tip for you, man."

"What?" Parker asked. "Are you talking to me?"

"Lose the cuff links," said Tom. "They're a bit much, don't you think?"

As soon as Tom and Julia disappeared into the elevator, Parker said, "Now let me get this straight — you loved that guy enough to have a child with him?"

"Apparently," said Katha.

"You willingly spent ten years of your life with him?"

"What's your point, Parker?"

"He looks like a homeless person," Parker said. "Like some guy you'd see waiting on line at a soup kitchen."

"His doctorate is from Stanford, you know."

"Obviously they never taught him the importance of avoiding frostbite," said Parker. "Jesus, even an animal knows how to keep himself warm."

"He always goes around like that," said Katha. "He's used to it, I guess." She stood at the expanse of windows in the loft's main room, looking uptown at the white lights of the Empire State Building. She imagined Julia and Tom walking hand in hand, a tiny figure bundled in a ski jacket and scarf, a tall figure in beach shoes and a cloud of wild hair. People would stare at them suspiciously, she knew, wondering at the child's luminous face, her animated chatter, wondering if she could possibly be in danger. Knowing that she was not, that her child was merely going off to have dinner with the man she loved best, Katha turned away from the window.

"The man's brain is fried," Parker insisted, coming toward her with a drink in his hand. "Like an egg in a skillet. Really. And Ph.D. from Stanford or not, the day will come when he'll be sleeping out on the street over a heating grate somewhere, dressed in plastic bags, a shopping cart full of his worldly possessions at his side."

"That's enough," Katha said. "Enough." Sipping at the brandy he offered her, she said, "If he had shoes and socks and a new hairstylist, you'd feel differently, wouldn't you?"

Parker shook his head. "You can't miss the look in his eyes," he said. "You know, the look of someone who never quite got the hang of taking care of himself."

"He's a grown man," Katha murmured.

"Doesn't mean a thing," said Parker. "Not a thing." He took the snifter from her and set it down on the windowsill. Opening his arms to her, he smiled as she leaned into his embrace. He smelled faintly of expensive cologne; his cheek was smooth against her own. "This is so much better," he said in a whisper. "Better for you."

"Of course," said Katha. "Anyone can see that."

Now, standing alone at the kitchen sink, a wood-handled brush against her fingertips, she shut off the faucet with a little groan of impatience. She pitched the brush into the basin, held her hands up in front of her. Water dripped past her wrists all the way to her elbows; it was, she thought, as if her hands were weeping.

Her nails were as clean as they would ever be. Not clean enough by Parker's standards, but there was no helping that. Perhaps she would take a bath later, soak herself until she was soft and wrinkly and bleached looking. Or perhaps not. Ultimately, you simply had to satisfy yourself. If you couldn't do that, she thought, only then were you truly lost.

3

FOR THE FIRST TIME in her life, Lucy had actually paid to have her hair done, arranged in three dozen skinny braids for which she'd shelled out more than a hundred dollars on the beach in St. Martin. The island woman who'd fixed her hair for her, at three dollars a braid, had been walking up and down the beach selling a woven basketful of tiny, colorful bikinis, and also her services as a hairdresser. It was Buddy Silverman, Lucy's husband, who called out to her, waving her over to the pair of chaises longues where he and Lucy were sunning themselves on the last afternoon of their vacation.

"My wife would like to see what you've got there, s'il vous plaît," Buddy said pleasantly.

The woman frowned for an instant at the word *wife*, clearly unhappy that Lucy had attached herself to a white man. And then, apparently having decided to regard her as just another customer, the woman said, "Oui? I have many beautiful things pour Madame."

"Not this madame," Lucy said, and laughed. "No way this body of mine is going to fit into one of those tiny things."

"It's not like you're a toothpick," Buddy conceded, "but I still think you'd look terrific."

"Oui ou non?" the woman said. Beads of perspiration had collected at her hairline and above her lip, and she shifted the basket to her other arm. If she was wasting her time with these people, she wanted to know it. "I will do something très jolie with your hair, then, oui?"

"Go for it," said Buddy. "I say, 'oui.'"

So Lucy sat for nearly three hours under the beach umbrella Buddy had run off to rent from the hotel, as the woman transformed her into a self she'd never seen before.

Her sons, Jonah and Max, pronounced her "cool" when she and Buddy arrived back home in New Jersey that night. Her mother, who'd been taking care of the boys for the week Lucy and Buddy had been away, was of a different opinion.

Sitting on the leather couch in the den with her arms crossed, Florine said, "You want the truth? I'd like you better bald and that's the truth." Her own hair was a bubble of tight curls, dyed auburn. She was wearing a running suit that zipped up the front and new white sneakers. She looked, Lucy thought, like the suburban housewife she'd never been, someone who might have spent her time gardening in the backyard and loading up her station wagon with endless bags of groceries, stalks of celery peeking out over the tops, their leaves stirring in the breeze of an open car window.

"Or you could shave your initials right here," said Max, pointing to the side of Lucy's head, directly above her ear. "That would be pretty cool, too."

He had just turned twelve and had recently become a strict, uncompromising vegetarian, given to making impatient speeches at the dinner table to his unenlightened, meat-eating family. Like his brother, he had Buddy's pale green eyes; his complexion was so light that when he was born Lucy had been startled, almost unable to believe she had propelled him into the world from within her. But then, examining his miniature fingers and nails, she saw that they were shaped exactly like her own, elongated and quite lovely. He and Jonah, who was two years younger, looked very much like twins, and even strangers on the street had to comment on how beautiful they were. "It's all from my side of the family," Buddy liked to tease. To which Lucy would respond, "Don't kid yourself. My nightmare was that they'd turn out looking like your mother."

She'd always been, in fact, very fond of Eleanor, whose greatest fear had been that her son would remain a bachelor forever and that she herself would die without ever having achieved the exalted rank of grandmother. She'd welcomed Lucy into the family lovingly and until her death had spoiled her grandchildren shamelessly. Florine, however, generally treated Buddy like a second-class citizen. She introduced him to people as "the Jewish dentist" and ignored him whenever possible. Lucy had long since given up trying to reason with her and had abandoned her old habit of defending Buddy by enumerating his virtues, ticking them off rapidly on the fingers of both hands. (Her mother had always countered by saying, "He may be smart, but how about the way those ears of his stick out?" Or "All right, so he's hardworking, but doesn't he have the palest, scrawniest arms and legs you've ever seen?")

Once, feeling her customary mix of anger and amusement after hearing her mother out, Lucy said, "Why don't we get you on one of those talk shows — the theme could be 'I Hate My Daughter's Husband'. You could get up there in front of the TV cameras with a panel of other hostile mothers-in-law and let twenty or fifty million viewers know how you feel. How would that be?"

"When did I ever say I hate Buddy?" her mother asked, looking insulted. "I don't hate him. I just don't think he's suitable, is all."

"Ah," said Lucy. "How stupid of me. But I'm glad that's all cleared up. I feel one hundred percent better."

"Good."

Hearing now that her mother would have preferred her bald, Lucy laughed. "That's fairly harsh language, but I guess you can't please everyone, right?"

"I think your hair looks outrageous," said Buddy. "In the best sense of the word, of course."

Florine narrowed her eyes. "You're a dentist," she said. "What do you know about hairdos?"

"Take a chill pill, Grandma," said Max.

"Are you going to let him talk to me like that?" Florine said. "Are you?"

"He does have a point," said Buddy.

"I wasn't talking to *you*," said Florine.

"It's late," Lucy said. "Everyone's tired. And some people are speaking improperly to others. Let's order a pizza and call it a night."

"I want to go home," said Florine. "And I don't mean tomorrow morning."

When the telephone rang an instant later, Lucy and Max raced for it, nearly tripping over each other as they crossed the den floor. "Silverman's House of Nuts," Max said politely into the phone. "Which nut would you like to speak to?" Handing the receiver to Lucy, he warned, "Don't stay on too long. We have to call Domino's."

"It's me," said Katha as Lucy lifted the phone to her ear. "How does it feel to be back in the bosom of your family?"

"One forgets," said Lucy, "while one is on vacation. One forgets many things."

"Don't tell me," Katha said. "You've been home five minutes and already you're contemplating shooting your mother at close range with that registered weapon you've been keeping hidden away on the top shelf of your closet all these years."

Lucy carried the cordless phone into the living room and stretched herself along the rose-colored carpeting. She studied her hair in the mirrored wall across the room. "You know me so well," she said.

"And I'll be perfectly happy to testify on your behalf at the murder trial. I'd do the same for any of my freshman-year roommates, wouldn't you?"

"Actually," said Lucy, "you wouldn't recognize me. I had my hair done on the beach today. I've got about a thousand little braids. Thirty-six to be exact."

"Well," said Katha, and paused. "You had your hair done, and our old friend Susannah had a miscarriage."

"No," Lucy said. "Oh, shit. Poor Susannah. And she'd been trying to get pregnant for so long."

"She's fine, clean as a whistle. Didn't even have to have a D and C."

"Maybe she's too old to have a baby. I mean, basically, she's middle-aged. Just like the rest of us."

"I have news for you, kiddo, we're all in the prime of our lives. And as long as we haven't hit the big four-oh, we're not middle-aged."

"Dream on," said Lucy. "We're halfway to old age no matter how you slice it."

"Look, if she wants to have a baby, I think we should let her go ahead and try to have it."

"You think so?"

"And besides, it's none of our fucking business," said Katha.

"Whoa," said Max from the extension in the kitchen. "Run that by me again?"

"Get off the phone, Maxie."

"You didn't forget about the pizza, did you?" said Max. "We're like, starving out here."

"I didn't forget. The sooner you're off the phone, the sooner I'll be off."

"I'm obsessed with you, Mom," said Max. "I want to be with you every waking minute."

Katha laughed. "That is *so* touching," she said.

"I'm just that kind of guy," said Max. "And I'm hanging up now."

"Is he gone?" said Katha.

"I really mean it this time," said Max. "Listen for the click."

"He's gone," Lucy said.

"You think you'll survive his adolescence?"

"I fully intend to, but you never know."

"Well, good luck," said Katha. "Let me know how it all turns out. And remember to call Susannah."

"Tonight?"

"Tonight, tomorrow, whenever you have a chance. And don't sound so panic-stricken. I told you she's fine. Be a grown-up, Lucy. I know you're capable of making a simple phone call."

Lucy wasn't so sure. She imagined Susannah turning weepy in the middle of the conversation, and there *she'd* be, at a loss for how to comfort her. She already knew, in fact, that she'd probably never make the call. That in certain difficult circumstances she was just about useless.

"Right," she told Katha. "But let me get back to my adorable family first."

"See you," said Katha.

"See you, baby."

As they sat down to dinner at the kitchen table, Florine reminded Lucy with a scowl that she wanted to go home. "You pretended you didn't hear me the first time," she said. "If you don't want to drive me all the way back to Brooklyn, I'll call a car service. It'll cost me forty or fifty dollars, but it's a sacrifice I'll make if I've got to."

Lucy could feel a vein pulsing at the corner of her eye. She put her finger over it, but the steady beat continued. "I'll take you back first thing tomorrow morning," she said. "As soon as rush hour is over."

"You don't understand," said Florine. "I'm aching to go home. Aching."

She was right: Lucy didn't understand, would never understand. The three rooms her mother shared with Bebe, Lucy's grandmother, were in an ill-kept four-story walk-up that smelled of disinfectant and the decomposing garbage in the courtyard behind it. The hallways were dim and noisy and decorated with a mixture of innocent and obscene graffiti. The super had to be bribed to take care of even the most basic repairs and rarely made an appearance. Climbing the worn steps to her mother's apartment once a month, Lucy felt her legs grow heavy, her heart even heavier. Her childhood and adolescence had been spent in a similar building in the same dreary neighborhood, from which she'd waited endlessly, impatiently, to make her escape. A scholarship to Wellesley was her ticket out; her only regret was that she'd had to leave her mother behind. Yet Florine claimed to be perfectly comfortable, perfectly happy to stay put. She was still working as an aid in the elementary school down the street, as she had for almost twenty years, supporting herself since the day her husband died, shockingly, of a cerebral hemorrhage just before Lucy went off to college. Florine insisted that the neighborhood was safe enough as long as you knew which street corners the drug dealers had made their own, as long as you were smart enough to keep your distance.

Lucy's house was the house of her own dreams, at least, a white colonial with black shutters, set back an attractive distance from the street on a manicured lawn where, after school, her sons tackled each other good-naturedly. There were five bedrooms and four bathrooms, too many rooms, really, for a family of four, Lucy thought. Several times she had invited her mother to choose a room for herself and another for Bebe. The first time, tears sprang to Florine's eyes. "Thanks but no thanks," she said. "What are you looking to do, ruin my life *and* yours?" The second and third time around, she simply said, "Don't start that again."

Why force your generosity on someone who claimed, relentlessly, that there was nothing she needed, nothing she wanted, nothing you could offer her, Lucy wondered.

Still she made a point of never arriving in Brooklyn empty-handed. Over the years she had dragged chairs and lamps, vacuum cleaners, an air conditioner, a small TV set, up the four flights of stairs, her heart pumping furiously. Her mother greeted every gift with an insincere grumpiness that masked an uneasy gratitude.

"Now what am I going to do with this thing?" she'd said last summer, kicking with her slipper at the compact air conditioner at her feet.

"It's several thousand degrees in here," Lucy said. "I'll pay the super to get it into the window for you."

"Pooh," Florine said. "I spent sixteen summers in Georgia before I came up here, and if I got along without air-conditioning down there, I can surely get along without it here."

"That's ridiculous."

"Besides, we like it warm, don't we?" she asked Bebe. "And if sometimes we don't, we open up a window and let a nice breeze in."

"The super's a drunk," said Bebe. "Sometimes he comes in here for a minute or two and the whole room smells like a brewery."

"You know, I'm sure," Lucy said carefully, "that the heat can be very dangerous for older people."

"Pooh," Florine said again. "I'm fifty-six years old and healthy as an ox."

"I believe that's 'strong as an ox.'"

"And I believe you're a kindhearted fool," said Florine.

"I'm nobody's fool," said Lucy.

"Huh," said Florine. "If you think I'm actually going to enjoy the damn air conditioner, think again."

"So you're going to keep it?" said Lucy.

"Air-conditioning's unnatural — I hate it."

"But you *are* going to keep it."

"I'll never turn it on, I can promise you that," said Florine triumphantly.

The air conditioner was shut off, the windows open, the apartment stifling, whenever Lucy visited in the summer. Just as her mother had promised.

"I'll bring you home tomorrow," she told Florine now. "We'll all get a good night's sleep and start fresh in the morning." She shook her head at Jonah. "If you're going to pick those green peppers off the pizza, at least use a fork."

"I hate this vegetarian crap. We should have ordered half bacon, half pepperoni, and let Max starve."

"The smell of bacon makes me sick," said Max. "It makes me think of the squeal of the poor little pig as he's led off to the slaughterhouse."

"I thought we had a rule that we weren't going to use the word *slaughterhouse* at the dinner table," said Buddy.

"We trashed that rule while you were on vacation," said Max.

Florine sighed. "Lord, I'm so tired of listening to that boy's speeches. Lectures on why I shouldn't wear leather on my feet or carry a nice handbag, or why we have to stop exploiting the silkworm and the honeybee. All day long, yakkety yak. And you wonder why I can't wait to get home. No sir, I can't wait. I'm calling that car service tonight."

"You're driving your grandmother from this house!" Lucy cried, turning on Max in a sudden fury. "No one can stand listening to you anymore. You've got to put a lid on that stuff!"

Max's face looked ashy; his bottom lip wobbled. "You and me," he said slowly, "have the . . . worst . . . relationship. The worst."

"You should be ashamed of yourself," said Lucy, though she wasn't sure why.

"You should be ashamed of *your*self," Max told her. "And you know it." Scrambling from the table, he knocked over his chair and streaked from the room, Lucy chasing him, then changing her mind as he flew up the stairs to his bedroom. She waited at the bottom of the steps until she heard the predictable sound of his door slamming, then she headed for the front door, grabbing the blazer she'd worn on the plane.

Outside, her neighbors' houses and shrubs were blazing with Christmas lights, some pure white and others in primary colors that offended her taste even as they cheered her. Her own house, along with a few others on the street, remained dark, acknowledging that Jews lived within them and, in the cul-de-sac down the road, a family of Moslems from Pakistan. When she and Buddy had first moved into the house, almost five years ago, she had argued with him briefly about putting a wreath on their door, "nothing too Christmasy, just something seasonal," she told him. "The point is we don't want to send the wrong message," Buddy insisted, so she had given in. It was a small matter, not worth fighting over, surely, but every year she felt the slightest bit cheated, a sentiment she found childish and kept to herself. She would, in fact, have converted to Judaism if Buddy had wanted it, but she was grateful that he did not.

Life, she reflected, had treated them well enough, all things considered. But each of them had lost a few friends when they'd married, friends who refused to attend the wedding and then disappeared from their lives. "Screw them," Buddy told her. "If they're uncomfortable with us as a couple, I say, who needs them?" He had been right, of course. And later there had been the real estate agents who greeted them with clenched teeth, announcing that they were looking for trouble if they thought they could simply fall in love with a house, put down a deposit, secure a mortgage, and move in like anyone else. "I've got news for you," Buddy informed them, "we're exactly like anyone else." "Give me a break," one agent told them. "Wake up and smell the cross burning on your lawn," another had warned them. They'd been shown a score of houses on the North Shore of Long Island, in Westchester, and in northern New Jersey, and ended up buying directly from a gay couple who were so homesick for the city they couldn't wait to pack up and clear out and so were offering their home for a song.

"Don't get me wrong," Edward had told them. He was the younger of the two men, dressed that summer afternoon in cycling shorts and a tank top that showed off his smooth, orangy tan and the countless hours he'd spent on an Exercycle. "It's not that we don't love our acre of grass and the privilege of looking at the Big Dipper from the skylight. It's just that we miss the scurrying of roaches and the roar of the traffic past our window. And, of course, gossiping with the doorman about the new couple who moved into the penthouse upstairs."

"Really," said Lucy, shielding her eyes from the backyard sun. Already she was imagining a swimming pool and an extravagant swing set beyond the cedar deck. "And what's the story on the neighbors?"

"The neighbors are a snooze," said Edward. "A big bore, though quite friendly. They'll invite you to their barbecues and then put you to sleep with their stories about who said what to whom at the PTA meeting and how the high school production of *Gypsy* actually rivaled the original on Broadway. We're talking the next Ethel Merman here, right on the stage of our very own Fox Lane High School," he said, rolling his eyes so theatrically that Lucy had to laugh.

George, his lover, was elbowing him frantically in the ribs. He was a man in his fifties, easily twenty years Edward's senior; he had a silk scarf tied around his neck and a pained look on his face. "I'm sorry," he told Lucy and Buddy. "Sometimes the meaning of the word *inappropriate* seems to elude him."

"What?" said Edward. "What's inappropriate?"

"These people have children," George said. "They might *want* to know who said what to whom at the PTA meeting."

Buddy smiled. "Well, maybe we're a little boring," he said. "Just a tad."

"You don't look boring," said Edward. "If you did, I never would have gone on like that."

"The truth is, we're city people," said George. "My psychic

warned me not to settle down in a house in the suburbs, but I didn't listen to him."

"You didn't want to listen to him. Or to me," said Edward.

"Well, next time I *will* listen. And as soon as we're back in the city, I'm going to let him know what a jerk I was to have doubted his judgment."

Winking at Lucy, Edward said, "George and his psychic have a very special relationship. Victor talks and George listens. And after he's done listening, he forks over one hundred and twenty-five big ones."

"Victor is a gifted man," said George. "He's never led me wrong."

"He was wrong about us," said Edward. "He said we were a match made in hell, or something like that, didn't he?"

George tweezed a thread off the leg of his khakis and examined it closely, then dropped it into the grass. "Something like that," he murmured, almost inaudibly.

"Look," said Edward impatiently, "I can't *always* be on my best behavior. That would be too much to ask of anyone."

"Inappropriate," said George. "Impolitic."

"Shut up, George."

Lucy had known then that dishes and pans had been flung across the kitchen along with a thousand accusations, that sharply raised voices had been heard through open windows on mild spring nights, that a single desolate light had often burned here long past midnight while every other house in the neighborhood had darkened. She almost let the house go, thinking that George's misery had seeped through the walls of every room, tainting the air dangerously, like radon. And she had known that Buddy would laugh, that he would good-naturedly dismiss her fears as those of a lunatic. *Of all the reasons to turn down an opportunity like this, that is the flakiest,* she could hear him saying. So she kept silent, and the deal had gone through without a hitch.

Edward and George sent them a Christmas card every year, each with an updated photograph of the two of them posed in tuxedos in front of their fireplace in Greenwich Village, wrapped in an embrace, looking the picture of health and happiness. And this year, a little foolish, still in their formal wear but with elves' caps drooping from their heads. So much for George's psychic, who obviously had missed the boat. Or misread the tea leaves at the bottom of George's cup. Lucy still believed that the rage and melancholy she'd sensed five years ago in George and Edward's household was absolutely real, but she no longer worried that her family might be harmed by any of it. She was, after all, a person of reason, a math major in college, someone who even in high school had appreciated the perfect cold satisfying beauty of geometry and calculus.

If only her son could be fathomed as clearly as anything to be found in her old textbooks.

In her backyard now on one of the first nights of the new year, she walked to the far end of the swimming pool, covered in plastic for the season, and sat at the edge of the diving board, her legs folded under her. She looked up toward the lighted rectangle of Max's window, knowing that in all likelihood he had flopped onto the floor with a pillow under his head and was enjoying a video game, half-listening to the radio that played quietly in the background. He was probably engaged in a phone conversation as well, with one of his sullen pals who was only too happy to hear what a bitch Max had for a mother. The unfairness of the characterization nearly made her weep. For some reason, Max liked the sound of the word; she'd often heard it mumbled under his breath after they'd fought, and also used to describe the French teacher he hated for reasons he kept to himself. Sometimes, like Mlle. Charbonneau, Lucy was simply the mean bitch who made Max's life miserable; on other occasions, she was the person he loved most in the world.

Waiting in the dark of his room for her to come in and say good night every evening, he would bargain for more time with her the moment she stepped inside and settled at the edge of his bed.

"Stay until eleven fifteen," he begged her.

"Eleven oh three."

"Eleven ten."

"Eleven oh five, and that's my final offer."

"I love you more than anything," he said, and took her hand. "You think I'm jerking you around, but I'm not."

She couldn't resist stroking his still perfectly silky cheek. "I know."

"Do you love *me*?" he asked night after night.

"Absolutely."

"Why?"

"Because you're my child. And, of course, for other reasons, too."

"The first reason is the dumbest. That means that if I were a killer or a robber, you'd still love me, right?"

"That's right."

"That's so wrong. That's perverted." Turning away, letting go of her hand, Max fumed in the dark.

"You can't possibly understand," Lucy told him. "Not at this time in your life. You're just not old enough to appreciate the depth of a parent's love for a child. It's limitless, that's all I can tell you."

"So that means you'd love me even if I told you I was never going to go to college?"

"I don't want to hear this again, Max."

"I'm going to be a network sportscaster. Going to college would be a big waste of time."

"We have years to discuss this, baby. We're not going to talk about it now."

"Fine. I want to let you know a little early so it won't be a big shock to you when everyone else is taking their SAT's and I'm somewhere else."

"Thanks for the advance notice."

"So now you'll have, like, four or five years to get used to the idea, OK?"

For only an instant, she'd wanted to seize him by the throat right there in his bed and let him know how much the sheer wrongheadedness of his thinking infuriated her. Instead, she sat on her hands, watching the digital clock radio on his dresser marking time in fluorescent turquoise numerals.

"It's not like I'm planning to grow up to be a murderer or anything," Max consoled her. "I'm just not going to college, that's all. And if I drop out of high school when I'm sixteen, that wouldn't be so terrible either."

"Good night, Max," Lucy said, and, meanly, left the room without kissing him.

Through the door she could hear him calling, "Hey, you forgot to kiss me, goddamnit."

The pebbled surface of the diving board had grown uncomfortable under her legs, and she began to shiver in the bitter cold. The tip of her nose felt icy against her palm; above her, a flat white moon glittered beautifully. Rising, she ran across the frozen grass to the far side of the fenced-in yard and hoisted herself onto the trampoline that stood on the lawn on short steel legs. She pulled off her shoes and tossed them overhead. As they disappeared somewhere in the darkness, she leaped into the air boldly, her toes pointed, her arms whirling. Exhilarated, ignoring every precaution she'd taught her children so well, she vaulted higher and higher. She was no longer earthbound; there was absolutely nothing to tie her to this earth.

In the moonlight, there was only the sound of her own breathing and the feel of the cold breeze under the windmill of her spinning arms.

4

IN HONOR of Lucy's birthday, Katha has arranged an appointment for her with Victor Mackenzie, the clairvoyant she'd heard about at Parker's office party at the end of the year. Seated across the table from Lucy at a tiny, antiques-filled Italian restaurant, Katha breaks the news excitedly.

"I made appointments for both of us," she announces. "We're taking a cab over as soon as we're finished with lunch." She smiles at Lucy, who doesn't return the smile. "Surprise!" she says. "Is that a fabulous birthday present or what?"

"A scarf would have been nice," Lucy says. "Or a pair of fur-lined gloves. It's been such a cold winter." Actually, she thinks, she would have loved theater tickets, would have loved to have seen *Crazy for You* or *Damn Yankees* or anything at all, really. What she certainly doesn't want is to have her palm read by some high-priced charlatan dressed like a sorcerer in a flowing gown and a pointed dunce cap emblazoned with stars.

Twirling ink-black linguini idly around her fork, she says, "I don't mean to sound ungrateful, but why do we have to do this?"

"For fun," Katha tells her soberly. "Perk up, will you?"

Lucy forces herself to swallow a sour bit of chevre from her salad plate. "What's so great about this guy that you're so hot to drag me over there?" she asks.

"The women at the party were raving about him. A couple of them even carried his business card in their wallets."

"What women?"

"Let's see," Katha says, "some were attorneys at the firm, a few were partners' wives who had careers of their own. They weren't a bunch of dummies, I'll tell you that. And they weren't flakes either. They all said pretty much the same thing, that this guy seemed to know their secrets, things even their husbands and boyfriends had no inkling of. What really got me was that he diagnosed breast cancer in one of them. Apparently he put his hand on her chest and said, 'You'd better get this taken care of right away.' She had to have three different radiologists read the mammogram before they finally found the tumor."

"So he saved her life, is that what you're saying?" Lucy asks.

"It does seem that way, doesn't it?" says Katha. "And then he phoned her weeks later to see how the surgery had gone."

"Does he make house calls, too?"

"Go ahead and laugh," Katha says. "I just don't think taking a narrow view ever got anybody anywhere in this world."

"What the hell," Lucy says, no longer in the mood to argue. "Take me to your leader."

When Victor answers the bell, he sees at once that the two women on his doorstep are disappointed at the sight of him.

"You'll have to forgive my appearance," he says, ushering them in. "My long, flowing robes are at the cleaner's. And to make matters worse, my crystal ball met an untimely end after it fell from a pair of soapy hands onto the kitchen floor."

"I assume you're joking," says one of them, a blond woman in a black cape.

"Nope. I never joke about anything. I have absolutely no sense of humor whatsoever."

Both women laugh at this, though a little uneasily, he notices.

Victor says, "Now, before we get started, let's decide who's going first. The other one will have to amscray, I'm afraid."

"Leave?" the blond woman says. "I thought this was going to be a group session. Why can't we both stay?"

"This is a one-on-one kind of thing," explains Victor. "It works best this way, for both me and the person I'm reading." A pair of gray cockatiels squawk vehemently from inside their wooden cage in the living room. "Come on, ladies," Victor urges. "Time's a-wasting." He turns away as the two of them confer in whispers. "And you guys keep quiet!" he yells at his papillons, who are leaping behind the gate in the back room, barking in their high-pitched voices. "I want you to calm down this minute!"

The tall black woman approaches Victor without enthusiasm, her hands clasped in front of her, as if in chains. "I'm your first victim, I guess," she says uncertainly. "But I really wish you'd let my friend stay. I could use a little moral support."

"Don't worry so much," Victor responds, and slings his arm around her. "If it will make you feel any better, we'll have her wait for you over there." He points to the long narrow room at the back of the house, whose windows look out onto a yard surrounded by a white picket fence. "All right?"

"She's the birthday girl," the blond says. "It seems appropriate that she go first."

"Adiós, amiga," Victor says. "There's a pile of magazines on the table back there and a couple of cans of Diet Coke in the refrigerator. The kitchen's to your right as you enter. And if the dogs try to jump over the gate and into your lap, speak to them in a comforting voice and they'll simmer down."

Seating herself at the oval table in the consultation room, the black woman asks, "Don't you even want to know my name?"

"Sure," Victor says. "But you don't have to tell me if you don't want to. The only thing you have to do is relax."

"I'm Lucy Silverman," the woman says, and sighs heavily.

"Well, Lucy Silverman, you're enshrouded in mist, did you know that?"

"What?"

"Well, usually I see images around a person, clues that tell me who they are. Like your friend with all the blond hair — I knew the moment she came in here that she was an artist."

"You're right about Katha. Score one for the witch doctor."

"What's with the sarcasm?" Victor says. "We're not exactly starting off on the right foot, are we?"

"I heard you diagnosed a malignant tumor in someone's breast."

"That was a few years ago. She's doing well, but who knows?"

"Don't *you* know?"

"I don't know everything, as a matter of fact." Victor smiles at her. "You think I'm a fraud, don't you? Normally that would piss me off, and I'd probably ask you to leave, but for some reason I'm willing to let it go this time. You're a challenge, I'd say, and that makes me all the more interested in you."

Lucy hands over the blank tape Katha had given her in the taxi. There are bits of lint clinging to it from the lining of her coat pocket; smiling, Victor brushes them away before he clicks the tape in place in the deck in front of him.

Turning toward the statue of Buddha, Lucy rubs its golden toes absently. She lifts one of the seven cups of incense lined up so neatly at its feet and sniffs. "It's not that I think you're a fraud, it's just that I'm not a believer," she says. "I was a math major in college — that ought to tell you something about the way I view the world."

"You don't scare me one bit," Victor says with a laugh, and steers her into her seat. "I've had engineers sitting in this very seat, biochemists, microbiologists, oncologists, you name it. And none of them was too much for me."

"There's always a first."

"You're not going to be the first," Victor says, taking her hand. "Trust me. And listen, you're very lucky. Your children are fine — they're terrific kids, both of them."

"Really. And how long have you known them?"

"You're worrying too much about the bigger one, he's what, thirteen or so?"

"Just twelve."

"He may need a little help, some extra attention, but there's no need to worry so much. Frankly, you've got bigger fish to fry."

"And which fish are those?"

"To be perfectly straight with you, what I'm seeing is a black cloud over your marriage, your husband under a lot of —"

"No way! That's bullshit, honey."

"That cloud is pitch black," Victor insists. Taking out his magnifying glass, he scrutinizes her palm in silence. "I'm surprised you don't have stomach problems," he says after a while. "You're a terrible worrier. And there's all this guilt, I see."

"What am I, a criminal? What am I feeling so guilty about?"

"Well, you have so much, you know. Too much, you sometimes think, while others whom you love don't seem to have nearly enough. But that guilt is unnecessary." Victor looks up at her. "Is any of this making sense to you?"

"Could be."

"Your love for your husband runs deep, but you're going to be disappointed in him."

"More bullshit," Lucy says cheerfully. "Your powers are failing you, hon."

Victor smiles. "You feel foolish, don't you, sitting here letting a stranger examine your palm, your life?"

"Of course I feel like an idiot," Lucy says, yanking her hand away. "Who wouldn't?"

"You'd be surprised," Victor says. "Most people are very receptive to the idea. Of course, there are always a few like you, who can't seem to get comfortable." He taps a water-filled wine goblet sitting next to the tape recorder. "Bet you didn't know your soul is trapped right here in this glass of water, did you?"

Lucy smirks. "Oddly enough, I didn't."

"I personally don't believe it, though many psychics do. But water seems to turn psychic powers on, like a faucet. When it rains or it's damp out, my powers are usually at their peak. Somehow it seems to open a valve in my head."

"What about snow or sleet?" Lucy asks mischievously. "They're forms of moisture, aren't they?"

"Look, you're not interested in a discussion of meteorology, and, frankly, neither am I. So let's see what the tarot cards say," Victor suggests.

In a few moments, when Lucy has shuffled them and laid them out, she begins to laugh. "The devil?" she says. "Scary-looking dude. How come he's got wings like a bat?"

"Never mind about that," Victor says.

"That's evil incarnate I'm looking at, right?"

"Evil, catastrophe, violence. And also disorder, which is probably the only thing you've got to worry about here."

"Well, great. Catastrophe just isn't my thing. Evil and violence, on the other hand, are my various breads and butters."

Victor is smiling. "One of these days I'm going to hear from you on the phone, apologizing away a mile a minute. But look, the disorder in your household is going to throw you for a loop, I'll tell you that much. It's apparently going to have something to do with your husband and his career. He'll be under considerable stress, and it's going to take great effort on your part to keep your marriage intact."

"What kind of stress? The number of root canals he does per

month is going to plummet sharply? His hygienist is going to trip over a spool of dental floss and break her leg and sue him for all he's worth? What are we talking about here?"

"Sometimes I don't have knowledge of the specifics, I just have a sense of things. And my sense is that Bobby —"

"Who's Bobby?"

"I thought he was your husband."

"That's Buddy."

"Sorry. Anyway, I have this image of Buddy in a warm-up suit, you know, the kind that's made of that shiny, slippery material and zips up the front, and he's running somewhere . . ."

"Where's he running, away from the office, away from me?"

Shrugging, Victor says, "Does he jog regularly, like every morning, or when he comes home from work?"

"Never. And that's why it occurs to me that you don't know what the hell you're talking about. And furthermore, this marriage of mine is as stable as can be. It's enviable, it's so stable. It's rock solid, it's exemplary, it's the one thing I can count on in this world!" Lucy's voice has quickly risen to a shriek; angry tears spring to her eyes.

"Don't yell at me," Victor says quietly. "And don't cry. See this card here — the woman petting the lion — this represents strength. And you're going to have it, I suspect. You're going to get through all this, one way or the other."

"And what's this card with the guy hanging upside-down from a tree?" Lucy asks, wiping away the tears with the inside of her wrist. "The hanged man."

"That's sacrifice, the sacrifices you may have to make as long as you and your husband are under this dark cloud."

"You know," Lucy says, "if I thought there was any truth to any of this, I'd be pretty spooked. I'd be frantic, in fact."

"I don't want you to be frantic," Victor says. "I just want you to be prepared."

"Prepared? I'm prepared to make dinner tonight and breakfast tomorrow morning and to work at the school book fair tomorrow afternoon, and beyond that it's the same old same old and, you know what, that suits me fine. I'm privileged, it's a privilege to take care of my family and to go to bed every night feeling utterly safe with my husband lying next to me, sometimes with his arm coiled around me and sometimes not. If my mother gives me grief from time to time and my son's love runs hot and cold from one day to the next, that's all par for the course. But don't you go telling me about a black cloud that I can't see or feel, because I won't buy it."

"I don't blame you," Victor says. "But would you rather I be dishonest with you and tell you that your son's going to graduate summa cum laude from Harvard and your mother's going to be won over by your husband and decide he's the best thing that ever happened to you?"

Lucy's head snaps back, as if she'd been slapped. "Why would you say those things to me?"

"You know why," Victor says. "It's what you want to hear, isn't it?"

"You couldn't possibly know that."

"It's what I do," Victor says. "It's what I am. Look at it this way, you opened up to me and I eavesdropped. Some people are closed as tight as can be, and then it's like I'm up against a brick wall, I'm locked out. Don't you know people like that, people who reveal nothing of themselves? You talk with them for an hour or so and come away with nothing, because they can't bear to give anything away."

"It's Robert," Lucy says, sounding dazed.

"Pardon me?"

"Buddy. His name is actually Robert. It's where you got 'Bobby' from."

"Well, thank you," Victor says. "I was waiting for that."

"It was stingy of me not to tell you."

"You weren't ready, that's all. Just like you're not ready to accept what I've told you about you and your husband."

"Listen, it's completely off the wall. It's preposterous."

"I wouldn't have told you if I thought it was too much for you. Sometimes I do that, withhold information or water it down if I think, gee, this person's not going to be able to handle this right now, if ever. But *you* can and you will."

"Me?"

"You know you're pretty tough."

"If I'm so tough, how come I feel so worn out? I feel as if you've seduced me, somehow. And the idea of coming to see you every once in a while seems very seductive."

"You know, this is the first time I've seen you smile since you came in here," Victor says.

Lucy's smile lingers. "If Buddy knew where I've been today, he'd think it was absurd."

"So you're not going to tell him, then."

"I guess not. And of course," Lucy says, giving him a smirky look, "I wouldn't want that black cloud to descend any sooner than it's going to."

"Keep an eye out for the warm-up suit. And some very expensive running shoes."

"Nikes? Reeboks? What am I looking for?"

Victor knows she is humoring him; he can't resist drawing her back, dazzling her with a little something just before she leaves. "You know someone named George who died recently," he says.

"Nope," she says instantly. "Definitely not."

"This George is in your dreams and he's in your house. Look around for him sometime."

"What's he doing in my house if he's dead?"

"I suppose it's his ghost we're talking about," Victor says nonchalantly.

"What's he doing in my house?" Lucy repeats.

"He probably lived there once upon a time. That's what ghosts do, you know, return to places that have some meaning for them."

"George!"

"So you do know him," Victor says. "Of course you do."

"I think you know him too," says Lucy excitedly. "You're the one who told him never to move to the suburbs. You told him to stay in the city, but he didn't listen to you. He was miserable in that house, so miserable he couldn't wait to get out of there. We bought the house from him, Buddy and I. George had lived there with his lover, some guy who didn't like you very much. You told George they were a match made in hell."

"George Macklin, Macklowe, something like that," Victor says. "Small world."

"Macklowe, that's it. You didn't know that this guy you claim is haunting my house was one of your clients?"

Shaking his head, Victor says, "I haven't heard from him in a year or two. The last time he came over, he brought his lover with him, and the guy was so hostile I couldn't wait to get rid of him. After he left I realized this lover of his had stolen something from me, a little carved ivory Buddha. George never came back after that; maybe he was too embarrassed."

"And now you think he's dead? Poor George."

"Poor George is right. Why have you been dreaming about him?"

"I haven't," Lucy says. "I've already told you that."

"Well, he's in your subconscious somewhere. Where else would I have gotten his name from?"

"I don't know and I don't care. I met the man twice, so what?"

"He obviously made quite an impression on you."

Lucy looks into her lap. "Not really."

Victor knows she is lying, but he decides not to pursue it. She has more important things to worry about than the ghost of George Macklowe. He hopes she will be up to the challenges awaiting her, though he doesn't know for sure. Sometimes people surprise him, surprise themselves, drawing strength from unexpected sources. And she *looks* strong, Victor thinks; under the thin skin of the leotard she's wearing, he can see that her upper arms are quite muscular, as if she's been working out. Her dark eyes are clear and penetrating, with no trace of the angry tears he witnessed. Perhaps her anger will serve her well — he would like to think it will. When she leaves, a few minutes later, to summon her friend, he has a vision of her springing endlessly into the air, her bare feet beautifully arched, her head thrown back toward the darkened sky.

As she settles into the cane-backed chair left vacant by Lucy, Katha tosses her mane of pale hair behind her and immediately knocks over the wineglass filled with water.

"Go to your room!" Victor teases, mopping up the water with a dish towel. "And you can count on going to bed without your supper tonight, Miss."

"I am *so* sorry," says Katha, who sounds far more contrite than necessary, Victor thinks. "It's all over your beautiful rug. You think it'll stain?"

"It's only water," says Victor. "And it's not your fault that somebody shoved the glass over to your end of the table." Still squatting beside Katha's chair as she bends toward the floor for a closer look, he feels her hair swish across his face.

"Oh, sorry," she says again.

"I'd say we've had enough apologies." Victor watches as she casts her hair behind her again and finds the gesture alluring. Though she's not conventionally pretty by any means — her chin is a bit too sharp, her cheeks a bit too full — her face is lively and interesting, he thinks. And he'd enjoyed the soft sweep of her lovely long hair in his face.

Under her cape, which she flips over her head now, she's dressed in black jeans and a black turtleneck, with a double strand of colorful glass beads against her chest.

"So you're an artist," he says, and switches on the tape recorder. "Painter, sculptor, what?"

"What? Oh, of course you can tell by my hands, can't you? I never can get the paint out from under my nails."

"I didn't even notice your hands. It's the vibrations you send off, the aura that surrounds you. I can almost always recognize artists or writers from their vibrations, and sometimes the actual images they bring with them. Often when I've got a writer in here, I can actually see paper around him, sometimes with writing on it, sometimes not."

Katha narrows her eyes. "Come on."

"Really. I usually don't make mistakes in that area, though I once mistook a hairdresser for an artist. A lot of hairdressers have three small marks under their little fingers — the stigmata of a healer. And they *are* healers in a way, aren't they? Think of what they do for you. You walk out looking and feeling better after they're done with you, as if you'd been healed in some way."

"I personally haven't been to a hairdresser since the seventies," Katha says.

"Your hair is quite beautiful," Victor hears himself say. And then, "Sorry, that was very unprofessional of me."

"Don't apologize," says Katha. "You think I don't know my hair is my greatest asset?"

"Did you know you're a little crazy? You've always been a little crazy, haven't you?" He says this pleasantly, smiling as he speaks.

"I'm a very levelheaded person," Katha protests. "You're way off base on that one."

"Well, then, it must be the man whose name begins with the initial *P* who's making you crazy. Or crazier than usual."

"Mind your own business," Katha says. "Really."

Victor can feel her closing up, snapping shut like a hinged jewelry box. "What did you come here for, if you wanted me to mind my own business?" he says.

"I thought it would be fun, if you can believe that. Entertaining, like going to the theater."

"I'm not an entertainer," Victor says, insulted. "I suppose that explains why you're not having fun."

"Frankly, I'm a little bit overwhelmed at the power of your perception."

"I *am* sort of successful in this business," he admits.

"I don't doubt it."

"Do you begrudge people their successes?"

"Why?" Katha says. "Because I'm a failure of sorts myself?"

"You're not a failure, you're in a slump, that's all."

"A ten-year slump qualifies as your basic failure, wouldn't you say?"

"You continue to have faith in yourself. And you should."

"Why should I? Maybe I'm utterly self-deluded," Katha says.

"The only thing you're deluded about is your relationship with Mr. P."

"His name is Parker," Katha volunteers.

"Whatever," says Victor. He hands her the cards. "Shuffle," he orders, and looks on as she shuffles them distractedly, chewing hard at the corner of her bottom lip. "Cut the cards three ways."

"What for?" says Katha.

"Just do it. And use your left hand if you're right-handed, your right if you're left-handed."

"Who makes up these scientific rules, anyway?"

Ignoring this, Victor says, "Now turn over the top card in two of the three piles."

The moon appears at the top of the first pile; a yellow disk with a pained face across its surface, gazing downward at a howling dog and a wolf with rabbit ears and a bushy tail. "We're looking at deception and disillusionment here," Victor says. "You're warned not to trust in appearances. But you have to trust me when I tell you that the problems between you and your Mr. Parker are only going to worsen."

"What problems? And you can stop calling him Mr. Parker. Parker's his first name."

"I think that a friend of yours is going to tell you that Parker recently . . . approached her, if you know what I mean."

"What friend? You don't mean Lucy, do you?"

Victor shrugs. "You would do well to listen to what this friend has to say. She'll talk to you truthfully."

"Great news, huh. And too far-fetched to think about."

"Well, here's the Fool," Victor says, pointing to the second card, which depicts a man in a short dress and yellow boots, a single white rose in his hand, the sun in his eyes as he's about to step over the edge of a cliff. "Now that, I think, is a blunder you've made in the past, an old relationship that's still a part of your life in some way. An ex-husband, perhaps?"

"Could be," says Katha, and Victor envisions a barefoot man in an alleyway, crystals of snow shining in his eyelashes, his hair a graying, iced-over fright wig.

"This ex-husband of yours is heedless," he says. "Improvident. His future is very uncertain." Victor is having trouble imagining Katha in love with this man, clearly a man on his way down. And Parker, who has already attempted to betray her. Victor is jealous of them both, he is surprised to realize, jealous of all the times each of them has awakened with Katha's hair draped across his pillow. But Katha's instincts are all wrong when it comes to men, a failing she hasn't yet perceived in herself. He looks up at her, a worried figure engrossed in twisting her necklace around the knuckles of one hand.

"Let's see what the last of the three cards looks like," he says, and waits, holding his breath as she turns it over. "The world," he says, relieved. "There's a triumph of some sort somewhere in your future."

"A one-woman show at an influential gallery?"

"I don't know," Victor says. "But I suspect it might be a different kind of victory, like the discovery of a new love, the kind that makes for lasting happiness."

Her smile is polite; she seems unconvinced. "Are you making this up as you go along?" she says.

"I'm the real thing," Victor says. "If I weren't, I would have been out of business long ago." Taking her palm and his magnifying glass, he finds himself searching eagerly for good news. He shuts out the sounds of one of the papillons barking, of the cockatiels' cranky squawks, of the phone ringing three times before the answering machine picks up.

"You have what is called an old soul," he says after a while. "That means you've had many lives. You've been here before and you'll be here again."

"As a human being or as an insect?"

"Insect, squirrel, porcupine, human being, whatever."

"Somehow I don't find that particularly comforting," Katha says.

"So it's the here and now you're interested in."

"That's about the size of it." She eyes the superdeluxe show guppies lightly twitching their bushy crimson tails, the neon tetras, the kissing gouramis with their pulsing lips, all gliding serenely in the tank built into the wall. "They're as calm as can be, aren't they?" she says.

"Sometimes I come down here at night and sit in the darkness watching them. There's no light at all except the light in the tank, and the longer I sit here watching them, the more tranquil I become. I can feel my body going limp, my mind emptying; it's almost as if I'm in a trance."

"Sounds very therapeutic."

"It's wonderful therapy, all right. You might try it sometime, try sitting here with me in the dark and just losing yourself."

"Well, I might or might not," Katha murmurs.

"You know, I'm not too worried about you," Victor says. He doesn't want to let go of her hand, which lies cool and steady in his own. He lets the magnifying glass slip from his grasp to the carpet and cups both hands around her palm. "All in all, you're in fairly good shape, I'd say. Given the circumstances."

He wants to drop a single, soundless kiss into her palm and watch her fingers slowly fold around it. It takes all his will to control himself, to keep his lips from touching her.

So he talks and talks, assuring her that her life line is deep and sharply etched, signifying health and energy, a good, long life. And he sees by the way her heart line points upward as it ends that she takes great enjoyment in physical pleasure.

"Is that so?" she says, her pale skin blushing.

"Well, that's what's suggested here, anyway. The lines change as one grows older, so nothing is absolutely certain."

"Only death and taxes," Katha says.

"Not a good idea to dwell on either of those."

"Right." She is silent for a moment; then she says, "We can talk about my daughter, can't we? Is there anything you want to tell me about her?"

Victor points to a line running down to the base of her finger. "There she is, right there. Got a photograph I can look at?"

He studies the snapshot she hands him of a dark-eyed child with red cheeks and full lips, her dark hair drawn back in a flowered headband.

"She doesn't look anything like you," Victor says, "but she's an old soul, just like you. And she's an artist or a writer, perhaps both."

"No mention of how beautiful she is?" Seeing Victor's frown, Katha says, "What? You don't think she's beautiful?"

"Her unhappiness is going to become more of a problem for you both if you don't take the appropriate measures."

"What are you talking about?" Katha demands. "I show you a picture of a smiling little girl, and this is what you come up with?" Seizing the snapshot from him, she examines it closely — as if he had damaged it somehow — before slipping it back into her wallet.

"I don't know the cause of her unhappiness, though I'm sure you do," Victor says quietly.

"I'm a perfectly good mother. As good as they come, in fact."

"Did I say you weren't?"

"You implied it."

"Don't be so defensive," Victor says.

"Don't be such a know-it-all."

"Look," Victor tells her, "no one says you have to take my advice about anything. It's strictly volunteer. If this Parker character is the great love of your life, then go ahead and marry him, for all I care." He suspects she will not; it's the line in her palm stretching from the line of destiny toward the heart line, without quite meeting it, that makes him skeptical.

He folds his arms across his chest and stares her down. "Feel free to do as you damn please," he says.

Rapping her knuckles against the side of her head, all at once Katha begins to laugh. "I'm spending my time arguing with a fortune-teller?" she says in amazement. "You must be right, I *am* a lunatic." Reaching across the table, she pulls Victor's hand toward her. "Want to know what I see in *your* palm, wise guy? I see arrogance and a healthy bank account and mucho trouble with women, one woman after another leaving you to marry doctors and lawyers and periodontists, normal, ordinary guys who couldn't predict rain on a cloudy day. And you know why they've left you? Because nobody in her right mind would want to be involved with a man so fucking abnormally perceptive."

"Shut up," Victor says and, recklessly, stretches toward her and matches his lips with hers, tasting the sweet, waxy finish of her lip gloss, breathing in the faintly perfumed scent of her hair. And then, pulling back slightly, seeing her bewilderment, he tells her that he has never done such a thing in the middle of a reading, that he hasn't any idea what led him to that kiss.

"I just felt compelled," he says lamely. He is threading his fingers through a thick handful of her glittering hair, which, he notices with surprise, is mixed with a bit of silver here and there. "It's not what you think," he adds.

"And what do I think?" Delicately she pries his fingers apart and reclaims her hair.

"I don't know . . . that I'm someone who's in the habit of leaping before I've taken a good long look."

Katha shakes her head. "I can't imagine why you like me. I've been extremely rude to you, haven't I?"

"Who said I like you?" he says evenly.

"For your information, I don't much like you either," Katha says.

"Well, too bad for both of us then."

"It *is* too bad, isn't it? Because despite the fact that I don't really like you, I like your beautiful aquarium, and your big, fat, gold-leaf Buddha over there, and those noisy birds in their wooden cage, and especially the sound of your voice."

The tape deck has shut off automatically with a startling click.

"So . . . I've got your voice on tape," Katha says.

"You should listen to it once or twice."

"But not when Parker's around," Katha says with a small laugh.

"I would hope not. In fact, I tell all my clients never to play their tapes in the presence of their spouses or lovers, and it's good advice, believe me."

Sighing, Katha asks, "What the hell did you do to me, anyway? I feel so shaken, as if I don't know what I want anymore, or where I'm heading. Or with whom. Do you make everyone feel this way?"

"I didn't mean to unnerve you."

"Just don't kiss me ever again," says Katha, slowly pulling herself out of her seat.

Victor shoots up, nearly knocking his chair over. "I wouldn't dream of it."

"Well, that's a relief."

"If I did, there's no telling what would happen."

"Utter disaster," Katha predicts.

"Catastrophe," Victor agrees.

"Wrack and ruin."

"Never darken my door again," says Victor, approaching cautiously, his feet barely moving across the rug.

"Don't worry, it's the farthest thing from my mind."

"Smart girl." Victor's hands are at either side of her face now; her eyelids flutter and close. "Actually, I'm thinking of kissing you one more time," he warns. "Something short and sweet and entirely harmless."

"Better not," says Katha. "I'm in enough trouble already."

"Not as far as I can see."

"And how far is that?"

Victor doesn't answer; drawing her into a leisurely kiss, he feels her heart beating swiftly against his chest, feels the tip of her tongue circling the outline of his mouth, her hair swinging forward and draping over his shoulder like a silken scarf.

There's so much he doesn't want to know too soon. And so he prays for a dimness of vision, a thousand nights of dreamless sleep.

5

WANDERING THROUGH the soft drink aisle in the supermarket a half hour after Katha has left with her friend, Victor slams his shopping cart head-on into a wagon belonging to a shrunken old man.

"They ought to give you a speeding ticket," the man grumbles. He's wrapped in a long woolen coat, and a fluffy white earmuff sits at either side of his head.

"Are you all right?" Victor asks.

"No, I'm not," the man tells him. "I have shingles, you know what they are? It's a horrible thing, comes from the same virus that gives you chicken pox. I've got welts all over my stomach, and you wouldn't believe the pain. And then I leave my sickbed to go get a couple of bottles of seltzer, and what happens — I'm almost knocked over by some maniac who thinks he's in the Indianapolis 500."

"If Sylvia were still here, she'd be making you those baked apples you like so much," Victor hears himself say.

"Sylvia's dead," the man says angrily. "We buried her last summer."

Victor nods; he doesn't need to be told this.

The man is peering at him, bewildered. "You knew Sylvia from the neighborhood? She used to shop right here in this store Mondays and Fridays. Usually in the morning, before it got too crowded."

"No," says Victor, "I didn't know her." Why can't he mind his own business? Why is it always so hard to keep silent, to simply clamp his teeth together and make a clean, fast getaway? He pats the man on his small, rounded shoulder. "You have to stop being so angry," he says. "She didn't want to leave you, but that's the way it worked out."

"I miss those baked apples almost as much as I miss her," the man confesses. "And I miss the nice, neat way she folded my underwear for me when it came out of the dryer. She had the magic touch when it came to laundry."

Victor smiles. He wonders whether Sylvia would appreciate being remembered as a laundress extraordinaire. He sees her hand half-circling an apple, the other hand coring it meticulously. Her short gray cap of hair shines in a stream of sunlight. He sighs, sorry for the inevitability of the old man's loneliness.

"Take care of yourself," he offers, and heads for the meat and poultry department, where he picks out two Cornish hens for dinner tonight. Dan, his oldest friend, is in from California on one of his rare visits. He and Victor go back all the way to junior high school, where they dissected a fetal pig together in their biology class; when the project was completed, the two smuggled the pig out in a plastic bag, stuffed its abdominal cavity with cherry bombs, and let it explode high over Victor's backyard. (They must have thought it amusing at the time, but now it strikes Victor as gruesome, an act of inexplicable, mindless cruelty.)

At the checkout counter, he tries to tune out the vibrations he's getting from the cashier, a woman in her midthirties whose nails are bitten to the quick. Her young son is home from school, feverish and drowsy. He's propped up on the living room couch, watching endless hours of MTV, all alone except for the cat snoozing at his ankles.

Can't you get a baby-sitter to keep him company? Victor wants to ask. Take a few days off from work, he pleads silently.

Paying for his few groceries with a fifty-dollar bill, he leans over the counter and whispers, "Keep the change."

The woman thinks he's crazy. "I'm not a waitress," she says, and counts out a pile of bills into his hand. "I'm not allowed to accept tips," she hisses.

"He's too young to stay without a sitter," Victor murmurs, leaving the money behind on the counter. He grabs his paper sack and flees, feeling guilty for interfering, hoping at least his money was well spent.

Victor throws his arms joyously around Dan, who's grown chunky at the waist, he notices.

"I love you, man," Dan says. "I wish you'd ditch this town and move out to San Diego. You could join my softball league and hang out with my pals and me. Doesn't that sound inviting?" There's a puffiness about his face that Victor finds disconcerting, hard to look at. Dan's eyes are bright and glittering, blinking at him rapidly.

"Want a beer?" Victor asks. "Dinner won't be ready for a while." From the foyer they progress toward the kitchen, where he can check on the Cornish hens and baste them with duck sauce every so often.

"I guess you're staying in New York, huh?" Dan says, shaking his head at a bottle of Tsingtao. "The only thing I'm drinking these days is H_2O."

"Come on, just one beer," says Victor, who hates to drink alone. "Please."

"I'm on lithium," Dan reports cheerfully. "Best medicine in the world for us manic-depressives."

"Ah," says Victor. "So that's it." He knows the long history of

Dan's troubles, the profound, mysterious sorrow, the endless search for a good shrink and an accurate diagnosis.

"Don't look at me like that, man. I'm doing OK. I get up, go to work, do my job like a good little drone, go home to Wife Number Four and a nice warm hug. Except on softball nights, I'm in bed by nine, up at five, and so it goes. I feel nothing, but at least nothing hurts. I'll tell you, though, I miss those manic episodes, those moments when I believed I could do anything."

"Anything?"

"I wrote *poetry*, man. Dozens and dozens of poems, most of which, in the light of day, truly sucked. Love poems, nature poems, lyric poems, narrative poems, you name it. I was fucking inspired." Dan rubs his palms together vigorously. "Forget that shit," he says. "What about you?"

"I've never written a poem in my life," says Victor.

Dan laughs. "Anything else you'd like to share with me? Any women in your life?"

"Not exactly," says Victor, and he finds himself thinking longingly of the flutter of Katha's heartbeat against his chest, a secret unexpectedly revealed to him.

"You lonely, my man?"

"It's not as if my days are empty," Victor says. "I'm a busy guy. But maybe I'm a little afraid of being alone years from now, when I'm old and feeble and in the habit of talking to myself at the dinner table."

"Ever think about having kids? A couple of psychic toddlers offering you advice when you need it most? Sounds awfully appealing, doesn't it?"

Victor remembers a conversation he had with his last girlfriend, Sarah, the oboist, one night after they'd made love on her lumpy futon. They'd been seeing each other for three or four months, and he had recently declared his love for her; for the life of him, he couldn't figure out why her response had been nothing more than a faint smile. He knew she loved him,

knew it from the ardent way she greeted him after every concert he so faithfully attended, the way, in bed, she tightened
her legs around his, the eager way she questioned him about
his workday, begging him to leave out nothing. That night, as
they lay entwined lazily around one another, Sarah began to
talk about her niece, a three-year-old who was already playing
Suzuki violin.

"We're an incredibly musical family," she told Victor proudly.
"You can be sure I'd be devastated if my own children didn't
have some kind of musical gift."

"Of course," said Victor. And before he could stop himself,
he added: "Imagine if they turned out to be musical *and* clairvoyant . . ."

Even in the darkened bedroom he could see the look of horror that stiffened her beautiful face.

"You don't love me?" he said in a whisper. "Is that what
you're trying to tell me?"

"Of course I love you."

"Could you say that a little more sweetly, please?"

"I love you," Sarah told him gently. "OK?"

"OK, then." Relieved, he kissed her eyes, her mouth, the
knobs of her collarbone.

Sarah let out her breath slowly. "But it's not as if we can
spend the rest of our lives together."

"We can't?"

"I want children someday, but not with you, Victor. I'd hate
the thought of them living a life like yours, distracted by visions, seeing into the near and distant future of every person
who brushed past them on the street, their heads crowded
with other people's lives, other people's worries. I'd want them
concentrating on their music, on their own worries."

"First of all," said Victor coolly, "if we did have children together, it doesn't necessarily follow that they'd be clairvoyant.
Neither of my parents was, as it happens, so there's solid evidence right there that it seems to skip a generation or two.

And even if these hypothetical kids of ours *were* like me, they might choose to turn their backs and ignore the gift they'd been born with. People do, you know."

"Listen to me," said Sarah, but she stared up at the ceiling, as if the person she was talking to was floating somewhere above her. "Being with you is a trip. A trip and a half. But the world you inhabit isn't one an ordinary person like me belongs in." She paused. "This can't be news to you, Victor — you have to have heard this before, I just know it."

"I may have heard it once or twice," he admitted. He rolled away from her and onto his side. He couldn't bear hearing it all over again, couldn't bear being made to feel like some unearthly freak, some misfit who might father a couple of freakish kids of his own. Shutting his eyes, he saw the man who would take his place in Sarah's life, a husky, bearded guy in a tuxedo, a cello balanced between his knees. Victor's heart fell low in his chest; he knew the guy, Rick something, a cellist with a sweaty handshake and an annoyingly talkative fiancée. So Sarah was going to break up the guy's engagement and eventually give birth to some extremely musical children. Wonderful.

He was so angry, so bitterly disappointed, that he left Sarah's bed at three in the morning without a word. And when she called the next day, asking to be forgiven, begging to see him again, he foolishly gave in, deciding to let the affair wind down on its own. It made no sense, continuing to sleep with her, continuing to take pleasure in the murmured "I love yous" that came his way. It made no sense at all, knowing he was doomed to lose her, but she was lively and impassioned and beautiful, so he indulged himself for two full months, which flew by with heartbreaking speed. In the end, his only consolation was that he would, at least, be a good deal smarter the next time around.

"Kids?" he answers Dan now. "Who's ever going to want to have kids with *me?*"

"Well" — Dan laughs — "I'm no prize, and look at all the

kids I've got. In fact, I could loan you a couple if you'd like. My fifteen-year-old, for instance. He's almost entirely self-sufficient, even does his own laundry. And the two-year-old is cute as can be, except, of course, she's not toilet trained yet, which might be sort of a problem for you."

"I think I'll pass," Victor says. "But thanks for offering."

In the middle of dinner he puts down the tiny wing he's nibbling on and excuses himself from the table. "Got to make a quick phone call," he explains. "I'll be right back."

"What's the hurry?" Dan says. "Can't you eat your dinner first?"

"Just a little unfinished business I have to take care of." He shoves a bowl of wild rice in Dan's direction. "Help yourself," he says. "There's more of everything."

He hurries up the stairs to his office on the third floor, goes straight to the Rolodex of clients on his desk. He pulls Katha's card from the wheel and dials her number. Delicately, he licks duck sauce from the tips of his fingers as the phone rings four, five, six times. If she doesn't answer on the next ring he's going to hang up, he decides. His heart thumps, his palms turn slick with sweat.

"Calm down," he says into the phone just as Katha picks up.

"What?" she says. "Who is this?"

"Victor Mackenzie," he says cautiously. "I hope I haven't caught you in the middle of anything . . . like dinner, I mean."

"Did you just tell me to calm down?" she asks. "And if so, why?"

"Me? Of course not. Why would I say that?"

"I don't know, but you did. I heard you."

"Oh, that," Victor says. "That was me talking to myself."

"Were you afraid to call me?" Katha says.

"Why would I be afraid to call you?"

"I have no idea," says Katha softly.

In the background he hears a child's voice say, "Not *Yoo-Hoo*. I said orange juice."

"Well," says Victor, and clears his throat.

"Well . . . what?" She sounds amused, but also patient, as if she'd wait for him all night if she had to.

"There's something I forgot to tell you this afternoon. And it's very favorable, actually."

"Are you going to tell me what it is, or am I going to have to guess?"

"You couldn't possibly guess," Victor says.

"That's grapefruit juice, Mom. What are you *doing?*" the child's voice says, all exasperation.

Victor hears the refrigerator door slam shut. He imagines the dark-haired girl in the snapshot watching impatiently as Katha pours her juice. Her legs swing back and forth under the table; the tiny toenails on her bare feet are painted royal blue.

"Katha?" he says.

"Don't tell me you want juice too," she says. "The fact of the matter is, you're just going to have to get it yourself."

"Can you come over?" he asks. "The news I have for you can't be delivered over the phone."

"Really. And why is that?"

"It needs to be delivered in person, take my word for it."

"I'm intrigued," Katha says, "but I can't come right now. Maybe tomorrow."

"Tomorrow might be too late."

Katha considers this. "Why is it you're so desperate to see me?" she asks finally.

Victor's face feels scorched; his eyes burn. "You're embarrassing me," he says. He wonders out loud if it was a mistake to have called her.

"I don't think so," says Katha.

"Get off the phone!" her daughter orders in her sweetly pitched little-girl voice. "You promised you'd play Scattergories with me."

"I have to go," Katha says.

"Will you come tomorrow, then? Around noon, all right?"

"Around noon? she says. "I don't know. I'm not sure I'll be able to. In fact, I don't think you should count on my showing up, Victor."

"Your daughter will be in school, won't she? And Mr. Parker will be at work," he says soothingly.

"Even so."

"I need to see you," Victor says. "It's a professional matter."

"And I have to go play Scattergories," Katha laughs, and hangs up.

She arrives twenty minutes after twelve, looking rather severe, her hair twisted tightly in a French braid. Sauntering toward Victor in pointy-toed suede boots, she says, "What am I doing here, anyway?"

"Hello to you, too," Victor says. He nearly cries out in disappointment at the sight of that perfectly braided rope that lies so stiffly against her back. He wishes her hair were loose and flowing behind her shoulders; already he can imagine burying his face in it.

"If I'm here on business," Katha says, following him into the consultation room, "I hope you'll be willing to take a credit card. I forgot my checkbook."

"Have a seat," Victor urges. "Make yourself comfortable. And don't worry about money — this one's on the house."

Katha stares at him suspiciously. "You're all flushed, like you have a fever. Are you sick?"

"As a matter of fact, I've never been better."

"Let me feel your forehead," she says, and presses her palm against his brow familiarly. "A little warm, not too bad."

"Sit down, please," says Victor, pulling out a chair for her. "Park yourself right here."

"Do I have to?" she says as she sinks into the seat.

"Look," Victor tells her, "what I neglected to mention yesterday was that you're under divine protection, which means that someone who's died is watching over you. I suppose that would be your mother."

"She's watching over my shoulder?"

Victor nods. "Her name begins with the initial *C*?"

"Claudia," Katha whispers and clutches the edge of the table with both hands. Her face is bone-white, her sea-blue eyes wide open in astonishment.

One of the cockatiels squawks rudely in protest; a dog laps water from its dish in the kitchen. Moments later, on the street, there's a piercing squeal of brakes and a voice that sounds as if it were coming from a loudspeaker bellowing, "Move *over*!"

"I don't like this," Katha says. "Not that I necessarily believe a word of it, of course, but if she's been spying on me, I'd like her to cut it out right now. I mean, give me a break."

"She's not spying," Victor says. "She's simply a loving presence who wants to make sure no harm comes to you."

"She was always so nosy — it makes perfect sense that she'd be spying on me from beyond the grave. Can't you get her to take a hike or something?"

"It's a gift, being under divine guardianship," says Victor. "It's a blessing. Why can't you accept it graciously?"

Katha swivels her head over her shoulder. "Is my mother actually hanging around here?"

"She's here."

"Can't you talk some sense into her?"

"No, I can't," says Victor. "She's all yours."

"Oh sure. I can just see myself having a conversation with a ghost. We *are* talking about a ghost, aren't we?"

"Well, I don't see her, but I do feel her presence. And what I do see is the letter *C* floating behind you."

Upper case or lower case?"

"What?" Victor says in annoyance. "It's just a plain old *C*." He takes a stroll around the table to his golden Buddha. He rubs its shining belly and lights a cup of incense at its feet. "Look," he says, "if it will make you feel any better, my mother's a pain in the rear too."

"Is she alive, at least?"

"Long gone," Victor says. "But still sending me messages from the other side."

"Well, you of all people ought to know how to tune her out."

"Don't I wish," says Victor.

Katha gives him a long, searching look. "Who *are* you?" she says. As he sits down beside her, she lifts his arm, examines it back and front. "What have you got up your sleeve?" she says.

"Nothing much," Victor says. "In fact, nothing at all."

"Then how did you get me to come here? I didn't want to, you know."

"Part of you didn't want to," Victor tells her. "The other part apparently found me hard to resist." He smiles at her. "Admit it."

She responds to his smile with a sigh. "The only thing I'll admit to is total confusion," she says. "It's like when I get out of the subway in a neighborhood I'm unfamiliar with and I'm all turned around, so disoriented I can't tell east from west. What it is, is that I've lost my bearings, I guess."

"Don't be afraid of me," he says gently.

"I'm not," she says. "But you know what I was doing last night? I was lying in bed trying to imagine you engaged in the most ordinary things, making yourself dinner, brushing your teeth, going to the post office to buy stamps, trying on a pair of pants in a department store . . ."

"And?"

"And it was impossible for me to picture any of it. I mean, let's face it, you're not exactly —"

"Come on," Victor interrupts. He reaches for her hand. "Come upstairs with me and I'll brush my teeth for you. I'm very good at it, very meticulous. And I floss every night, how do you like that." He has forced himself to sound casual and good-natured, but inwardly he is boiling over, so frustrated that he would like nothing better than to put his fist through a pristine sheet of glass. What will it take to convince her he is of this earth, flesh and bone like everyone else?

"I believe you," Katha says, locking her hands together to avoid his. "A demonstration won't be necessary."

"No, no, come upstairs with me," he insists. "You can see my toothbrush and my tube of Crest and the razor I shave with and the blow dryer I use on my hair. And maybe I'll even let you check out my closet. There are quite a few pairs of pants in there, which, you may be surprised to hear, I put on one leg at a time."

"Victor," Katha says in a whisper. Now her hands are crossed at her throat, as if she believes herself to be in danger.

"The one thing you won't find in my closet," Victor says fiercely, "is that big pointed dunce cap like that ancient guy wore in *The Sorcerer's Apprentice.* You know the guy I mean?"

Katha nods. "The sorcerer," she murmurs.

"That's right," Victor says. He is breathing so heavily he can almost believe he's just raced up five flights of stairs. "That's absolutely right."

"What's wrong with you?" Katha asks. Before he can answer, though, she says, "Forget it, I really don't want to know." Rushing from the room, leaving Victor behind, she bumps into Dan at the foot of the stairs.

"Excuse me," he says, and watches as she fumbles with the doorknob. "May I get that for you?"

"You must be clairvoyant," Katha says. "I mean, how else would you know I can't wait to get the hell out of here?"

"Clairvoyant?" Dan laughs pleasantly. "Not me. I'm manic-depressive."

"I'm sorry to hear that," says Katha, before she lets the door slam in his face.

6

NEARLY A MONTH AFTER after her visit to Victor, when the air has finally warmed and almost everyone is walking through the streets of the city in shirtsleeves, jackets hooked over their thumbs or draped casually across their arms, Katha finds herself booking one birthday party after another, the loft filled, two and three times a week, it seems, with chatty little girls in their private school uniforms. She is happy enough that business is booming, though this leaves her, of course, with less time for her painting. And the less she paints, the edgier she feels. Her painting, her real work, the work she is sometimes proud of, is something she simply cannot live without. She has been laboring, for several years now, on a series of muddy-colored paintings of tunnels, most of them leading to fiery, hellish places. Parker finds them gloomy and utterly mystifying; from time to time he asks why she can't switch to still lifes or portraits, "paintings people might actually want to have hanging in their homes. I mean, face it," he tells her, gesturing to one of her canvases, "who would want such depressing stuff in their living room?" "Fuck you if you don't know the answer to that," she responds, which only makes him shrug and back silently out of the little studio she rents on the third floor of a cream-colored brick building just across the street from where they live.

It is Julia, her nine-year-old, who studies her work with a painterly eye, circling the canvases with her hands in a knot behind her back, offering comments in her childishly pitched voice about light and shadow, comments that make Katha want to cry out in gratitude and love. Julia has her own set of watercolors and oils in Katha's studio, her own small easel and collection of coffee cans filled with brushes. Sometimes, after school, while the light is still good, they paint side by side, Julia in a frayed old oxford shirt of Parker's worn backwards and reaching below her knees, mother and daughter saying not a word for, perhaps, a quarter of an hour at a time, as baroque music plays on a portable tape recorder set on the windowsill. These are the richest, happiest moments of Katha's day, time that Parker has never shared, scenes he has never caught even a glimpse of.

On this spring day that feels so close to summer, Katha is busy with one of her parties, arranging the bright clay beads of a dozen necklaces on a tray that is about to go into the oven for exactly twenty-two minutes. While the beads are cooking, the party guests eat their iced cupcakes and drink their Hawaiian Punch from paper cups patterned with Barbies and Kens. Allison Fraser, the mother of the birthday girl, refills the cups of punch and hands out party bags filled with chocolate kisses and boxes of pebbly candy inexplicably called Nerds. She is a casual acquaintance of Katha, a PTA buddy who calls occasionally to chat about school, often passing on gossipy bits of news in which Katha feigns interest as she prepares dinner or loads up the dishwasher. Allison wears tortoiseshell headbands in her frosted blond hair and nearly always seems to be dressed in tailored skirts and flat shoes in pink or green — the kind of neatly arranged outfit that makes Katha a little nervous. Divorced for several years now, Allison was rumored, most recently, to have been dating the owner of a chain of movie theaters, or so Katha remembers.

"Look, I don't know if this is the appropriate time or not," Allison says, approaching Katha at the oven, "but there's something we probably ought to talk about." She smiles at Katha, then licks her lips slowly. "Actually, I'm a bit embarrassed about this."

"Don't be embarrassed," Katha says. She opens the oven door to check on the beads, which are cooking nicely. Turning back to Allison, she says, "Let's hear it."

Allison moves toward her and pulls away a wisp of hair that's stuck at the corner of Katha's mouth. "There we go," she says.

"That's it?" Katha asks. "You wanted to tell me I had hair in my mouth?"

"Not exactly." Then she flashes a look of pity mixed with triumph so Katha can see that it's bad news and also that Allison is taking the slightest bit of pleasure in delivering it. "It's your friend Parker," she says. "I wish there were some way I could say this tactfully, but the fact is he sent me his business card. In the mail, I mean."

"His business card? I'm supposed to be upset by that?"

Speaking just a little too loudly and with an exaggerated deliberateness, making sure that Katha gets it, that she understands that this is the worst possible news, Allison says, "He was responding to an ad I'd placed in the personals column of a magazine."

Katha feels her arms and legs stiffening; her stomach curdles. "I see," she says. "And what did it say on the card?"

"Oh, he scribbled 'call me' above the telephone number. With an exclamation point at the end, I think."

"And did you?"

"Katha! I'm surprised at you," Allison says. "And highly

insulted. I'm a nice person. I'd never steal someone's boyfriend right out from under her. So to speak."

"You wouldn't?"

"What's the matter with you? Of course I wouldn't. Though
I'm sure there are plenty of women in my situation who would.
Listen, I've been carrying this secret around for weeks. I honestly didn't know whether to tell you or not, and then finally I
thought, this is ridiculous, you have the right to know what's
what."

"Excuse me, did you say 'weeks'?"

"It's been about four weeks, I guess."

So this was what Victor was warning her of, she thinks, as the
skin at the back of her neck prickles with a strange, sickening
excitement. "What do you know," she murmurs. The truth is,
she has thought of him often, fantasized about showing up at
his doorstep unannounced, late at night, and asking to sit in
the dark with him in front of the lighted fish tank. And, too,
she has hoped that he would call her and maybe even offer her
another look into her future. It is a disappointment that he has
not but one she can live with, she figures. Because the last
thing she needs is another difficult man in her life, even one as
attractive and mysterious as Victor. But her first impulse now is
to rush to the phone and call him, to let him know that she is
overwhelmed by the absolute accuracy of his vision, that nothing in her life has ever astounded her quite like this, or struck
her as so remarkably uncanny. Exhilarated, her heart jack-
hammering madly, she holds her hands in front of her, palms
up, and watches as every one of her fingers trembles.

"I'm truly sorry," Allison says, but with the faintest of smiles
that suggests some part of her is enjoying this. "I can see what
terrible shape you're in."

"I'm not."

"You're in denial," Allison tells her. "And you know what, if
Parker sent *me* his business card, you can bet there must be

plenty of other ads he responded to. I mean, there's got to be more than one that caught his eye, wouldn't you think?"

"Probably," Katha says. "I mean, I have no idea, really."

"So what are you going to do about it?" Allison asks.

"I have no idea."

"Well, you can either pretend this conversation never took place, or you can do your best to make him feel like the pond scum he obviously is."

"It's that obvious?"

"Sweetheart, the love of your life is actively perusing the personals. I'd say 'pond scum' doesn't do him justice."

"That bastard," Katha hears herself say. "Maybe I'll kill him when he gets home tonight."

"Now that's more like it," Allison says approvingly. "You've got to get yourself all worked up so you'll be in the right frame of mind when he walks in the door. You've got to let him know how disillusioned you are, how betrayed you feel. And above all, you've got to make him feel guilty."

"And then I kill him?"

Allison gives her a funny look. "I assume you're being facetious. Because if you're not . . ."

"Get a grip, Allison."

"*Of course* I know you were joking," Allison says, smiling now, her relief evident. "It's just that you never know what wild ideas people will get into their heads in times of great stress."

"True," Katha says. "And murder seems so uncivilized. And then, too, all that blood in the apartment would infuriate Parker. He's so meticulous, and bloodstains are so hard to get out."

"You're really angry, aren't you," Allison says, impressed.

"I'm fucking incensed," Katha murmurs, as a girl in a wrinkled gray pinafore and white blouse approaches. "And what can I do for you, young lady?"

"Well," the girl says, "this party's kind of boring. When are our necklaces going to be ready? We can't wait forever, you know."

"You can't?" Katha says. "Well, you won't have to. They'll be ready in a couple of minutes."

"Do you have any Janet Jackson tapes?" the girl asks, and then belts out something about having come too close to happiness to have it swept away.

"I'm afraid we don't allow music by any of the Jacksons in our home," Katha says. "They're a highly dysfunctional family, and I find their music very dishonest."

"Go back to your seat, Raleigh!" Allison tells the girl.

"All right, but the cupcakes were gross. There were nuts in the frosting," Raleigh says, making gagging noises. "Some children might even be allergic to them. And also, how come you didn't have, like, any magicians or fortune-tellers or anything? At my party last year, we had a gypsy who looked at everyone's hands. She told us cool stuff like we were going to grow up to be ballerinas and have rich boyfriends."

"And did you believe her?" Katha asks.

"She was wearing too much makeup and her breath smelled like cheese, so I only believed her a little. But at least I had fun at that party. This party sort of sucks, though."

"Go back to your seat, Raleigh!" Allison shouts. Lowering her voice, she adds, "And if you tell anyone else this party sucks, I'll tell your mother you said the F curse today."

"But that would be a lie."

"Go," says Allison, and then to Katha, in a whisper, "Her mother's found herself a new husband, and I hear it's a disaster."

Katha shakes her head, imagining Victor at a children's party, reading their small, grimy palms, predicting losses of all kinds, disappointments, dreams unfulfilled. She shivers in her hot kitchen. She thinks of Parker, falling, so inappropriately, in love with his brother's wife. And running his eye up and down the columns in the back pages of *New York* magazine, *American Lawyer,* *The New York Review of Books,* sorting through the listings of all those bereft Single White Females. And maybe the married ones, too. She wonders what he found so compelling in Allison's ad; she imagines him framing his business card between his manicured fingers, pausing for an instant or two before he slips it into an envelope and seals it, then placing it in his out box, a satisfied smile on his lips.

Why? she asks herself. She can't remember whether she loves him, or why she should. Is it possible to love someone who would betray her in so calculated a way? If he came home and reported that he had fallen in love with a colleague or with a waitress in the coffee shop in the lobby of his office building, would that hurt almost as much as this? She doesn't think so. She understands that sometimes love isn't sought but simply happens, like a sudden rainstorm, an avalanche, two people colliding head-on as they round a corner. Or it blossoms so slowly that the couple isn't even aware that they are caught up in something whose loss they would mourn. But to search for it in the pages of a magazine is something entirely different, and her anger flares thinking of it. She waits for the sickening feel of humiliation to spread within her like an ink stain in water, and it does, just as she is bending over the open stove to retrieve the tray of beads. The tears that fill her eyes blur the sight of all those vivid colors and, beyond them, the dozen light and dark heads at the table swiveling toward her in anticipation.

"Check it out, girls," she says in a choked voice, and hears the sweet, high-pitched oohs and aahs as she carries the tray to the table. "Look what a beautiful job you all did."

Once the beads have cooled, the girls string their necklaces on lengths of nylon thread, their faces bent toward their task, fingers working clumsily, cries of both frustration and satisfaction filling the room. Katha moves from child to child, offering praise and assistance, her own hands still a little shaky, the flesh across her cheekbones pulled taut by the tears that have slowly fallen and then evaporated along the planes of her face.

Near the party's end, as the girls are scooping up their spoils, arguing over what belongs to whom, Allison takes Katha aside at the window and says, in a breathy voice, "I just had an idea, and it's actually quite brilliant. You'll either love it or you'll hate it, I'm not sure which."

Outside the window, ten stories below, a man in a yellow rain slicker is picking through a garbage can. A woman pushing an empty baby stroller saunters by, a cigarette between her fingers. Drifting past them both, over their heads, a black plastic bag catches in the branches of a flowering Japanese cherry tree.

"Let's hear it," Katha says.

"Here's the thing," Allison begins, "let's say I respond to Parker's invitation, using an assumed name, of course, and agree to meet him for a drink somewhere. I give you the time and place, and you show up at the perfect moment. You'd catch him red-handed, and he wouldn't be able to deny a thing. Wouldn't that be the sweetest revenge?"

"It's tempting," Katha admits. "But public scenes aren't my style. I'd probably feel more comfortable letting him have it in the privacy of my own home." Sweeping her arm through the space around her, she says, "Or whatever this place is."

"You're sure?" Allison says, clearly disappointed.

"Besides," Katha says, "it sounds like some scheme cooked up by Lucy and Ethel, if you know what I mean."

"But that's the fun of it."

"Fun?" says Katha. "Isn't this my goddamn life we're talking about?"

"Well, give me a call if you change your mind."

"Don't count on it," Katha says wearily. She stares at the other woman's crestfallen expression and thinks that perhaps

Allison and Parker deserve each other, that perhaps a date with Parker would suit all three of them.

Sitting stiffly on the couch hours later, watching Parker walk through the door, Katha feels her cheeks blaze with shame, as if the news of his betrayal was absolutely fresh, an arrow that had just gone straight through her.

"Hey there," he says, attaché case still in hand as he leans over for a kiss. "How'd the party go?"

"Hey, Parker," she manages to say, allowing herself to endure his brief kiss, clenching her fists at her sides. "The party went fine, thank you very much."

"Where's Julia?"

"Having dinner at a friend's."

"On a school night?"

"She seemed to want it so desperately, I didn't have the heart to say no."

Shrugging out of his jacket, loosening his tie, he regards her with a puzzled frown. "Maybe it's my imagination, but you're looking at me as if you'd never seen me before."

"Maybe I haven't."

"What?" He slips off his shoes and goes into the kitchen for a beer, then tries to sit down beside her.

"I'd rather you didn't," she says coldly.

"I can't sit next to you?"

"That's right, you can't."

"Let me guess," he says, and tilts the bottle toward his mouth, taking one long sip. "I yelled at Julia last night for getting the bath mat all wet after her shower, and she was so humiliated she couldn't get out of bed this morning. Is that why you're mad at me?"

"This has nothing to do with a fucking bath mat."

Parker cringes. "You know I hate it when you talk that way."

"You find it offensive? Well, I find *you* offensive."

"What did I do?" Parker asks, sounding so desperate, so bewildered, that she almost pities him.

"You tell *me*."

"I'm not a mind reader," he says.

Hearing this, Katha laughs. "Now that's funny, because someone who is, sort of, predicted this very conversation."

"I'm absolutely lost here," Parker says.

"Go sit over there on the love seat. Make yourself comfortable."

Parker hunches over the edge of the leather seat and grabs his knees. "So what's the deal on this person who predicted we'd be having this conversation?"

"He's a clairvoyant," Katha says breezily. "No one you know."

"You went to see a clairvoyant?" Parker says in disbelief. "What the hell for?"

"It doesn't matter. We're getting off the track here."

"You tell me you went to see a clairvoyant, and it doesn't matter? Why would you do such a weird thing? It seems to me that's like consulting a witch doctor or a faith healer, something only a truly desperate woman would do, right?"

"Oh, I'm desperate, all right. Desperate to find out why you'd send your business card to Allison Fraser after reading her ad in a personals column somewhere."

"Who's Allison Fraser?" Parker asks innocently, but Katha is pleased to see his pink-cheeked face has already lost some color.

"Just a wild guess, but tell me if this sounds familiar: 'DWF, late thirties, mother of two, looking for nonsmoking, drug-free SWM, preferably an MD, JD, MBA, or CEO to share romantic dinners, moonlit walks along the beach, piña coladas, tennis and golf at your club or mine,' et cetera, et cetera, ad nauseam."

"Who's Allison Fraser?" Parker asks again, his voice cracking slightly this time.

"PTA vice president, short, blond hair, a little too perky for my taste, but maybe not for yours."

"Oh, Christ," says Parker, and claps his hand over his eyes.

"Your goose is cooked, buster."

Parker considers this for a moment. "Maybe," he says, "I wanted to get caught. Maybe, subconsciously, I wanted you to find out so that you'd stop me before I wrecked everything between us. Who knows, maybe my picking Allison from all those dozens and dozens of ads will ultimately prove to be the best thing for us."

"Or maybe you're full of shit," says Katha, and she begins to cry, which surprises her. She had planned to be steely and ice-cold, dignified and self-possessed, making Parker look all the more vile as he tried to explain away the indefensible.

"Get away from me," she barks as he slips to his knees on the floor, slithers over to rest his head in her lap. Neither of them moves, then Parker begins to speak to her, as softly as if he were soothing a small, whimpering child.

"It isn't that I don't love you," he tells her. "It's just that I have this need to play these games every once in a while. To prove to myself that I'm still desirable out there in the market-place and all that."

"And that's supposed to be some sort of consolation to me? Tell me, how many dates with Allison and all the other Allisons does it take before you have the proof you need that you're still desirable?"

"There haven't been any other Allisons."

"I'm not *that* stupid, Parker."

"Well, there may have been a couple here and there." Parker sits on his heels and looks up at Katha. "I hate to see you cry," he says gently, though she is no longer weeping.

"A couple is two or three," Katha says. "I wouldn't think that would be proof enough." She doesn't know why she is doing this, encouraging him to be absolutely open, to provide statistics that will only fuel her anger and disappointment, when really all she wants is a deeply felt apology. And also the strength to wring his neck.

"Maybe it was more like half a dozen or so," Parker says, eyes lowered.

"Did you sleep with any of them?"

"These days," Parker says, "you need a doctor's note to get any action at all. Not that it's a bad idea, but I can't imagine ever going to the doctor's office and asking for one, can you?"

"Action?" says Katha, turning the word over in her mind and finding it utterly distasteful. "Weren't you getting enough action at home?"

"Sure," Parker says. "I mean, I guess so."

"I guess not."

"Look," says Parker, "how bad is the damage here? Is it irreparable?"

"I don't live with guys who go out on dates while I'm here keeping the home fires burning. I don't marry them either."

"Do you *want* to get married?"

"To you or to someone I can trust?"

"From this moment on I'm going to be someone you can trust," Parker says and puts two fingers together like a Boy Scout.

"Just like that, huh?" Katha says. "I'm supposed to believe in magic, is that it?"

"You believed that clairvoyant, didn't you?"

"I didn't, actually. Or I didn't want to."

"What else did he tell you?" Parker asks her.

"That you would beg for my forgiveness," Katha lies.

Arranging himself on his knees, Parker presses his palms together. "I'm begging you," he says. "What else?"

"I hate the sight of a grown man begging like that," Katha says. "It's pathetic." And also rather gratifying, she thinks.

"Did he say you should have faith in me when I give

you my word that I won't be mailing out any more business cards?"

"He didn't mention it," Katha answers as Parker eases himself onto the couch and casts his arm around her shoulders. "He did recommend that I watch you like a hawk though."

"He'd be better off minding his own goddamn business," Parker says.

"Minding other people's business *is* his business."

"Not unless he's a licensed shrink, it isn't."

"Victor's quite a remarkable guy," Katha says. "Not that I would expect you to understand the nature of his gifts."

"And how much did you have to spend for the privilege of hearing this guy's bullshit?"

"You're the one who's on trial here, not me," says Katha. "You don't have the right to ask questions. You're the one who's got to bend over backward to try to win me back, if that's what you're hoping for, anyway."

"Have I lost you?" Parker asks warily.

"Put it this way — you're walking on eggshells, buster. Just watch your step."

"I read you," he says. "And it looks like I'm going to have to be on my best behavior for the rest of my life."

Katha laughs. "Why does that sound so awful?"

"Like a prison sentence."

"So you want a pardon from the governor?"

"I'd be very grateful," Parker says.

"Sorry, you'll have to earn it."

"There's always a catch, isn't there."

"Always," Katha agrees.

"I really do love you, you know," Parker says.

Katha is silent, wondering why this declaration fails to move her.

"If I didn't love you, I wouldn't be feeling so guilty, would I?"

"You're asking *me*?"

"Who should I be asking, your psychic?"

"I don't *have* a psychic, and I don't want to talk about him anyway."

"Well, I do. I think he tried to turn you against me, telling you things that couldn't possibly do either of us any good."

"He's on to you, Parker. And so am I."

Parker plays with the keys in his pants pocket awhile, then pulls them out and dangles the sterling silver ring from his finger. "He's a dangerous guy. It seems to me you ought to stay away from him."

"You sound frightened."

"The only thing I'm afraid of is your becoming the kind of person who would actually rely on a quack like that for advice on how to live your life."

"First of all," Katha says, "he's not a quack. And, second, I don't need advice from anyone, including you."

"Suit yourself," Parker says and stalks off to the kitchen, carrying his key ring and shoes. He fills a little Pyrex cup with a solution of water and ammonia, into which he drops his keys. He swirls the liquid with the tip of his finger, as if it were a mixed drink. Taking a sponge from under the sink, he pours a capful of bleach onto it, then scrubs the soles of his shoes, humming jauntily as he works. When he is finished, he sets the loafers upside-down on the counter to dry. This has recently become a nightly routine, performed as faithfully and automatically as brushing his teeth or washing his face.

There's dangerous bacteria everywhere, he's warned Katha. *Why not minimize contact with it as best you can?*

She sits motionless on the couch, pretending that she doesn't know what Parker is doing; pretending that if she averts her eyes for a moment, a man looking exactly like Parker, and dressed in Parker's clothes, will be standing in the kitchen preparing dinner, sautéing broccoli in oyster sauce, steaming rice, presiding over a small frying pan crowded with chicken cutlets. With her eyes closed, she can taste the salty tang of the oyster sauce, hear the hiss and pop of the chicken frying in olive oil. What she sees when her eyes are open and staring straight into the kitchen is Parker standing at attention, arms at his sides, keeping watch over his keys as if they were something precious.

Walking in great angry strides to the kitchen, she offers him the tinkly chime of glass shattering as she pitches the Pyrex cup into the sink. *Why?* he wants to know. In all the world, Katha thinks, he alone doesn't have a clue.

She helps him pick the largest shards from the sink; across the countertop are barely perceptible splinters of glass, the ones Parker says are too dangerous to touch bare-handed. Ignoring him, she collects them in her palm, pricking her fingertips here and there, droplets of the most vivid red blood appearing like tiny, brilliant ornaments against her skin.

"I *told* you," Parker says, shaking his head at her. "You're crazy." She sees then, in his clear hazel eyes, that he is afraid of her, and that she has been transformed into someone fearless.

7

THE PALM Victor is studying under his magnifying glass is small and dry and full of old news; the client it belongs to is ninety-three years old, a well-groomed woman with surprisingly thick white hair arranged in an elegant twist. She'd arrived alone in a taxi and, in big ugly Space Shoes made of midnight blue suede, had slowly walked, arm in arm with the cabdriver, up the steps to Victor's door.

When Victor tells her she has an exceptionally long life line, both of them laugh.

"My mother was buried one day short of her hundred and first birthday," Mrs. Novogrod says. "That was all very well and good for her, but to tell you the truth, there's such a thing as living too long."

"Maybe so," Victor acknowledges.

"I'm tired," Mrs. Novogrod says. "Sometimes I'm so tired I can't even read the newspaper. I stay in bed all day with the television playing, but that's only because Gemma — that's the woman my daughters pay to keep me company — loves those soap operas of hers. And if she happens to miss an episode, she calls one of those nine hundred numbers, a soap opera hot-line, they call it, and they fill her in on whatever she needs to know. She's an ignorant woman, this Gemma, she can barely read or write, and she doesn't know her numbers very well. 'Shame on you,' I tell her, 'a grown woman and you can't even pick up a *TV Guide* to see what's playing.' I'm going to leave her a little money when I go, and I want her to use it to hire a tutor for herself, but I know she won't."

"How about some tea?" Victor suggests.

"Thank you kindly, but I'm too tired to lift the cup to my mouth. It was such an effort getting here, you know. I came all the way from Riverside Drive in the cab. There was so much traffic, I must have been in that backseat for almost an hour. Not a comfortable ride, I'll tell you that. The driver was an Indian, I think, and he told me all about his daughter, the doctor he's so proud of. She works in the emergency room somewhere in the city, I can't remember where, and I had to hear all the terrible stories about the gunshot victims and the stabbing victims and all the rest of it, and finally I said, 'Mr. Cabdriver, sir,' — because I didn't quite catch his name — 'you're tiring me out with all these sad and terrible stories, so I'm just going to sit back here and close my eyes and rest.' And he didn't say another word after that, but I could tell that he took it very personally, that he was insulted I didn't want to hear more about his daughter and her work. I gave him a nice big tip to make up for it, and he barely thanked me, and that was that."

"Sometimes it's hard to listen," Victor says. "I know."

Mrs. Novogrod purses her thin pale lips. "I wish I weren't afraid to die," she confides. "I'm like that Old Man River song, tired of living and scared of dying. I've outlived a son and two husbands, and some days it's very bad. I lie there in bed at one o'clock in the afternoon and think of the ones I've lost and it's just too much. It's been thirty-two years since I lost my child, and sometimes it seems like yesterday that I was sitting at the kitchen table drinking my coffee and the call comes from my daughter-in-law that his appendix had burst, and there she is a widow, like me. He was such a smart young man, an economics professor at Cornell University. I held the phone in my hand for a long time after my daughter-in-law hung up — I was in shock, I suppose. 'What?' I kept saying into the phone. 'What's this? What did you say to me?' I was angry because it was so unfair, and I'm still angry after all this time. And I'm still in mourning, because when you lose a child, the mourning is never complete. It goes on and on for as long as you live. He'd be a senior citizen today, my son, isn't that something?"

"Arthur," Victor says. "He was a chess player; he did very well in the tournaments."

Mrs. Novogrod nods calmly; she doesn't seem at all impressed by Victor's knowledge of this. "He could have been another Bobby Fischer, but he gave it up when he was sixteen, who knows why. He just didn't want to play anymore." Looking into Victor's eyes, Mrs. Novogrod says, "It's clear you're a very smart man yourself, Mr. Mackenzie. Have you found my son for me?"

"He's gone," Victor says. "I was aware of his presence, but he's gone now."

"He didn't even want to talk to me for a minute?"

"I'm sorry."

"Can't you bring him back?"

"I'm truly sorry," Victor says. "He's a little worried about someone named Lois, that's basically all I know."

"That's my older daughter," Mrs. Novogrod says coolly. "I don't wish to discuss her."

"He's worried that she's taking too much vitamin E and not enough beta-carotene. And there's also something about a television set."

"He came all the way here to talk about vitamins and a television set? Doesn't he want to let me know how much he misses me?"

Victor considers the possibility of lying, which he's done in only the rarest of circumstances and nearly always regretted. He clears his throat, preparing to offer Mrs. Novogrod exactly what she wants to hear, but then she saves him the trouble.

"Of course he misses me," she says. "That's obvious. I suppose he didn't want to waste time on the obvious."

"Absolutely," Victor agrees, relieved that he's been let off the hook.

"Now, could you write down the information about the vitamins for me? My short-term memory isn't what it used to be. When you get to be my age, you're lucky if you remember how to put one foot in front of the other to get from here to there and back again."

"It won't be long," Victor murmurs.

"Speak clearly," says Mrs. Novogrod. "My hearing is still good, so I know you must be mumbling."

"I was saying that some doctors believe strongly in the importance of vitamins. But not all. Some of them refuse to commit themselves on the subject."

"Well, these vitamins may be fine for my daughter, but they can't be of much help to me. Since of course I'm not going to be around much longer."

"You're not?" Victor asks, as if this were a surprise to him.

Mrs. Novogrod looks at him darkly through her bifocals. "What kind of a clairvoyant are you, anyway? Not a dishonest one, I hope."

"Not everyone needs or wants to know the truth. For those who don't, I hold back a little."

"Don't waste my time, Mr. Macintosh."

"Just call me Victor."

"Oh, but that wouldn't be right. We hardly know each other."

"I *do* know you," Victor insists. "I know you've traveled all over the world. You've been to Russia and Japan; your last trip was a cruise to Alaska. You've written books and —"

"Only two, and no one would publish them."

"Well, maybe they will. And one of your husbands was in the fashion business and the other sold fruit, was it?"

"You make it sound like he had a pushcart on the street," Mrs. Novogrod snaps. "He was an importer — he sold to all the cruise ships and made a small fortune. He happened to have been a very refined gentleman."

"And most recently," Victor continues, "you've been hanging up on your daughter Lois every time she calls. It has something to do with a television set?" Smiling, he shakes his head. "I assume that's the TV your son was worried about."

"Don't laugh, because it's not one bit funny. This daughter of mine bought me a new television even though the old one wasn't too bad at all. Well, it had a few problems, but I wasn't going to pay $187.50 to have it fixed. So Lois bought me a new one, after I specifically told her not to, and then tried to stick me with the bill, which was $399.00 plus tax. Actually, she put it on her credit card, and now she expects me to reimburse her, which of course I refuse to do, because what do I need a brand-new television set for when I won't even be here to enjoy it?"

"You want her to remember you lovingly, don't you?"

"Frankly, I don't care one way or the other, Victor."

"I'm afraid I don't believe that."

"Well, Lois says she'll stop asking for the money if I apologize. For what, I'd like to know. I told her not to buy the damn television but she went ahead and did it and that's her folly. And anyway, I don't apologize to anyone. I never have, and that's the way it's always been."

Victor covers her hand with his own. ''When you pass on," he promises in a near-whisper, "she'll be at your side. She'll be getting out of the shower at someone's house — I don't know whose — when the call comes, and the back of the blouse she puts on will be wringing wet because she won't even take the time to dry off before she rushes out. It's her voice that you'll

hear just before you pass over to the other side, her hand that
will be in yours. Whether you apologize or not, that's the way it
will be."

"Are you sure?"

"It's what I see," Victor says. "Whether you apologize or not,
her voice will be the last that you'll hear."

"Why do you think I'm so afraid?" Mrs. Novogrod asks tearfully.

"Of apologizing?"

"Of leaving this earth, Victor." From the pocket of her dress,
she pulls out a handkerchief and a dispenser of Tic-tacs.
Silently she hands a couple to Victor and takes one for herself.
"My children and grandchildren aren't much interested in
me, the men who loved me are gone, I'm too tired to take pleasure in anything, really, but I still want to stay. It's puzzling,
isn't it?"

"Not at all," Victor says.

"My life doesn't seem worth holding on to, and yet somehow
it does."

"You'll be ready when the time comes," Victor says, "you'll
see."

Mrs. Novogrod doesn't seem reassured. She takes off her
glasses and blots her eyes with the folded-up handkerchief.
"Every morning, the moment I wake up, I find myself wondering if today's my last day on earth. Sometimes I'm almost sure
it is, and then there I am the next morning, wondering the
same thing all over again. Maybe if I were a religious woman, it
would be easier for me."

"It's the television set," Victor says. "You won't be at peace
with yourself until you resolve that business with your daughter."

"I have nothing to apologize for," says Mrs. Novogrod, gently sliding her glasses back on, using the fingertips of both
hands, exhibiting a daintiness that Victor finds touching.

Then her lips are pursed again, her steel gray brows drawn together in exasperation.

"Apologize anyway."

"I've never done it; I wouldn't know how."

"Let's practice," Victor urges. "'I'm sorry, Lois,' you say. 'I know you were only trying to be helpful, and I wish I'd been more gracious.'"

"I'm sorry, Lois," Mrs. Novogrod says, completely deadpan.

"You can do better than that."

"I can't."

"Sure you can. Make the effort. Put some emotion into it."

"Haven't I finally earned the right not to have to do anything I don't want to do?"

"Do it for Arthur, then, so he'll stop worrying."

"I could do *that*," Mrs. Novogrod says, brightening. "I could say, 'Lois, I'm doing this only because Arthur wants me to, not because of you, don't flatter yourself. If it's so important that even Arthur's worrying about it, I'll swallow my pride right now and admit that the new TV is a whole lot better than the old one and that it was very nice of you to go all the way over to Macy's and pick one out for me even though I specifically told you not to waste your time.'" Helping herself to another Tic-tac, she says, "How's that, Victor?"

"Better, but it still needs work."

"You're awfully hard to please," Mrs. Novogrod contends, as the papillons begin barking frantically from the living room chairs where they've been lounging. There's a banging at the front door now, a rude, impatient pounding that Victor would like to ignore, along with the bad news he suspects will accompany it.

"Do you *mind*?" he shouts at the dogs.

"If you're going to answer the door," Mrs. Novogrod says, "you'll have to tell your visitor to come back later. My hour's not up yet, and he'll just have to wait his turn."

"You bet he will," Victor says, and then, "I'll be right back." Opening the door, he finds himself staring at a bulky, red-headed man in a beautiful dark suit, a rolled up newspaper under his arm. The stranger takes the newspaper and points it at Victor in a decidedly unfriendly way. "Are you Victor Mackenzie?" he says, as if he were accusing him of something unspeakable.

"Do you have a search warrant?" Victor says.

"Nope, but I do have a bone to pick with you. Are you going to let me in or what?"

"That all depends on who the hell you are."

"Sorry," the man says. "I thought that someone with such great psychic gifts would have recognized me in an instant, but obviously I was wrong."

"Oh, you're one of those. Get lost, will you," Victor says, and starts to close the door.

Yanking the door back open, stepping over the threshold, the man says, "I'm Parker Allen."

"You'll have to give me a little more than that," Victor says, puzzled.

"What more can I tell you? I want you to stay out of my girl-friend's life, you asshole."

"And that would be Katha?" Victor says. "Of course. A lovely woman with unfortunate taste in men." He conjures up, as he has so often, that kiss, her glorious hair, the heat of that odd, exciting first encounter. He has been waiting to hear from her, hoping for the sound of her voice, the sight of her standing shyly at his doorstep, nervously pushing her hair from her face as she apologizes for insulting him, diminishing him, unintentionally or not.

"You smug bastard," Parker says. "Where the hell do you think you're going?"

Striding through the parlor and into the dining room where Mrs. Novogrod is waiting, Victor says, over his shoulder, "Back to work. And incidentally, how dare you interrupt me while I'm in the middle of a consultation. If you want to talk to me, you'll have to wait out in the hallway until I'm done."

"This can't wait," Parker says, and follows closely behind.

"I thought you'd forgotten all about me," says Mrs. Novogrod plaintively. "And who's *this* dapper gentleman?" she asks. "That's a lovely suit you're wearing, sir," she tells Parker. "That's a very fine wool, isn't it? The top of the line, I'd say. My first husband was in the business, so I know all about it."

"It's the top of the line, all right," Parker says. "You have a very discerning eye."

"Thank you," says Mrs. Novogrod. "Flattery will almost always get you everywhere, you know. Now tell me, whoever you are —"

"Parker Allen. And it's a pleasure to meet you."

Mrs. Novogrod smiles coyly. "Tell me, Mr. Allen, do you believe in apologizing when you know in your heart of hearts that it's the other party who should be offering the apology? I don't, personally, but Mr. Mackenzie here thinks otherwise."

"I think it's important for you to know," Victor says, "that you're talking to a man who has a lot to apologize for."

"Really?" asks Mrs. Novogrod. "And he looks like such a gentleman. What's he done?"

"What's he done? Let's see," Victor says. "Well, to begin with, he helped ruin the marriage of someone closely related to him, a brother, I believe, or maybe even a twin brother. And then he betrayed an exceptionally lovely woman not once but many times over."

Parker's well-scrubbed, pink-cheeked face glows red. "Shut up, you miserable shit," he says and, lunging forward, slugs Victor in the stomach. Mrs. Novogrod lets out a shriek. The papillons bark in unison; the cockatiels scold disapprovingly in their cage; the kissing gouramis plunge to the bottom of the fish tank in confusion. Victor is on the floor, his arms wrapped around his middle; the pain, initially shocking and worse than he could have imagined, has already begun to subside a bit, so he forces himself up until he is standing face to face with Parker.

His arms are still pressed against his waist, and he's breathing arduously. "You're playing a dangerous game, my friend," he says.

"I'm not your friend," says Parker.

"That's right, you're not."

"Maybe we should call the police," Mrs. Novogrod suggests. "And if there's going to be any more violence, I'd like to pay my bill and go home."

"I'm sorry you had to witness that," Parker says. "But a man can be pushed only so far."

"Don't forget that goes for women too," says Mrs. Novogrod. "No one's ever treated me disrespectfully and gotten away with it. My husbands could both attest to that, if only they were still among the living. They were both faithful to me, thank God. And if they weren't, at least they were discreet about it. Discretion is nine-tenths of the law, as they say."

"And if it's not, it should be," Victor says, smiling. He's never been slugged like this before, he realizes, and has the feeling that this is a first for Parker too.

"So, did you enjoy it?" he asks, eyeing Parker curiously.

"Enjoy what?"

"Hitting me."

Parker is busy fiddling with his gold watch, shifting it back and forth on his wrist. "It was pretty satisfying, actually." He shakes his head at Victor, saying, "I didn't mean to hurt you."

"It hurts like hell."

"Look, I'm sorry," Parker says. "You're the first guy I've hit since . . . junior high, when I beat up Angelo Sermonetta in the boys' locker room for stealing my baseball glove. It was a great moment for me, even though I got suspended for two days and it went on my permanent record."

Victor nods. "Uh-huh, uh-huh. You're lying."

"I am *not*," Parker says indignantly. "The guy was on the football team and built like a tank. No one could believe it when they saw me go after him. I was no match for him, but somehow that day I was."

"In your dreams," Victor says.

"What?"

"You may have dreamed about beating him up, but that's about the size of it."

Hanging his head, Parker says, "That glove was my prized possession. I took such good care of it — I actually rubbed it with a stick of margarine every night all season to soften it up. I wouldn't even let my brother near it. It was mine — I bought it myself with money I'd saved up for months and months. And then that prick Angelo Sermonetta broke into my locker and took it. And there was no way I could get it back without getting my head crushed."

"That's a very sad story," says Mrs. Novogrod. "I'm exhausted just listening to it. If one of you gentlemen would be so kind as to find me a cab, I'll go home and put myself straight to bed."

"I still owe you a little time," Victor says.

"Give it to Mr. Parker," she says, as Victor helps her to her feet. "He needs it more than I do."

Easing her into a taxi on the street, Victor tries to make her promise to call her daughter.

"I will or I won't," she says. "But we all know you can't teach an old dog new tricks."

"No one's so old that he can't be taught something," Victor says, and watches as the cab pulls away from the curb and vanishes around the corner. He sighs, massaging his stomach with both hands.

In the living room, Parker holds up his palm for inspection. "Want to give me a reading?"

"Forget it."

"I've got a blank check on me."

"I don't like you," Victor says flatly. "And that's that."

"I'll register a complaint with the Better Business Bureau. Even better, I'll get the IRS in here."

"Be my guest," Victor says.

"You're a fraud and a crackpot," Parker says. "All you guys are frauds."

Victor grabs Parker's hand. There's no time to find what he's looking for there in his palm. But the vision that comes to him is just as helpful for Victor's purposes. "I wouldn't be making any car trips to New Jersey or Connecticut if I were you," he says darkly. "I see serious damage to that car you love so much. On the driver's side. About six or seven thousand dollars' worth, I'd say. Possibly more."

"Oh God," Parker says, anguished, "not the BMW. Look, can you give me a time frame here? Are we talking about tomorrow? Next week? Next month?"

Releasing Parker's hand, Victor says, "Consider yourself warned, that's all I can tell you. Be careful."

"Well, thanks," says Parker. "I appreciate it."

Victor nods. "What do you think, am I a fraud or not?"

"I'm not taking any chances with my car, that's for sure." Parker leaves in a daze, without another word, lingering on the street for a while, looking up at the hazy sky with his hand at the back of his neck, his mouth hanging open slightly. Victor spies from his window, peeks through the slats of silver Levolors; he can't help feeling triumphant, despite the ache deep within his stomach and another, more oppressive ache floating somewhere above his chest. Silently, he wishes Mrs. Novogrod a speedy, painless departure from this life. Her fears are his own, of not wanting to take leave when his time has come. At least Mrs. Novogrod will have her daughter at her side. If *he* fell into a coma tomorrow, who would he have watching over him? Who would turn pale with grief as he drifted toward death? Of all the women who have come and gone in his life, there's not one he can still count on for anything. It's true that women have fallen for him easily enough, but they've always been the wrong women. Women who wanted too much from him or not enough. He considers why he hasn't called Katha again; like a fool, he supposes, he'd been expecting her and her apology, as if at just the right moment she'd appear and they'd connect again, effortlessly. He listens to himself laugh out loud, hurting his bruised stomach, as he thinks of the good fortune that brought Parker to his door.

A story to tell his children someday: *Your mother's boyfriend socked me right in the guts, which was exactly what I needed to get me moving, really. And the rest, as you know, is history.*

Or, more likely, fantasy.

He finds her number and calls with a lollipop jammed into a corner of his mouth, a substitute for the cigarettes he once smoked endlessly. The answering machine comes on immediately; it's Parker's voice. Hanging up, he bites down on the lollipop so hard that it splits in two.

He calls again, unsuccessfully, between clients, and then again around dinnertime.

Saying only the single word "yes?" she sounds nettled, as if he's caught her at just the wrong moment.

"It's Victor Mackenzie," he says. "You know, the one who's not in the habit of leaping before he's taken a good long look?"

"You never called me," she complains.

"As I see it, you're the one who was supposed to call me to apologize."

"*What?*"

"It doesn't matter anymore," he says impatiently. "Look, I'm calling to tell you your friend Parker punched me in the stomach today. But rest assured I came through beautifully."

Her voice freezes over. "That's not a particularly funny joke."

"It's no joke, especially since I was with a client at the time.

An old lady, who, incidentally, was a real admirer of Parker's good taste in clothing."

"I can't believe this!" Katha cries. "I'm sick just listening to this."

"Well, it could have been worse — he could have given me a black eye or a broken wing. Instead he went straight for my guts."

"Ironically, he was supposed to be on his best behavior for the rest of his life."

"Well, he blew it.'"

"*He* may have, but you didn't," Katha says. "He'd been a busy boy behind my back, just as you said. I almost called you, in fact, to let you know you'd been right on target. I'm so impressed, really."

"Don't be," Victor says. "It wasn't difficult to see — any clairvoyant out looking would have caught it."

"Speaking as a mere mortal previously blinded by false hopes, please accept my gratitude."

"We're all mere mortals," says Victor. "Every last one of us."

"OK," Katha concedes, and then sighs. "Do you know what I'm doing right now? I'm cooking chicken in butter sauce with shallots," she says, "for a man who deserves to go to bed hungry tonight."

"And I'm having tuna fish on a hamburger bun," Victor says, oozing self-pity. "A stale hamburger bun, to be precise."

"Do yourself a favor and throw it out. I'm coming over with my chicken," Katha says and then she hangs up.

She arrives with her daughter and several fragrant packages wrapped in aluminum foil. The three of them dine outdoors in his fenced-in backyard; on the glass-topped wrought-iron table, Victor arranges a pair of tapered candles and a vase of bright yellow forsythia. From time to time, one of the dogs appears at the window, its face held yearningly against the glass.

"What's new in third grade?" Victor asks Julia, a diminutive nine-year-old who sits sideways on her chair, as if she's about to take off at any moment.

"A boy in my class tried to choke me while I was eating lunch today," she says casually. "He came up behind me and put his hands around my neck and squeezed really hard. He thought I stole his lunch box, but why would I do that?"

"Why didn't you tell me?" Katha asks, leaning forward to examine Julia's neck in the candlelight. "Who was it, sweetie?"

"Stefan." Julia shrugs. "There were red marks on my neck, but then they went away. Mrs. Kirkpatrick screamed at him and sent him to the office, and he stayed there for the rest of the day. Stefan gets child abuse, you know."

"He's abused at home, you mean?" Katha frowns. "Well, that's pretty awful."

"Yup, and he has one blue eye and one brown one."

"You have to tell me these things," Katha says, stroking the crook of Julia's arm. "You have to let me know what's going on."

"What for? I'm fine."

"Because a mother always has to know everything."

"Well, did you know I'm writing a script for *Seinfeld*? It's about lesbians."

Victor isn't sure if it's all right to laugh, but he can't help himself. "Can I read it?" he asks.

"It's a big mess," Julia admits. "I have pretty terrible handwriting, especially when I'm writing really fast."

"I *knew* you were a writer," Victor says. "I told your mother that, before I even met you."

"Some of my stories aren't very good," Julia says. "But the script for *Seinfeld* is going to be great. And you know what, the word for *lesbian* is almost the same in Spanish. It's *lesbiana*."

"Where'd you learn that?" Victor asks her.

"On the subway, of course. They had a poster in Spanish and

in English that said if your lesbian girlfriend is hitting you, you should call this number for help."

"I guess you don't spend much time playing with Barbie dolls, do you?"

"Hate 'em," Julia says. "And anyway, I'm too busy."

Katha wipes away the shine of butter sauce from her daughter's lips. "Why the sudden interest in lesbians?" she asks.

"I don't know, I saw it in the subway."

"So what were *you* up to in third grade?" Victor asks Katha. "Writing scripts for *Howdy Doody*?"

"I was sitting at the kitchen table doing endless rows of long division, if I recall correctly. And mooning over Dr. Kildare, probably."

"What, no fantasizing about being a major league baseball player?"

"None whatsoever."

Victor swiftly passes the tip of his index finger back and forth through the flame of the candle. "I was in third grade when I saw my first ghost," he says.

"Cool!" says Julia. "Were you, like, so scared?"

Shaking his head, Victor responds, "It was someone I knew, a man who'd always been nice to me. Maybe that's why I wasn't frightened."

"Well, that makes perfect sense," Katha says coldly.

"Is there a skeptic in our midst?" Victor says. He's hurt by her distrust, by the ease with which she dismisses him. It's going to take some doing, he knows, to bring her around. If he ever can. "Don't disappoint me," he says. "Don't close yourself off to all the things there are to see out there."

"I don't want to see them," Katha says. "I have a hard enough time seeing what's right in front of me."

"Would you prefer that I change the subject?"

"What was the ghost wearing?" Julia asks. "Was his face all white but with a tiny bit of green?"

"He was in his pajamas. Which I guess was what he'd been wearing when he died in his sleep that night. And I don't remember his face, except that he gave me a little smile before he disappeared."

Julia's dark eyes are luminous in the candlelight. "You are so lucky," she says. "And I'm so jealous. If you were my friend in school, I'd invite you over every day and make you tell me about the ghost a hundred or a thousand times."

The pleasure he takes in her enthusiasm is enormous; he tries not to look at Katha, who's leaning away from him, one side of her face sunk into her palm, as if she has a toothache.

"I used to lie in bed waiting for him," he tells Julia, "but I never saw him again. He owned the one candy store in town, and after he died, it was never the same. The Hershey's bars weren't as smooth and sweet, the bubble gum was stale and harder to chew, the Life Savers cracked as soon as you put them into your mouth. Maybe I was the only one who noticed — my friends never mentioned it. We went there after school every day and bought the same stuff we always had, but it just wasn't the same. Once Murray was gone, his brother ran the store. He yelled at us for hanging around and for looking over the comic books and the *Mad* magazines, which we loved to do. 'This isn't the goddamn public library, boys,' he said. 'If you want to read, that's where you belong.'"

"Murray would never have been mean like that," Julia says. "He would never have made you feel so bad."

"I would have given anything to see him again. There were quite a few things I wanted to tell him."

"You wanted to complain," Julia says. "Maybe that's why he never came back."

"Sounds good to me," says Katha, speaking up at last. "Not a bad theory."

"Not bad at all," Victor says. "And the chicken was just wonderful."

"You're welcome," says Katha.

Tentatively, Victor begins to caress her hair. "So, will you cook for me every night?"

"Where'd you get that idea?"

"Close your eyes and imagine it," Victor instructs her. "You can make as big a mess as you need to in my kitchen, and I'll clean up every bit of it while you sit around relaxing or checking Julia's long division."

"We're doing fractions now," Julia says. "The lowest common denominator and all that stuff."

"You'll never have to scour a sink again. That's my department," Victor says. "And the spaces between all the dials on the stove? I'm the one who'll be in charge of keeping them grease-free."

"Was it after Parker punched you or before that he told you what an inferior housekeeper I am?"

"No one told me anything," Victor says. He passes his finger in and out of the flame again. "But you shouldn't let him make you crazy about things like that."

"Could you love someone who cleans the soles of his shoes every night with bleach?" Katha asks. "Or would you have to be crazy to love someone like that?"

"Don't ask questions you already know the answers to."

"Can I go inside and play with the dogs?" Julia inquires.

"Sure you can," Victor says. "And by the way, you can always ask me anything."

"What about me?" Katha says.

"You're a different case altogether," Victor says, and moves to kiss her as Julia opens the back door and slips inside the house. The kiss goes on and on, long enough for Victor to feel as if love is somehow within reach. In the yard behind them, a neighbor steps out, smoking a pipe. He's speaking to someone animatedly, saying, "I *told* you she was fucked up beyond belief, didn't I?" The smoke drifting across the fence is sweetly scented, the sky overhead cloudless, showing off a perfect slice of moon and silvery white stars. Victor's fingers travel the curve of Katha's ear to the soft flesh of her lobe, where a small gold heart dangles from a wire. His hand continues down the side of her neck into the V of her T-shirt.

"What are you doing?" she says, but gently.

"Trespassing," he says, and withdraws his hand, tucking it safely behind his back.

"I left a note for Parker," Katha says. "I told him we were at the movies."

"We?" he asks, as if, absurdly, he were included as well.

"Julia and I. He'll know it's a lie because I'd never take her anywhere like that on a school night."

Victor is silent. What he remembers most clearly of Parker is that stricken look when he heard his car was in danger. Oddly, he thinks, Parker hadn't even asked about his own safety. Or Katha's.

"Don't ride anywhere in his car with him," he says now. "It might be dangerous."

"He's going to be in an accident?"

"It looks that way. An expensive fender bender, probably."

"Probably? What good is 'probably'?"

"Look, it's not as if I saw an ambulance and lots of flashing lights, I only saw a car colliding with something that looked like a fire hydrant. I told Parker to be careful, and I'm sure he will."

"He didn't laugh at you?"

"He was pretty shaken, actually."

"How can you stand knowing these things?" Katha cries. "How can you live like this? How can it be anything other than a burden?"

"A burden?" Victor says. "It's a gift that sometimes may seem like a burden, but it's still a gift. Think of that client of mine with breast cancer. She had to work hard to convince a doctor that there was actually a tumor there, but they finally found it and she got the treatment she needed. Of course I wish I'd been wrong, but it was the greatest luck that she came to me when she did, wasn't it?"

"Of course," says Katha. "But every time you see disaster approaching someone else's life, don't you want to weep for them?"

"Sometimes, but I've got to maintain a professional distance. If I can't, and I'm overwhelmed, it's just no good for anyone."

"If it were me," Katha says, "I'd turn my back on the whole business and pretend I was just like everyone else, that all I knew was that darkness would fall at the end of every day and that the sky would lighten again in the morning."

"You don't think you'd find it hard to be so selfish?"

"Everyone has instincts to protect themselves. It's not selfishness, it's self-preservation," says Katha.

Giving her a half-smile, Victor says, "You *are* a little afraid of me, even though you say you're not."

Katha gnaws at the side of her finger; she looks up at him for an instant, then turns away. "Well, you know, it's just that I'm utterly mystified."

"Don't be afraid," Victor says as she leans against him and their arms fall in a tangle around each other. "I'll never tell you more than you want to know."

That night he dreams he is back in his childhood bed, with Katha lying beside him. They are two grown-ups clinging to each other in a narrow twin bed as the ghost of Murray Weinbaum appears, dressed in his plaid pajamas.

Say hello to Murray, Victor urges Katha.

I don't talk to ghosts, says Katha. I just don't.

But this is Murray! Victor says. I haven't seen him in more than thirty years.

I don't care if he's John Lennon himself, Katha says, rolling over and turning her back to Victor. If he's not made of flesh and blood, I have nothing to say to him.

How can you be so rude? Victor asks. What's wrong with you?

Don't worry about me, I'm used to it, Murray says. You wouldn't believe the things my own son says to me.

I'm sorry, Victor says.

Murray holds up his hand in protest. Don't be sorry, he says. It's too soon, that's all.

Too soon for what?

See you around, Murray says.

Awakening, Victor opens his eyes to the sight of Murray hovering above him, his bare feet fluttering, as if he were treading water.

"You still in those pajamas?" Victor asks, more astonished at the pajamas than at the sight of Murray himself. And he has no idea if he's speaking aloud or if it's just Murray reading his mind.

Murray shrugs his shoulders in response.

"I was talking about you tonight at dinner," Victor says, raising himself up on his elbows. "And just now I was dreaming about you. But of course you know that, don't you."

"Your mother and father think it's still not too late for you to go to medical school," Murray reports. His voice, in Victor's head, is absolutely soundless, a mere ghost of a voice.

"My father's never visited me, you know, since he passed away. And I haven't heard from my mother in months. Which is probably all for the best. What are you, anyway, their messenger boy?"

"You sound awfully cranky, Victor."

"I'm too old to be getting career counseling from my parents, don't you think?"

"That's not for me to say, buddy."

"And besides, I already have a career I'm committed to."

"According to your parents, you're capable of better."

"So I'm still something of an embarrassment to them, what else is new?"

"I hate to see you this way, buddy."

"What way?"

"Well, you don't seem very happy to see me."

"I'm delighted to see you," Victor says. "I just wish we didn't have to talk about *me*."

"Your mother, especially, would love to see some grandchildren, you know."

"See, that's exactly the kind of thing I don't need to hear. Can't we talk about the old candy store?"

"My brother burned it to the ground for the insurance money years ago," Murray says. "What's to talk about?"

"Damn," Victor groans. "Did he get caught?"

"Nope. He took the money and bought a condo in Florida right on the golf course."

"He spoiled everything after you were gone, you know."

"I don't want to hear about it," Murray says. He crosses his arms behind his head and floats on his back, as if he were relaxing in a pool. "So will you give it some thought, at least?"

"What?"

"What your parents suggested, medical school and all that."

"Absolutely not," Victor says. "And you can tell them I resent the implication."

"In that case," Murray says, "good-bye and good luck." And turning to glittery dust, a lovely metallic confetti, he vanishes.

Victor punches his pillow, exasperated. He hates knowing that his parents still haven't given up on him, that even now, years after they've been gone, they're capable of making him feel their disappointment. After college he'd gotten a little work as an actor and then done lucrative voice-overs for radio and television commercials, which had pleased his mother but not his father, who wouldn't even make the effort to run to the

TV to hear Victor's voice hawking diet soda and cat food, antidotes to dishpan hands and sour stomach. He never understood what all the fuss was about, Hank claimed; the thrill that Lila felt hearing her son's voice broadcast out into the world eluded him. He'd begged Victor to go back to school and take some premed courses. To devote his life to something worthwhile. And when Victor had saved up enough money to go into business for himself as a clairvoyant, as he'd been planning all along, Lila seemed almost as bewildered and disenchanted as his father. This can't be the way a person actually earns a living, she said. A summa cum laude graduate of Columbia University, no less? She sent him clients, though, friends she had in the city, and friends of friends, and nearly every one of them offered glowing, admiring reports, from which Lila took some small solace. There was no comfort for his father in Victor's success, only embarrassment and disbelief. But if Victor hadn't earned his father's respect, at least he had his love. Which was surely worth something, his father had reminded him.

"Surely," Victor says out loud.

He tries to fall back to sleep, but it's hopeless, he soon realizes. He makes his way downstairs in the dark and goes straight to the refrigerator. Careful not to wake the dogs, he fixes himself a chocolate egg cream, one of Murray's specialties. Syrup dribbles from the countertop down the silverware drawer and onto the floor. He observes this with interest, too tired to clean it up, too exhausted to enjoy his perfect egg cream.

If he doesn't see another ghost until the time he becomes one himself, it would suit him just fine.

8

OVEN MITT IN HAND, attending to a half-dozen hamburgers smoking on the gas grill, Lucy waves a red plastic spatula in Buddy's direction. He and the boys, along with a couple of the neighbors' kids, are in the pool, two teams tossing an orange Nerf Ball back and forth, shrieks of pleasure punctuating their game. From where she stands on the deck, she can see the swirl of flattened curls on Buddy's chest, the sun on his shoulders, his hand sweeping over the long, wet flap of hair that has fallen into his eyes. His voice, so much more powerful than any of the boys', cries "point!" while his arms rise over his head in triumph as he catches the ball. Everything, Lucy notes with satisfaction, is as it should be. The sun is high in an aqua-blue sky, the backyard grass is a rich, healthy green, the round, white table with a striped umbrella blossoming from its center is crowded with bottles and jars of speckled mustard, rust-colored barbecue sauce, bright ketchup. The ice cubes dumped into a deep aluminum bowl have not yet begun to melt, the pile of paper napkins patterned with an assortment of hockey uniforms sits undisturbed by the faintest of breezes.

"Anyone waiting for a rare, medium, or well-done burger, come and pick up your order right now!" Lucy calls, hanging over the deck's railing, signaling energetically with her spatula.

"How's my soy burger?" Max asks.

"As well as can be expected, kiddo."

"If you loved me," he yells over the water, "you'd throw me a can of Coke so I could drink it right here in the pool."

"Fat chance." She walks to the pool and hands out towels as everyone except Max hoists himself over the ledge and onto the concrete deck.

"What exactly are you saying?"

"No eating or drinking in or around the pool, that's what I'm saying."

"You ever hear of hoping against hope?"

"If you're not at the table in the next sixty seconds, I'm sending your ugly little soy burger straight to vegetarian heaven."

"I hear you," Max says and climbs out of the water.

After lunch the boys retreat to the pool, drifting on floats or practicing their dives. Jonah sunbathes alone on the trampoline, flat on his stomach. On the tennis court belonging to the neighbors, a little girl in a bikini serves a bucketful of balls into the net. Lucy contemplates going for a swim later, when the boys have cleared out and she can have the pool to herself. She stacks the remaining paper plates and drops them into a trash bag, screws the lids onto jars and bottles, collects crumpled napkins and soiled silverware.

Buddy sits at the table watching her, his eyes hidden behind mirrored sunglasses. "You ever fantasize about selling the house, moving to some quaint town in the middle of nowhere?" he says.

Sinking into a chair made of ropes of white vinyl, Lucy curls her bare toes around the warm aluminum bar at the bottom. "Can't say that I have."

"Well," Buddy tells her, "there I am in the city in the middle of probing around in a patient's mouth, and you know what I'm thinking? I'm imagining some stone cottage on a lake in Vermont or New Hampshire, someplace lovely and quiet, as far away from my office, as far away from here, as I can possibly be."

Lucy asks, trying hard to keep her voice from sounding anything other than reasonably curious, "What would you have there, what do you expect to find there?"

"Something different than what we have here."

"Which is what?" she presses.

"Everything. We have everything, our kids have everything, but sometimes my heart is numbed by it all. I find myself feeling numb and anxious at the same time, if that's possible. I stand at the edge of the soccer field with all the other parents, watching the boys play every Saturday, I take them to Roy Rogers for lunch afterward, and to the mall so they can buy yet another CD, another Super Nintendo cartridge, another T-shirt with Pearl Jam lyrics on the back, another baseball hat to add to their collection. And then Saturday night there's Chinese food for dinner, breakfast at the diner every Sunday, and Monday morning I'm back prowling around in someone's mouth."

"OK," Lucy says. "But what exactly is it that's wrong?" Little bubbles of panic rise from the depths of her middle all the way up through the back of her throat; she swallows hard, as if she could disperse them in a single, determined effort.

"I don't *know*," Buddy says.

"You do."

Still hiding behind his sunglasses, Buddy says, without any affect at all, "It's as if my self, whatever I am, is fading, thinning out, losing substance. Like a man becoming a ghost."

"I don't know what you mean," Lucy says. She knows that she should move toward him, take his hand, lean over and press his head against her shoulder, but all she wants is to keep her distance. And then, without warning, the muscles in her stomach contract sharply and she is out of her seat, rushing to shove aside the sliding glass door that leads to the kitchen. In a sink filled with plastic mugs and vegetable peelings, she vomits violently, her heart shuddering. Sweaty and tearful, she drinks straight from the faucet, remembering too late that even water might make her sicker.

She staggers up to her bedroom to sleep away the rest of the afternoon.

That night, after she and Buddy have made love, he clings to her with a fierceness that seems to have less to do with deeply felt affection than with fear.

I'm the worrier in this family, she wants to remind him. I'm the Jewish mother.

George Macklowe enters her dream uninvited, helping himself to a cup of coffee and sitting down at her kitchen table as casually as if he owned the place.

I don't mean to be rude, Lucy tells him, but I believe breaking and entering is still a crime in this state.

A man's home is his castle, is that it? George asks pleasantly.

Nodding, Lucy says, I love this house.

That's unfortunate, he says. Because there's bad karma in every room, as I'm sure you've already figured out. So there's nothing to be gained and everything to lose for anyone who's foolish enough to hang around here. In other words, you can kiss your happiness good-bye, lady.

Enraged, Lucy knocks the coffee cup from his hand, watches the china splinter against the kitchen floor. That was my good china, she tells him.

George brushes away a shard thin as eggshell from the shelf of her shoulder.

And this is only the beginning, he announces.

*   *   *

Staring dumbstruck at the clock radio at her bedside, unable to believe that everyone in the house is still sleeping soundly, Lucy lets out a scream as piercing as a siren.

"It's eight-oh-four!" she shrieks. Rudely, she yanks the pillow out from under Buddy's head. "What time is your first patient?"

"What? I don't know, eight forty-five, maybe," Buddy says, slipping the pillow back under his neck. He doesn't look particularly concerned; he looks, in fact, oddly serene.

"Get up!"

"Stop screaming," Buddy says. "It's not as if this is a disaster that's going to rock the world."

"There's no hope of getting the boys to school on time. And what about the patient who's going to be sitting around waiting for you?"

"Oh, it's only Mrs. Fishbein. She's got nothing better to do. She'll wait."

"Buddy!"

"All right, I'm calling the office right now and leaving a message on the answering machine."

"Damn straight you are."

Rousing the boys from their beds, shoving Pop-Tarts into the toaster oven for their breakfast, fixing their lunches like the most efficient of short-order cooks, she wonders at Buddy's utterly placid demeanor, the way his hands reached automatically for the pillow she'd pulled from him so frantically. But she doesn't have time to worry about him — a grown man perfectly capable of getting himself dressed and out of the house in record time.

"Eat your breakfast in the car," she tells her sons. "And don't forget to brush your teeth."

"If I brush my teeth before I eat," Max points out, "my breakfast will taste terrible."

"Just do it!" Lucy roars.

"Chill, Mom," says Max, backing away from her. "Jesus."

She's in the car with the engine running when she remembers the committee meeting for the school's spring fair, scheduled to begin in exactly fifteen minutes in the cafeteria. She wishes she had put on the slightest bit of makeup and something more presentable than sweatpants and a souvenir T-shirt from St. Martin. And she isn't sure if she washed her face or not, though she does remember rinsing her mouth with Listerine.

"God, I hate starting off the day like this."

"Any day that starts with school is a day I can do without," Max offers.

"Me too," says Jonah.

"Give me a break, will you," Lucy says, and lets them off at the circular drive in front of the building. She parks the car in back and smiles, as she enters the school, at the security guard seated inside the doorway.

"Don't worry about no hall passes," the guard says in a friendly way. "You think I don't know who you are by now?"

"Thanks."

Hurrying toward the cafeteria, Lucy brushes past a young woman, murmurs "Excuse me," and continues down the hallway for only a moment until the woman calls after her.

"Bonjour, Madame." It's Max's French teacher, who's smartly dressed in a short leather skirt, high heels, and a silk blouse. Instinctively hanging her head for the lecture she's about to hear, looking down at her toes, Lucy notices she's wearing two mismatched sneakers, one plain white, the other decorated with stars made of thickly woven silver thread.

"Bonjour, Mademoiselle."

Mlle. Charbonneau looks at her gloomily. "What are we going to do about Max?" she says in lightly accented English. "He's very bright, *bien sûr*, but there's no way around it — he's

got to sit down and memorize those irregular verb forms.
Sometimes it seems he can barely conjugate the regular ones,
the simplest ones. He's been making no effort at all lately, and
I don't know why."

"I'm sorry," Lucy says.

"*Moi aussi,* because he should be one of my best students. I
want to help him, you know, but he resists me. He doesn't want
my help — he'd rather just scrape by."

Lucy is close to tears. "But why?"

"Well, you know, the hormones are raging in these seventh
graders. We have to be understanding."

"But perhaps not too understanding."

"It's a delicate balance, oui?"

"Oui," Lucy agrees, and listens to the purposeful click of
high heels marching past her now on the shining linoleum
path. "Shit," she says, and stamps her plain white sneaker.
Her son will not come close to failing French or anything else,
because she simply won't allow it. And she knows what
he'll say when she delivers the bad news: *Why do you care when I
don't?*

She drags her feet to the cafeteria, where a group of well-
dressed mothers have spread themselves out along a row of
lunch tables, some of the women with equally well-dressed babies in their laps. They greet her warmly; she's a dependable
volunteer, someone they can count on to make four dozen
cupcakes at the last minute or two dozen phone calls begging
for contributions to whatever PTA fund needs replenishing.
They're overflowing with suggestions this morning, as enthusi-
astic as if each one of them were planning her daughter's wedding instead of the annual school fair.

Lucy is empty of ideas; she's too angry at Max and unnerved
by her mismatched sneakers to concentrate on the pros and
cons of hiring a hot dog cart or renting a cotton candy machine. She stares at a dark-faced baby with a shockingly bright

yellow pacifier plugged into his mouth. His mother, the only other black woman in the room, and one of the school's few black parents, has never been particularly friendly toward Lucy; she has, in fact, refused Lucy's invitations to join her for a cup of coffee or lunch. This can only be because of Buddy, she assumes and has decided that, in any case, the woman isn't worth pursuing. But she smiles at the baby, who smiles back so broadly that the pacifier pops out of his mouth and onto his plump little thighs.

The head of the committee is calling for a vote in favor of the cotton candy machine or against the hot dog cart, and Lucy raises her arm absently just as all the other arms go up.

"Make up your mind, Lucy," the chairwoman says. "It's either yes or no, you can't have it both ways."

"I can't?" Lucy says. She laughs along with the rest of them, though she can't imagine what it is that's so amusing.

Buddy is reading the newspaper, slouched in a chair at the kitchen table, when she arrives home. He's wearing boxer shorts and a V-necked undershirt, and there's a spot of raspberry jam lingering at his collar.

"Don't tell me," she says. She looks pointedly at her watch and then at the jam stain on his white shirt.

"I'm playing hooky," Buddy says. "I'm taking a mental health day."

"And may I ask why?"

"I'm entitled, I guess. And you don't have to look at me so disapprovingly."

"Wipe your mouth," Lucy says.

"Want to go back to bed with me? Take advantage of some unexpected free time together?"

"No thanks." She clears the table, stands at the sink with her back toward him. When, a few moments later, he sneaks up behind her and puts his hands on her shoulders, she flinches.

"What's with you?" Buddy asks.

"I've never been much for mental health days."

"Sorry you feel that way," Buddy says, sounding utterly unconvincing. On his way out of the room, he adds, "I guess I'm going back to bed for a while. See you whenever."

He gets up an hour later than usual the next morning and indulges in a leisurely shower that fills the bathroom with a thick, fragrant steam. Knocking against the frosted glass of the shower door, barely able to control her anger, Lucy says, "How about canceling that Beatles concert and hurrying up out of there?" She listens as he finishes his rendition of "Please Please Me" and starts on "Norwegian Wood."

She makes their bed, dusts their dressers with Buddy's pajama bottom, tosses it on the floor. She envisions herself throwing open the shower door and pulling Buddy out by the elbows, ignoring his protests and the spray of hot water in her face.

She hears the faucet being turned off and Buddy climbing out. She gives him a minute or two, then peeks in. There's a towel knotted at his waist and manicure scissors in his hand.

"What are you doing?" she says.

"Shocking though it may be, I'm about to cut my nails."

"Your nails are perfect," says Lucy. "And anyway, you're already an hour behind schedule."

"Relax," says Buddy. "I canceled my first couple of appointments."

Lucy seats herself in the doorway, holds on to the doorframe with both hands. "I don't understand," she says.

"Sure you do. I'm running late so I canceled a few appointments."

"It's two days in a row, that's what I don't understand."

"Apparently I'm not all that hot to get to work."

"Apparently."

Spraying a pure white cloud of shaving cream into his palm, applying it meticulously to both sides of his face, Buddy says, "Before you stopped teaching, before you decided you'd rather stay home and be with the kids, didn't you ever wake up in the morning and tell yourself, 'I just can't do this today'?"

"Well, I might have felt the urge, but I'd never indulge myself that way."

"There's the difference between us," Buddy says. "I'm a self-indulgent slacker and you're not." Taking the razor to his jaw-line, he clears a path through the shaving cream. "Simple, huh."

Through the skylight in the bathroom ceiling, Lucy can see the green leaves of an enormous oak tree surrounded by white sky. She remembers the hanged man, the figure dangling upside-down from a flimsy-looking sapling on one of Victor Mackenzie's tarot cards. She can hear Victor explaining, in his quiet voice, about sacrifice, the sacrifices she would have to make as long as the black cloud was overhead. The black cloud she could neither see nor feel. It cannot be, she thinks, that Victor was on to something that day, it cannot be that the future he revealed to her was anything more than a fantasy he'd conjured up as easily as any gifted storyteller. Some things simply cannot be; surely she is smart enough to know this. So she ignores the hackles that have risen all along her spine and looks away from the skylight and back toward her husband.

"The thing is," she tells him reasonably, "the thing is that you have a family depending on you."

Buddy stares at himself in the mirror, checking for any stray whiskers he may have left behind. "Tell me about it," he says, and she understands that of course he does not have to be told, of course he will not disappoint her.

"I love you," she says gratefully.

"Let's hope so," he says, and shakes out the razor, scattering tiny blue-black hairs everywhere in the sink.

*　　*　　*

When, a few days later, he calls from work, interrupting her lunch, she takes the magazine she is reading and shoots it sharply across the kitchen table.

"Am I glad you called," she says. "This article I've been reading was making me sick. Literally." She waits for Buddy to ask for further details, and when he doesn't, she fills him in anyway. "It was all about an execution by lethal injection in a Texas prison, and what really made me queasy was that this particular prisoner was so eagerly looking forward to his meeting with Jesus that he could barely wait for the moment of his death. Can you believe it?" The absolute silence at the other end puzzles her; at first she thinks there is something wrong with the line. "Buddy?" she says. Now she hears something that sounds like a deep, poignant sigh. "What's going on, Buddy?" she asks. "Are you there or not?"

"I'm nothing," Buddy says in the faintest whisper. "I'm no one."

These few words are too agonizing to appraise, so all she can say is, "What?"

"That's who I am," says Buddy. "Now you know."

"What are you talking about?"

He breathes in sharply, convulsively, once, twice, and then again, and she guesses that he is weeping, guesses because in all the years of their marriage he has never once wept in her presence.

"Listen to me, Buddy," she says, holding her hand against her heart, as if to prevent it from shattering. "This is who you are — the best kind of husband, a father any boy would be crazy about, a professional with all sorts of diplomas on the wall and a thriving practice. Do you understand?"

"Don't patronize me," Buddy says. "Do you think you're talking to a child?" His anger is unmistakable; Lucy welcomes it, certain that it must be a favorable sign.

"I don't know *who* I'm talking to," she says.

"You're talking to no one," Buddy informs her. "So I'm going to hang up now, OK?"

"And then what?"

"And then I'm going to read some X rays, fill a couple of cavities, finish up a root canal or two. Because, as you know, that's what I'm here on this earth for."

"Come home, Buddy."

"Why? Because you think I'll fuck up and find myself with a big fat malpractice suit on my hands?"

"Because I think you're . . . tired. Too tired to work today."

"I *am* tired," Buddy says. "Sick and tired of being no one."

"I'm going to drive in and pick you up," Lucy says. "Wait for me."

"Don't forget to bring my pillow," Buddy tells her. "I can't wait to put my head down and go to sleep."

"Jesus Christ Almighty!" Lucy cries as she hangs up. "Oh Jesus."

Jasmine, the receptionist, and Patti, the hygienist, are conferring in Jasmine's glassed-in corner when Lucy arrives. Buddy is nowhere in sight, and the waiting room is, for the moment, empty.

Making an enormous effort not to appear frantic, Lucy says, "Where is he?"

"In with a patient, where else?" Jasmine answers, so casually that Lucy knows Buddy must have pulled himself together in time. "Want me to let him know you're here?"

"Don't bother him. I'd love some coffee, though." Patti offers her a Styrofoam cup with her right hand and thrusts out the left dramatically, showing off her engagement ring. "I personally think pear-shaped stones are the most elegant, don't you?"

"Lovely," Lucy says. "Congratulations."

"Just because this is Phil's third trip to the altar doesn't mean I should be cheated out of all the good stuff, right?"

Lucy nods. "Listen, can I ask you something?"

"I'm listening."

"It's Buddy I'm wondering about," Lucy says. "Does it seem to you he's been more than a little depressed lately?"

"Some of us," Patti says, "have been having trouble getting into work on time this week, but other than that, it's been business as usual."

"Really? You're telling the truth?"

"Actually, I'm lying," says Patti. "The truth is, Buddy's hell to work for and Jasmine and I would be out of here in a minute if only we could find someone to hire us." She studies Lucy's worried face, then winks at Jasmine. "Gotcha!" she tells Lucy.

Smiling weakly, Lucy enjoys their laughter. "You got me, all right."

"What's the matter with you, girl?" Jasmine says. "Don't you know we love Buddy? He's a boss from heaven. We've got no complaints about him."

"Except for the Beatles tapes he plays all day long."

"I believe that's just a stage he's going through," says Jasmine.

"I wouldn't be so optimistic if I were you," Patti warns. "Those tapes may mysteriously disappear one of these days, that's all I'm saying."

"If they do, it wouldn't be the worst thing in the world."

When Buddy turns up, wearing a long, pale blue lab coat over his jeans, he's leading an elderly patient down the hallway, bending slightly as he speaks into her ear. "Remember: nothing to eat or drink for the next forty-five minutes or so, Mrs. Fishbein," he says loudly, and waves at Lucy.

Mrs. Fishbein taps her hearing aid and complains, "This damn thing is almost useless. Frankly, sometimes I think I'm better off not hearing half the things people say to me anyway."

"I know what you mean," Buddy says in a booming voice. "Here, let me write down the instructions for you."

"Don't I get a kiss?" Lucy says. "Or even a simple hello?"

"Hello," Buddy says. "And here's your kiss."

Mrs. Fishbein looks on curiously as Buddy sweeps his mouth across Lucy's. "Is that your lovely wife?"

"Sure is."

"What do you know," says Mrs. Fishbein. "You learn something new every day."

"You do, don't you," Buddy says.

"So how do you like being married to a nice Jewish boy like Dr. Silverman here?" Mrs. Fishbein asks Lucy. "The gentiles always say it's the Jewish men who make the best husbands, but I, unfortunately, would beg to differ. Mr. Fishbein, my ex, was a disappointment in so many ways. He did give me two very lovable children, though."

"Well, that's something, anyway," Patti shouts.

"It's something, all right, but it's not everything." Addressing Lucy, Mrs. Fishbein says, "You didn't answer my question, young lady."

Lucy slips her arm through Buddy's. "He's a wonderful husband."

"Pardon me?"

"I said, he's a terrific husband."

"Be sure and hang onto him, then. But if by some chance you decide not to, I might take him home with me."

Lucy smiles. "I'll let you know."

A silver-haired man and woman appear as Mrs. Fishbein is leaving. The man looks gaunt and utterly miserable, the woman exasperated. "I'm positive he has an abscess," she says. "He's been in pain for two days, but you know how he feels about dentists, no offense."

"Not feeling too well, Mr. Ferrell?" Buddy says sympathetically. "Come on in and let's take a look."

The man grunts at his wife, who says, "The big baby wants someone to hold his hand."

"In that case, you can come in too," Buddy says.

"I'd really rather not."

"Thanks a lot for nothing," Mr. Ferrell says and shuffles off behind Buddy.

"I practically had to drag him here kicking and screaming," his wife explains. "I think I've earned the right to stay out here and read some magazines, haven't I?"

No one answers her. She shrugs and picks out an old, limp copy of *Glamour* from the rack. "You really ought to update your selection here," she says, then falls silent.

Lucy stands at the door, unsure of where to go or when to return. Clearly Buddy has recovered; if he hasn't, he's putting on a convincing performance. It's almost as if their conversation a few hours ago is something she imagined, however vividly. She'd been so frightened then, she nearly phoned Victor, who, she remembered, had predicted she would someday call to apologize for having doubted him. Remembering this had frightened her even more. The only call she made was to a neighbor, who promised to look in on the boys as soon as they arrived home from school. And then she had backed her car out of the driveway and took off, making the trip all the way to the Lincoln Tunnel with her hands clenched fiercely around the steering wheel. She'd half-expected to find Buddy coiled up on the couch in the waiting room, his tearstained face hidden beneath his arm, Jasmine and Patti standing over him with paper cups of water, expressions of bewildered concern across their faces.

It occurs to her that she could be angry with Buddy if she weren't so relieved. He'd suffered a few moments of heartrending self-doubt and then he'd come to his senses. It happened to the most accomplished people, she knew; it could happen to anyone at all. Perhaps this was what Victor had foreseen, a few difficult moments that he'd mistaken for something far more dramatic and ominous. The man wasn't God, after all; he didn't know everything. What he knew was just enough to stir even a skeptic like her.

She's grateful now for whatever it was that had kept her

from making the call. If she'd phoned him, it would only have been out of weakness, something she has always been impatient with. It's laughable, really, to think that she had even contemplated calling him. She hears herself giggle out loud now and clamps her hand over her mouth as she leaves the office, unable to say where she is going or what she is looking for.

She walks out onto Fifth Avenue and stops to buy a soda on the corner from a street vendor who says, "How are you, today, nice girl?"

A homeless man, thin and grimy, eyes her ruefully. He follows her down the street, saying, "Could I have a sip of that Pepsi?"

Ignoring him, she crosses Fifth Avenue in a crowd that takes flight as soon as the traffic light changes in their favor.

"I'm only asking for one sip," the man says. He's wearing a filthy yellow Ralph Lauren polo shirt that's several sizes too small for him, revealing his ribs and navel. "What kind of person are you that you can't give a thirsty man one sip?" he says. "It's not like I'm asking for the moon."

Shamefaced, she hands over the Pepsi in the middle of the street and then disappears inside Lord & Taylor, where she pretends, for over an hour, to be interested in leather handbags and costume jewelry and finally an endless variety of perfumes so overwhelmingly sweet that after a while she feels faint and abruptly sinks to the pink marble floor. A flock of saleswomen instantly surround her and not one of them believes her when she repeats three times that, really, she is perfectly all right.

9

O F ALL THE CLIENTS who have come through Victor's door over the years, of all the lives that have been opened for his inspection, there has never been one as luckless as the young woman seated before him now. The moment she appeared on his doorstep, wearing the skimpiest of summer dresses that revealed the frail bones of her limbs, the pallor of her skin everywhere, he'd wanted to retreat from her, to bolt the door securely, sending her back from wherever she came.

"You have no appointment," he'd said reasonably, standing behind the screen door while the papillons growled in fear against his ankles.

"You've got to see me anyway," the woman told him. "My friend drove me all the way from Connecticut, and I can't go home without seeing you. It's as simple as that."

There was no aura surrounding her; it was as if she did not exist. When she stepped inside the foyer, the damp summer air turned bitterly cold, as icy as the hand she offered him.

He had no need to study her palm or read even a single card for her. He knew that she had no future, and also why she had come.

Sipping tea now from a white china cup, she looks slightly stronger, more firmly tethered to the earth.

"You have great reserves of strength, Elizabeth," Victor tells her. "It's your love for your son, isn't it?"

Elizabeth smiles bleakly. "The thought of leaving him is the most painful of all."

He knows the little boy's life will be brief, though not brief enough. "Don't you think his father will make sure he gets the best of care?" Victor says.

"His father's an asshole," Elizabeth says. "He's got a new wife and baby, and all Zachary's going to be to him is a once-a-week inconvenience when he drives out to visit him at the rehabilitation center every Sunday."

Victor stiffens; he sees a car swerving off a narrow two-lane road, and shattered glass glinting in early-morning sunlight all along the dashboard and front seat. "The boy was in an accident?" he says.

"I fell asleep behind the wheel," Elizabeth says. "If only my life and Zachary's had ended then and there . . ."

"I understand," Victor says. "Your son is unable to move, he's hooked up to machines, but he's still a bright boy. He's reading books, I see, one after the other."

"Nothing has gone right, and I don't expect to ever know why," Elizabeth says. "Do you understand *that?*"

Anxiously, Victor clears his throat, searching frantically for a word of consolation. "Do you believe in God?" he asks.

Elizabeth looks at him incredulously. "Are you out of your mind?" she cries. "My child is hooked up to a respirator and a feeding tube, his lovely neck broken because *I* fell asleep at the wheel, and you ask me a question like that?"

"I know there's more," Victor murmurs.

"That's right, there is. That's only Part One. Part Two is that these next few months are all I've got. If you think there's any chemotherapy out there, any therapy at all, that can save me, you're wrong." Seizing Victor's wrists, she says, "I'm Job, get it, but without the faith. Without anything at all."

"Listen to me," he says, his eyes burning as he looks straight through her, "if there's no consolation for you in this life, there will be in the next. You'll be able to watch over your son for as long as he needs you. You won't be abandoning him, I promise you."

"How am I supposed to believe that? I have no faith in anything, I've already told you that."

"Find it," Victor says sternly. "I've given you some good news; all you've got to do is welcome it. I know it's what you came here for."

"I came here because I had nowhere else to go."

"Well," Victor says, "you came to the right place." He's so weary, he can barely keep his head up. He's heartsick, utterly enraged at this stranger's fate. She is lighting a cigarette now with no ashtray in sight, fiercely blowing smoke out the side of her mouth.

"You know," she says, "I have very few friends in this world. I'm not an easy person to like, apparently."

"You're not?" Victor says, reaching behind him to yank open a drawer. He places an ashtray in the shape of a miniature tire next to her, saying, "And why do you think that is?"

"Well, my ex-husband said I was too critical, that I never gave anyone the benefit of the doubt."

"Was he right?"

Shrugging her fragile shoulders, Elizabeth says, "It's a little late to start figuring these things out now."

"Forget it, then. Concentrate on something else."

"I've been thinking a lot about the funeral, actually. The one where yours truly is going to be the guest of honor."

Victor looks away. He stares at the fish in his tank, willing himself to be mesmerized by their darting movements, the slight shuddering of their fins as they glide so aimlessly.

"No matter what anyone in my family wants, *I* want my son to see me in the coffin. He has to understand why it is I've stopped visiting him; he can't be allowed to think I've deserted him intentionally." The cool steadiness of her voice convinces Victor that she's been over this a hundred times, a thousand times, that no one will ever dissuade her from this.

He feels himself recklessly crossing into dangerous territory, leaving his professional self behind as he says, "I can make sure of it."

"What?" Elizabeth says. The cigarette has burned down to her fingers; grasping it from her, Victor singes his thumb.

"I'll be there," he says. I'll weep for you, he adds silently.

Her mouth arranged in what could pass for a faint smile, Elizabeth says, "If my ex-husband happens to show up, tell him I'll be watching him every step of the way. You might just scare him a little. In fact, scare the shit out of him," she says eagerly.

"With pleasure," says Victor.

"Well, this is cool," Elizabeth says. "I haven't felt this together in a long while." She shakes a finger at Victor. "And you didn't want to let me in the door. You were afraid of me, weren't you? You were afraid I was beyond help, even yours."

"I wasn't," Victor says.

"You can't lie to a dying woman. It can't be done. I'm smarter than I've ever been, my senses are sharpened like you wouldn't believe. If I concentrate, I can see through almost anyone."

"So," Victor says, "I'm game. What do you know about me?"

"You," Elizabeth tells him, "are as transparent as a pane of polished glass. You're in love with someone, but you're not sure that you can win her over. You want to move quickly, but she won't let you. She's very cautious, this woman; she disapproves of you, in a way."

"All right, that's enough," Victor says. "Stop right there."

"Ah, so you can dish it out but you can't take it, is that it?"

"That's it, exactly."

"You're a funny guy, Victor. You're sweet, too. If I weren't in such lousy shape, I'd probably summon up the energy to flirt with you." Tugging at the tip of his ponytail, Elizabeth says, "How come you're so nervous about this woman? You're not about to let her get away, are you?"

"Absolutely not."

"Take it slow, then." She looks at him wistfully. "You've got all the time in the world, haven't you?"

He yearns for something life-affirming, something to heal the open wound Elizabeth has left him with, the pain of bearing witness to life at its cruelest.

He leaves the house without an umbrella on this oppressively hot afternoon, ignoring the echoing claps of thunder and darkening sky as he races the half dozen blocks to Katha's studio, ignoring, too, the premonition that she will not be particularly happy to see him.

"Come on up," she barks through the intercom and buzzes him in.

The elevator clanks and wheezes as it carries him uncertainly to the third floor, and he vows to take the stairs on his return trip. Walking down the long, gloomy, linoleum corridor, he prepares an explanation for his visit.

She doesn't want to hear it.

She greets him at the doorway, paintbrush in hand, a narrow slash of dark green across the bridge of her nose. "I'm working," she says brusquely. "It isn't that I don't want to see you, it's that I can't right now." Her hair is tied back in a bright silk scarf; Victor notices with amusement that her bare feet are spattered with paint.

"Oh, all right," she soon says. "I'm not going to send you out in the rain, am I?"

"I think not," Victor says and, after a moment's hesitation, kisses her mouth.

"Have a look around and don't talk to me," she says. "If you talk to me, you'll have to leave."

The small, high-ceilinged room is cluttered with canvases stacked everywhere against the walls; except for a number of lovely still lifes done in opaque watercolors, most of what he sees are dark, disturbing portrayals of tunnels leading to places clearly resembling hell. On a skinny-legged card table three glass bottles of sparkling water stand; beside them lie a half-eaten banana, a partially peeled orange, and two dusty plums. Victor washes off a plum at the sink in the corner and stands silently at a bank of tall, dirty windows, watching the driving rain. In his pocket is an index card with the name and telephone number of the hospice Elizabeth will be entering when she can no longer care for herself. He takes out the card and folds it into tinier and tinier rectangles, then jams it deep in his pocket.

Selfishly, moving toward the center of the room, tossing the plum back and forth between his hands, he gives away her story bit by agonizing bit, as Katha continues to paint. After a while he hears her moan, and then she is turning to face him and pitching her brush at her feet. At the easel, taking her into the shelter of his arms, he feels her tears dampen the side of his neck.

"I *told* you not to talk to me," she sobs.

"I'm inconsolable," he says apologetically. "It's the things she said to me, the facts of her life — I can't get them out of my head."

"If I were her," Katha says, sniffling, "I'd throw myself in front of a fast-moving bus. And that would be the end of it."

"I'd probably take a dive off the Triborough Bridge."

"Listen to us," Katha says. "What a pair of hopeless cowards."

"It seems like far too much for any one person to bear, doesn't it, and yet *she's* going to hang on until the bitter end," he marvels.

"To think you almost sent her away without listening to her."

"Even the dogs were afraid of her," says Victor. He trembles slightly, remembering the way the air had turned icy in her presence. "It was that moment I realized she had no future — it was horrifying, impossible to accept." Tightening his hold on Katha, he draws something like hope from her warmth.

They have slipped to the floor now, their backs against the easel, their hips touching. Victor reaches up and wipes at the smudge of paint on her nose.

"I'm not going to cry anymore," she says. "I'm done for the day." She rests one small, paint-spattered foot against his ankle.

"That's a cute little foot you've got there," Victor says.

"And I've got another one just like it."

"So I noticed."

"Really?"

"I've noticed many things about you," Victor says. "I've taken a good long look."

"And?" she says.

Slowly she unties the silk scarf holding back her hair. She smiles at him shyly, expectantly, he thinks. He imagines all that glorious hair skimming the surface of his bare chest, his stomach, his thighs. He lets out a muted groan of longing. Eyes half closed, Katha's combing her hair back with her fingers now, so slowly and deliberately, that in the simple act of watching her, Victor feels an electric current traveling through him. He moves toward her, stopping her hands in midair, matching his palms with hers. Gently he lowers her shoulders to the floor. Above her, he slides his hand into the generous gap between two buttons of her shirt.

"No bra?" he says.

"Must be your lucky day," Katha murmurs.

On the slickly varnished wood floor, under a bare lightbulb, he makes love to her urgently, moved by both desire and a trace of despair. *I'm Job,* he hears Elizabeth saying. *But without the faith. Without anything at all.* It seems to take all his will, and most of his strength, to silence her voice; then at last he feels a lightening, an unburdening, that gives way to something purely exhilarating.

"Hey," Katha says in a clear, bright voice. "Did you know I'm feeling the slightest bit better?"

Arching his head back and away from her, he sees her dazzling smile. "You're not the only one," he says. It's as if he'd come to her ill, weakened and feverish, and has just now begun to feel his health at least partially restored to him.

"Although I must say these accommodations are far from deluxe," she acknowledges.

He rolls up his shirt and pants, and places them gently under her head. "I guess you could call that an afterthought," he says.

"Carpeting would have been nice."

"Satin sheets on a king-sized bed would have been even nicer."

"Well, I wasn't expecting you," Katha says. "More to the point, I wasn't expecting this."

"Me either." Laying his head on her stomach, he lets his fingers travel down her thigh and behind her knee.

"What? You didn't look into your crystal ball before you came over?"

"Nope. I merely acted on impulse, as we all do from time to time."

"How can I trust you?" Katha asks, sitting up abruptly, drawing her knees together so that Victor is displaced, his head bumping uncomfortably hard against the floor. "How do I know you're being straight with me?"

"Ouch," he says.

"Well?"

"How can I trust *you*," he says, "not to pull away from me like that?"

"Did you hurt yourself?" she says, leaning over him and caressing the top of his head.

"I'll live."

"Good. But you still haven't answered my question."

"Look," Victor says, "you know perfectly well there's no crystal ball. I haven't looked at my palm in years, and I've never sought out another clairvoyant. If I happen to see a ghost now and then, I can ignore him if I want to."

"Him?"

"Or her. And sometimes they don't even bother with me, they just hang around for a while and disappear, like the old woman who used to live in my house when it was first built, around the turn of the century. The people I bought the house from had seen her too. They described exactly what she was wearing, the way she fixed her hair, the bracelet around her wrist, the cameo at her throat. Their description was accurate, as it turned out."

"Really."

"That's right," Victor says. "Really. And please train that icy stare on someone else, if you don't mind."

"Sometimes you're so thoroughly normal," Katha says with a sigh. "You look normal enough, your feet touch the ground like everyone else's. And then I hear you saying so casually that your house is haunted, and I start to feel like I'm in the presence of some screwball." Gathering her clothes, she begins to dress, struggling with the tiny buttons of her shirt, rejecting his offer to help.

"Have faith," Victor says. He pulls his T-shirt over his head angrily. "Oh, and by the way, how's Parker's broken wrist? When's the cast coming off?"

"What's the matter, your magic radar's in the repair shop? It's only a sprain," Katha reports, refusing to look at him.

"Anyway, he's got a plastic brace on it. And the car's going to be as good as new."

"I warned him," Victor says. "I did the best I could."

"When he called from the emergency room, he kept saying, 'Do you believe this? Do you believe I let this happen?' He'd been driving around for weeks at twenty miles an hour, trying to be careful. And of course it was someone driving the speed limit who rear-ended him."

"Well, it's over, anyway. He's got to be relieved."

"Actually, after he thought things over, he decided you were to blame." Katha laughs. "He's convinced you put a spell on him, that you're the one who somehow caused the accident."

"A spell? What am I now, a warlock?"

"He's been very irrational lately. He wants to transfer to the firm's L.A. office, and then he's hoping we'll get married out there. It seems he'd rather play it safe than live anywhere near you."

"So I'm a dangerous man. Interesting." Buckling his belt, slipping into his old, broken-backed loafers, Victor says, "A dangerous screwball."

"I seem to have a habit of falling for difficult men, don't I?" Katha says. On her knees now, she crosses her arms around his neck and hangs her head over his shoulder.

"Are you accusing me of being difficult?"

"I'm accusing myself of poor judgment."

"Moving to L.A. with Parker would be poor judgment," Victor says. "Falling head over heels for me, on the other hand, would be the smartest thing you've ever done."

"What do you think I am, someone who takes advice from a clairvoyant?"

"When it comes to you and me," Victor says, "I can't even predict whether we'll ever have dinner together again. My powers fail me, my vision is clouded, as if there's something obstructing the passage of light."

"Sounds like cataracts," Katha jokes. "Maybe you should have your eyes checked."

"You're laughing," says Victor, "but it seems to be the truth."

"And if it isn't, maybe I'll let myself believe it is anyway." Raising an imaginary glass, Katha says cheerfully, "Here's to your failing powers!"

Victor has fallen asleep on the couch in the parlor, the fingers of one hand pinched tightly around a single Ritz cracker. The box of crackers is lying open on the floor, alongside a jar of peanut butter and a spoon crusted over with low-fat Skippy. He licks his lips in his sleep, flutters his eyelashes, rolls over on his side toward the edge of the couch. Louis, the oldest and smartest of the papillons, stiffens in his corner near Victor's feet and lets out a low growl.

"Are you going to eat that cracker or not?" a voice says, and Victor is instantly awake, squinting at Murray in the dark.

"Go away," Victor groans, as Louis flees the room. "I'm too tired to talk to you or anyone else. Come back sometime in the next century, why don't you."

"Hard day at the office?" Murray says sympathetically.

"As a matter of fact, yes." Foolishly thrusting the cracker into his parched mouth, Victor chews and chews, lusting after a cold drink. "Would you do me a big favor and go into the kitchen and pour me some OJ?" he asks Murray. "Forget the glass, you can just bring the carton."

"Much as I'd like to, I'm afraid I can't," Murray says. "I don't have that kind of power over earthly objects."

Victor considers getting up, but an overwhelming sluggishness keeps him in place. Looking at Murray floating before him so expectantly, he suddenly turns hospitable. "Care to sit down?" he says.

"Can't do that either. I'm a drifter, as you can see. But thanks for the offer."

"So," Victor says, "what brings you to this part of town? Something on your mind, or are you just here to shoot the breeze?"

"Oh, a little of this and that."

"If I fall asleep while you're talking, don't take it personally," Victor says. "I've had a tough day."

"Maybe you ought to get out of the business and try something less stressful."

"Like medical school? Let's not start that again."

"Your mother had the idea that a Ph.D. in clinical psychology might be a good compromise."

"Doesn't she have better things to do than plan a midlife career change for her only begotten son?"

"Apparently not," Murray says.

"How come she's never shown up here to torment me personally?"

"She doesn't have the heart to argue with you. She's done with all that."

"And my father?"

"He's decided to let your mother handle it. Via yours truly, of course."

"Well," Victor says, "here's the way to handle it: buzz off, OK?"

"Victor, Victor, Victor," Murray says. "I'm surprised at you. Do you think I've come all this way to be dismissed like that?"

"Let's change the subject, shall we?" Victor suggests. "You ever going to get a new pair of pajamas?"

"You ever going to get a haircut?"

"That's one of the pleasures of being in business for myself — there's no dress code, no rule that says my hair has to be above my ears."

"And your girlfriend likes you just the way you are?"

"What girlfriend?" Victor tries to push himself up on his elbows but, inexplicably, seems incapable of the effort.

"The blond," Murray says. "The artist. Though from the looks of those paintings of hers, I wonder if a career change might not be in order for her too."

"First of all, who made you an art critic? And what were you doing looking at her paintings?"

"When it comes to art, I know what I like — I'm a big Rothko fan, in fact. Listen, your girlfriend's work is self-indulgent, to say the least. She'll never sell that stuff, trust me. She's got to move on to something else, something lighter in color and spirit."

"You were in her studio, is that what you're telling me?"

Murray begins to glow dimly in the dark. "You're under divine guardianship, buddy. Let's just say I'm around more than you know."

"This afternoon?" Victor cries. "Don't tell me you're some kind of celestial voyeur!" Outraged, he imagines Katha's response after he breaks the news to her. *Well, she says, convulsed with laughter, look at it this way: better Murray than someone with a pulse.*

"Now don't get all excited," Murray says. He shades his eyes with one hand. "I'm very discreet. I went through the paintings while you and your friend were . . . otherwise engaged. I had my back to you the whole time. I didn't see a thing, I assure you."

"How did you know what we were doing if you didn't see a thing?"

"I may be dead, but I'm not stupid, Victor. I could sense the way things were going between you two. So I got a good look at those canvases of hers and then I vamoosed."

"Get out of my house!" Victor shouts. "Get out of my life!"

"You're upset," says Murray calmly. "I understand that. But you need to think things through in a rational way. You need to —"

"Out!" Victor orders. "Now!"

"All right, all right, you won't have to ask again. Look, I don't want to alarm you, but —"

"I don't want to hear it."

"I've got to warn you that your girlfriend's got a soft spot in her heart for that guy she was married to, the one who needs a hairstylist more than you do."

"He does, doesn't he?"

Murray smiles. "At least we agree on something," he says. As the light around him fades, he vanishes obediently.

10

SOUNDING PREOCCUPIED, a trifle impatient, Lucy says, "This isn't a terrific time for me, Katha, can I call you back?"

"No," Katha says, "you can't. It's one of those now or never deals."

"Can we cut to the chase, then? I'm half an hour late picking up Max even as we speak."

"This isn't how I imagined this conversation," Katha says disappointedly. "I imagined I'd have the luxury of giving you the long version." She hears herself sigh theatrically, waiting for words of encouragement from her friend; getting none, she plunges forward anyway.

And then, shrieking like an adolescent girl, Lucy says, "You slept with Victor?"

"I think you just punctured my eardrum," Katha says irritably. "And what's worse, I seem to be falling in love."

"There *is* something very seductive about him," Lucy offers. "But of course you're living with someone who isn't exactly loaded with great personal charm."

"Let's leave Parker out of this, if you don't mind."

"I don't mind. I'd much rather contemplate the thought of you and Victor together. You know, the two of you out to dinner, you in your little black dress, Victor in a dark, floor-length robe and one of those dunce caps with lots of stars all over it."

"See, I'm not laughing," says Katha. "Are you trying to make me feel like I've fallen for some kind of freak?"

"There's something freakish about his powers, all right."

"It's all very confusing," Katha says vaguely.

"I'll bet."

"It isn't exactly that he's someone to be afraid of, yet I'm unnerved by him, slightly on edge, as if at any moment he might be looking straight through me, sorting out all my secrets, learning every last thing about me."

"You'll just have to trust him, I suppose," Lucy says.

"Sure. But part of me is drawn to him for the very reason that he's capable of knowing me inside out. And part of me wants to shield myself from the possibility of ever being *known* so completely by anyone in this world."

"Well," Lucy says, "the one thing I know for sure is that you've got at least one too many men in your life."

"True. And now that I've slept with Victor, it's creepy sharing a bed with Parker. Not that we've been sharing much of anything these days. Clearly we've lost whatever we once had, and the odd thing is, it's a loss I can't even mourn. Maybe if he'd made a real effort to win Julia over . . . I don't know."

"What are you talking about?" Lucy bristles. "He was on the prowl for other women, he never let you feel entirely comfortable in what was supposed to be *your* home, he's an anal-compulsive sicko — what's to mourn?"

"Are you finished?" Katha asks coldly.

"Did I step over the line here? I'm sorry," Lucy says. "I was trying to point out that —"

"I *know* what you were pointing out. It's as if I've got this internal compass that's led me in the wrong direction every step of the way. First there were all those druggies I dated in college, then Tom, then Parker. And now where do I find myself? Enormously attracted to a man who studies palms under a magnifying glass and apparently shares his house with a ghost or two. *Am I crazy or what?*" she yells.

Lucy laughs. "You know what I think? I think your compass is finally pointing you in the right direction."

"Oh, bless you, my oldest and wisest friend," Katha says. "Can I throw my arms around you and squeeze you tight?"

"Feel free. But in case I'm wrong, promise you'll only blame yourself."

"No problem. I always blame myself for everything," says Katha. "Or almost always."

Now that Parker has seized upon the idea of transplanting himself to Los Angeles, he knocks himself out trying to convince Katha to accompany him. Day and night, it seems, he promises her the works — a five-thousand-square-foot house in Mandeville Canyon (with more than enough room for her own glassed-in studio), a swimming pool with a mosaic floor, glorious weather, private school for Julia . . .

"Stop!" Katha says late one night, unable to listen to the familiar litany again. "Let's not forget the mud slides and the earthquakes," she says, preferring to blame the elements rather than her own dwindling affection for him. "And the smog out there is deadly." Sitting in an ice cold theater, they have just finished viewing the last movie they will ever see together; the only patrons remaining in their seats, they watch the final credits crawl by because it has always been Parker's habit to read every last one.

Waving his hand about impatiently, as if he might magically cause the smog to disappear, Parker says, "That's the wrong way to approach this deal. Why don't you think about how terrific it will be for Julia with all that space to roam around in?

She can swim and ride her bicycle all year round, and we can send her to camp in Colorado for the summer. Next summer, I mean." Seeing Katha's eyes narrowing in disapproval, Parker says, "What? What's the matter?"

"Are you her father?" Katha says. "Her legal guardian? You're sending her to Colorado for the summer?"

"Her father's a deadbeat," Parker reminds her. "He couldn't send her around the corner for an ice cream cone. And by the way, he still hasn't paid back the fifteen hundred dollars he owes me."

"You lent him money?"

"He happened to call one night a few weeks ago when you were out, and . . . we got to talking," Parker says. "I forgot to mention it."

"You and Tom?" Katha laughs. "I'm not even going to try to guess what he claimed to need the money for."

"We talked for a long while, and before you know it, there I am offering to loan him the fifteen hundred. He seemed very grateful. He's not a bad guy, actually," Parker says, sounding surprised.

"Well, neither are you."

"I'm not the easiest person to live with," Parker says as the house lights are switched on, revealing the spilled popcorn and flattened soda cups all around them. "I don't deny that," he continues, and kicks away a lone bonbon at his feet.

"But?" Katha says. "But what?"

"But I think I might be a new, improved version of myself on the West Coast. Someone who couldn't wait to get out of his buttoned-down shirt and tie and into his swimming pool as soon as he got home from work."

"You'd get bent out of shape by all the damp footprints all over the house," Katha says, hating it that she can predict this so confidently. "And then there are Julia's bathing suits lying in puddles on the bathroom floor."

"That's the part of me I'm going to leave behind," Parker says earnestly. "I'm going to make a heroic effort to chill out."

"Why?"

"Isn't that what you want?" Parker asks.

"I don't want anything from you."

"Nothing?"

Parker looks at Katha, startled. "You're not afraid of being alone, are you?" he says. And then, lowering his voice, "I thought all women were afraid of being alone."

"Where'd you hear that idiocy?"

"Oh, in some sweet French film about incest."

"Well, I'm afraid of plenty of things," Katha tells him. "But being alone isn't one of them."

A teenager in a maroon blazer and matching pants appears in the aisle with a broom and a tall garbage pail on wheels. "Excuse me," he says pointedly, and sweeps past the tips of their toes. "People are such pigs, I actually found a used condom back here once," he confides. "Can you believe that?"

"Well, better safe than sorry," Katha jokes. She gets no response.

Outside in front of the darkened marquee moments later, she stares at the winking lights of an ambulance reflected on the glossy surface of a black plastic bag left at the curb. She feels Parker take her hand, hears him offer, once again, to marry her. It pains her to reject him, and to refuse the comfortable life he is all too willing to share with her. She wonders if he will let her stay on in the loft until he sells it, knowing she can't possibly afford the monthly maintenance and mortgage payments. He has no reason to be generous with her, no reason to want to ease her worries as a single mother with a pitifully small savings account. She wishes she loved him, as she once did, though she can barely remember the particular feel of it, the heat she'd once felt in his presence, and also the contentment. She will miss the delicate scent of his expensive cologne, the attentiveness with which he'd listened to her. What else? she asks herself, and comes up short.

"You're making a huge mistake," Parker says as he helps her into the passenger seat of the BMW. He is at the curb looking down at her now, and his plump, boyish face sags with resignation. And then, as if remembering there's still a card or two up his sleeve, he brightens. "For a smart person, you're awfully dumb. No, I take that back," he says. "You're oblivious."

"To what?"

"Your psychic almost got me killed, that's what. And you can't even see how he tried to wreck our relationship with all the things he told you. You haven't been the same since you went to him. You've toughened up, you've lost your willingness to compromise, to overlook whatever failings you think you see in me. The first time I mentioned the idea of transferring to the L.A. office, of the two of us picking ourselves up and heading out there, you laughed at me. There hasn't been a single moment when you've even considered coming along. I know you dismissed the idea instantly."

"That's not true," Katha says lamely. "What I said was that I'd think about it. And the only reason I laughed was that I couldn't believe you'd let yourself be frightened off by Victor like that. You have to admit it's a little extreme," she says, rolling her eyes. "Not to mention entirely irrational."

"I don't care what you said — you've been stringing me along for weeks," Parker says. "What is it that you don't want to leave behind? What?" Met with utter silence, he says, "Feel free to say you no longer love me. It's going to kill me to hear it, but go ahead and say it anyway if you have to."

Hands clenched at his hips, eyes closed, looking as if he were readying himself for the firing squad, Parker waits. A woman walks by with a small dog on a leash, a small child in a stroller.

"You *cannot* continue to get up at midnight seven days a

week asking for your damn chocolate milk, Shawn," the woman tells her child. "You're three years old, for crying out loud, and I expect better of you."

Katha thrusts an arm out of the car and strokes Parker's knuckles, feels the knobs of hard bone under soft skin one last time.

"You've lost me," she says. "I'm already gone."

11

THE VACUUM CLEANER SALESMAN in Victor's parlor is a big, florid man with so much to say that Victor despairs of ever getting him out of his town house and back on the street again.

"Listen, Mel," he begins, "the truth is, I'm perfectly happy with the vacuum I've got. So it's extremely unlikely you're going to make a sale today." This is the third time he's said this in the forty-five minutes Mel's been pitching his miracle of a vacuum cleaner, and the third time he's been ignored. It was the sweat that's still streaming down the man's jawline that convinced Victor to allow him into his home; now, once more, he offers him a cold drink.

"I *told* you," says Mel, "I sweat like this every day of the year. I'm not hot and I'm not thirsty, I just want to talk to you about the microscopic world of common household dust. And there'll be a free gift for you if you let me finish up my demonstration."

"I don't want your free gift," Victor says. "How about if I give you a free gift instead — I'll read your palm for you and then you'll be on your way."

"You're not letting me do my job, Victor," Mel complains. "I have a super-duper product I'm trying to sell, and you keep interrupting my flow here. Don't you think my job is hard enough as it is? Don't you think I've got housewives and maids slamming doors in my face left and right? Do you know what that does to a man's ego? Take a guess, Victor."

Victor sighs. He imagines the word SUCKER stamped across his forehead in big block letters. "I believe you were discussing household dust," he says wearily.

"Yes I was. We're talking about dust mites, mold spores, pollen. It's disgusting, frankly, the stuff that lives in your carpeting and bedding. Now let me tell you about dust mites — did you know they're related to the spider and the tic?"

"Is that so," says Victor. "Look, I know you're a songwriter," he says, "a man with a poetic soul. So why are you selling vacuum cleaners, tell me."

Bending over to screw a plastic attachment onto the vacuum's hose, his face bloodred, Mel says, "Now how would you know that, Victor?"

"You'd be surprised at the things I know."

"Well, I'm interested, but not that interested. I'm more concerned with those nasty dust mites, those eight-legged, hairy creatures roaming your mattresses and carpets."

"And your daughter's married to a man who's nothing but trouble," Victor continues. "You can't keep lending them money — they're bleeding you dry."

Mel laces his fingers together and cracks his knuckles, making the sound of dry twigs snapping. "That's very impressive," he says. "But it's no concern of yours. Now, do you have any allergies?"

"None."

Looking disappointed, Mel says, "Well, if you did, this particular attachment here would be of special value to you. And do you know why?"

At the sound of the doorbell, Victor leaps joyfully from his seat. "That must be my next client," he lies. "I'm sorry, but I've got to get to work."

"Well, I guess I'm leaving," Mel announces. "Here's the deal: you buy a machine from me and I'll stop those handouts to my daughter and that bastard she calls a husband. I mean, what am I, made of money? A Rockefeller? I'm a vacuum cleaner salesman, for Christ's sake," he says, outraged.

"And a very good one, I might add," says Victor as the bell continues to ring. "Write up a bill of sale and I'll get my checkbook."

"That'll be twelve hundred plus tax," Mel says calmly. "Thirteen twenty-five, total."

From the front door, Victor calls, "For a *vacuum cleaner?*"

"Yeah, but this isn't any old vacuum," Mel yells back. "We're talking the Rolls-Royce of vacuum cleaners."

Parker stands behind the front door, his finger pressed against the bell.

"Take your finger off of there, please," Victor says. "And what are you doing here? I thought you'd already left for California."

Scowling, Parker says, "Do you think I'm an idiot? Did you know I skipped from second to fourth grade in grammar school? My IQ is one forty-six, for your information."

"There's more than one way to measure a man's intelligence," Victor says, opening the door. "And by letting you in, I'm probably proving my own stupidity."

"You told Katha not to come with me to L.A., didn't you?" Parker says, as he pushes ahead of Victor into the parlor. "Did you bill her for that brilliant piece of advice, or did you give it away for free?"

Victor is silent. He eyes the neatly ironed crease in Parker's jeans, the coat of clear polish on his nails. He can see Parker's house in the canyon, the endless, immaculate rooms of terra cotta and glass, the coyotes snapping their jaws just beyond the chain-link fence surrounding his yard.

"Don't you have a plane to catch?" he asks.

"If it weren't for you, a few short hours from now Katha would be leaning past my shoulder for a better view of the Grand Canyon."

Suddenly noticing Mel, Parker asks him, "Are you aware that you're in the presence of a dangerous man?"

"Let's make it thirteen hundred even," Mel says. He smiles at Victor. "Funny, you don't look like a dangerous man."

"Where's my free gift?"

"I'd like to see that check first, Victor."

"This man," Parker says, seizing Victor by the shoulders, "cost me my happiness. And thousands of dollars in repairs to my BMW."

"Take your hands off him," Mel orders.

Hearing this, Parker clamps an arm tightly around Victor's neck. "Who the hell are *you*?"

"You're choking me, you moron," Victor croaks.

"I'm one fucking good vacuum cleaner salesman," Mel says coolly. "And I've got arms of steel from dragging these babies all over town. Now you let go of Victor, or the next thing you know you'll be spitting out teeth and thumbing through the yellow pages for a plastic surgeon."

"We hadn't made love in God knows how long," Parker confides mournfully. "Did you tell her I had a sexually transmitted disease or something?"

The pressure against Victor's windpipe is almost unbearable; clenching his fist, he aims successfully for Parker's groin. And just as Parker releases him, Mel moves in, swings his arm back and then forward, and knocks him out cold, flat on Victor's floor.

"What did you do *that* for?" Victor yells.

"He deserved it," explains Mel. "And once he comes to, he'll be a whole lot less obnoxious."

"I really wish you hadn't done that," Victor says, on his knees now beside Parker. He slaps his cheeks briskly, calls Parker's name. He feels a surge of relief as Parker begins to stir. "There you go, buddy," he says gently, as if the two of them had a long, shared history they could look back on with affection. "You want a glass of water?"

"Did I say thirteen hundred? Let's make it twelve fifty, and that's as low as I'm willing to go," Mel says.

"Apologize to him, or the deal's off," Victor says. He helps Parker into an armchair and goes to the kitchen for some water. "Apologize for what?" he hears Mel holler.

"My head hurts," Parker complains.

Victor returns with a tumbler of water and two aspirin. The glass is from Disneyland, decorated with a pair of mouse ears and the name *Victor*, both etched in white.

"Cute." Parker outlines the mouse ears with his fingertip. "That water's not straight from the tap, is it?" he says suspiciously.

"It's from the tap, but the faucet's got a filter on it."

Hesitating, Parker stares at the chalky white aspirin tablets in his palm. "I don't know."

"And here I thought I'd knocked some sense into you," Mel says with a shake of his head. "Swallow the damn aspirin, would you. And, listen, I heard you had a plane to catch — you want a ride to the airport or something?"

"You viciously assaulted me without provocation and now you're offering me a ride to La Guardia? I don't get it."

"One," Mel says, "there was nothing vicious in the way I popped you. Two, you needed to be shown the error of your ways. And three, I'm a big-hearted guy." He turns to Victor. "It's kind of my way of apologizing, get it?"

Parker gulps down his aspirin, throwing his head back dramatically. "In all fairness, I have to tell you I'm contemplating suing you for assaulting me personally, and also my dignity."

"Cut the crap, Parker. You want a ride to the airport or not?" Victor says. He knows what's on Parker's mind, and he doesn't want to hear it. "Don't you have some carry-on luggage you've got to pick up at home first?"

"There's one more thing. You and Katha," says Parker slowly, "have something going, don't you?" He gives Victor a particularly soulful look. "I told you I'm not an idiot, remember?"

"I remember," says Victor.

"Do you happen to remember where you keep your checkbook?" Mel asks.

"I'd love to make your life miserable," Parker says wistfully. "But I'm a lot more civilized than you think. I'm even letting Katha stay on in the loft rent free until I sell it."

"Out of the kindness of your heart," Victor murmurs. He goes to the mahogany escritoire in the consultation room and writes out a check for the Rolls-Royce of vacuum cleaners, sucking in his breath as he signs his name.

"That's right," Parker says. "Out of the kindness of my heart."

"You may be a tad fucked up, but you're still a generous guy, is that what you're saying?" Mel asks. He smiles at the check and stashes it in the back pocket of his pale blue pants. "And by the way, who's Katha?"

No one answers him.

The papillons, locked away in the kitchen for too long, begin to yap querulously.

"There's an attachment here," says Mel, "that'll suck up that dog hair like magic."

It's only after his visitors have cleared out and Victor is all alone that he realizes he never did get his free gift.

"Damn," he tells the dogs, and listens gratefully as one of them offers what sounds like a sympathetic sigh.

12

THE MORNING that Buddy decides not to get out of bed at all happens to coincide with Max and Jonah's departure for summer camp in Vermont, where they are scheduled to remain until the end of August. Jonah is eager to spend another summer away from home; it is Max who has handcuffed himself to his bedroom doorknob.

"I swallowed the key," he reports grimly as Lucy stares at the metal cuffs illuminated in bands of sunlight, "so there's no point in taking my room apart to look for it." His expression changes, and he smiles at Lucy exultantly. "You lose," he says.

"Not quite," says Lucy. "Either I'll stick my fingers down your throat or I'll call a locksmith. And remind me to throw away your magician's set as soon as I turn you loose."

Jonah's eyes glitter. "Don't we have a power saw? Why don't we saw the knob off the door?" he says. "Tell Daddy to do it."

"Daddy?" Lucy says, so distracted it's as if she's having trouble comprehending exactly who Daddy is. "He's feeling under the weather today. Let's leave him out of this." As hard as she's tried, she hasn't been able to coax Buddy from their bed; worse, he's unwilling to offer anything resembling even a partial explanation.

"'Under the weather'? Sounds like total bullshit to me," says Jonah.

"OK, wise guy, you just lost fifteen minutes from whatever favorite TV show you were planning to watch tonight. Keep it up and you'll lose the whole show."

"What are you talking about? Ain't no TV where I'm going."

"Or Super Nintendo," Max adds. "Or clean bathrooms or carpeting or air-conditioning. It's a hellhole you're sending us to. Which is why I'm not going back there this year or any other."

"Don't waste your breath, Max," Lucy says. She knows that there's not much behind this drama he's so intent on playing out, except for an adolescent desire to leave his mark here, to manipulate her emotions one last time before he's gone for the summer. "Let's stop fooling around," she says sharply. "Where's the key?"

Patting his stomach in a clockwise motion with his free hand, Max says, "You don't believe me? Get a metal detector."

"I say we use the power saw," Jonah insists. Holding his finger horizontally across his brother's throat, he makes a rude buzzing noise.

"Shut up, asshole," Max says.

"Talk to him like that again and you'll find your TV missing when you come home at the end of the summer."

"Whoa," says Max. "Now there's a threat that's got me shakin' in my boots."

Lucy aches to slap him hard across the face; instead, in search of the key, she begins pulling out drawers from his dresser and flinging the contents behind her — boxer shorts patterned with emblems of various football teams, bandannas in an array of colors, a stick of deodorant, a bottle of cologne.

"Hey, don't do that, you're messing up my room," Max says, genuinely distressed at the disorder she's wreaked.

"I'm just getting started," Lucy says. "Watch me." Seizing a ceramic football that is, in fact, a bank loaded with change, she aims for the door and hits her mark. Split open, the football reveals, disappointingly, nothing but coins.

"It's not in there!" Max shrieks. "It's right here in my sneaker."

"I love doing things the easy way, don't you?" Lucy says, and bursts into tears.

"Don't cry, Mom." This comes from both her sons at precisely the same moment, an offering that sounds like an apology she has no choice but to accept.

"I wasn't crying," she tells them. "But thank you anyway."

Freeing Max's hand easily enough with the silvery key, she raises his narrow wrist to her lips and bestows a kiss upon it, as if it has just been rescued from danger. "I'm going to miss you terribly," she admits. "Both of you." It's the same every year; walking down the hallway toward their rooms on a summer evening near dusk, turning her head for a glimpse of a sweat-slicked Michael Jordan adorning a poster on Jonah's wall, or the cover of the *Sports Illustrated* swimsuit issue tacked above Max's bed, or the one stuffed animal sitting at each of her son's pillows, she sometimes felt a sorrowful lump rising in her throat. And it occurs to her occasionally that perhaps she loves them too much, too fiercely, that when someday they leave home for good, as they are meant to, the pain will be too much for her to bear.

"Excuse me, because I know you don't like to hear this, but that is such bullshit," Max says. "You're going to miss us? Maybe for like a minute or two when the bus pulls away, but that's it. After that you're going to go out and celebrate while my bro and me disappear into the sunset."

"Shut up," Jonah says helpfully. "Let's go, I want to get a good seat on the bus."

"See, you're not even answering me, Mom, because you know what I said is true and you can't think of a way to defend yourself."

"I'm not going to dignify that with a response," Lucy says. "Go say good-bye to your father, and then we can leave."

"He's not coming with us?" Max says, shocked. "What the hell is wrong with him?"

"Whatever it is," says Lucy, "he'll be out of the recovery room by tomorrow. Don't spend even a minute worrying about him, OK?"

"I think he's mental," Max says. "The only excuse for not coming with us is death. Or a massive stroke. And since we know he's still alive and kicking, he's got no excuse at all."

"Say good-bye to him anyway," Lucy orders. "And don't be such a tough guy, tough guy."

As the camp bus pulls out of the Kmart parking lot, a flurry of waving hands barely visible through its tinted windows, Lucy stares, horrified, at a graying mother of two who rises off the concrete to click the rubber heels of her sneakers together joyously. "I'm free!" the woman announces to the bevy of abandoned parents, some of whom are still waving forlornly as the bus picks up speed, traveling farther and farther north, and soon out of view, with its beloved cargo.

"Those kids of hers must be teenagers from hell," a man next to Lucy remarks, winking at her amiably. "Not that mine are all sweetness and light either." He waits for Lucy to offer something in kind, but she's choked with nostalgia, as if Max and Jonah's childhood were long past, irretrievable. She walks to the car with her head tucked between hunched shoulders, her feet kicking at bits of gravel, shards of amber glass from a broken beer bottle. In the pocket of her shorts are Max's handcuffs, which she pitches into a plastic drum stamped BOTTLES ONLY.

"Sorry," she murmurs, as if the sanitation worker who will find them there tomorrow might be listening.

On her way home, she stops at a favorite bakery for a bag of extravagantly rich croissants, which she hopes will get Buddy out of bed in a hurry. A man in his twenties with a shaved head and a distracted air, a man she's never seen before, serves her from behind the counter; he's the only employee in sight, and he looks at the croissants unhappily as he drops them into the bag one by one.

"That'll be it, thanks," Lucy says, reaching for her wallet, ignoring his frown.

"Do you know how much cholesterol and fat are in each one of these greasy things?"

Lucy steps back from the counter uneasily, suddenly aware that she is the sole customer in the store. "I probably don't want to know, do I?" she says. "I probably just want to pay the bill and get out of here."

"I'm trying to tell you that the stuff in this bag will probably kill you someday. But you people with your sun-dried tomatoes and your designer water and your designer luggage, you think you're all going to live forever. And that's a mistaken idea, see, especially if you're going to clog up your arteries with this crap."

Leaning against the cash register, Lucy sees, is an oversized postcard with a likeness of a haloed Jesus on it; He's wearing a white gown and a brilliantly red, bleeding heart in the center of His chest. "I don't expect to live forever," Lucy says, "and my luggage is Samsonite, for your information. So just give me the croissants, will you?"

"Well, have a nice day and all that," the man says mildly.

Hands trembling as she takes the grease-stained bag, Lucy flees to the safety of her car, where she cools her wrists against the wind blowing from the air-conditioning vents and contemplates the possibility that retreating to bed for a day or two might not be the worst idea that ever entered Buddy's mind. She imagines herself beside him, briefly avoiding the world, taking comfort in soft pillows and the familiar flesh of her husband, and offering comfort in return, a loving patience that will gently nudge him back into the clamorous swirl of life.

But, arriving home, confronted with the infuriating, bewildering spectacle of a healthy man refusing to leave his bed, she can only yank at her braids and howl, *"There's nothing wrong with you!"*

"Now there's where you're wrong," Buddy says in a small voice. He's lying on his side under the covers, his palms pressed together under his ear.

"This isn't a sickroom," says Lucy. "You don't have to whisper."

"You don't have to scream."

"Fine. If you promise not to talk in those hushed tones as if there was a dying patient in the room, I promise not to scream."

"Deal," Buddy says. "I assume the kids got off OK?"

"Do you care," Lucy asks, "or are you just making conversation?"

"You're not trying to make me feel any better, are you?"

"That's right, I'm not. I'm trying to make you feel contemptible."

"And doing a first-rate job of it," Buddy says. He draws his knees into a fetal position and shuts his eyes. "Go away," he says. "Come back when you're feeling more charitable."

Setting aside, with great effort, her disappointment and exasperation, a stubborn belief that he can will himself out of this mournful inertia if only he chooses to, Lucy curls herself around him and lets him feel her warmth.

"Will you stay with me?" Buddy says.

"If it helps."

"Nothing helps."

Lucy jerks herself upright. "You're frightening me, Buddy."

As if he hadn't heard her, Buddy says, "I need a new pair of shoes."

"What?"

"There's a hole in my sole," Buddy murmurs.

"Your soul?" Lucy says, in what she will presently see as a perfectly natural leap of misunderstanding. "I think I can understand that." Believing that this revelation of his will lead somewhere helpful, she adds, "I've heard the new rabbi's started all kinds of support groups at the synagogue — he's got one for cancer survivors, one for relatives of AIDS patients, one for widows and widowers. I bet he'd start up a support group just for you, and before you know it, there'll be a roomful of people with souls like yours meeting every Tuesday at nine."

"I don't need a rabbi," Buddy says impatiently. "I need new loafers, reddish brown — oxblood, I believe they call it, size ten-B. I want something different from my old ones, something with a tassel and a thicker sole. Can you go over to the mall and get me a pair?"

"I see," Lucy says. "I see we no longer speak the same language."

"What's this about a rabbi, anyway?"

"I thought you could use some spiritual counseling."

"Oh," Buddy says, "*that* soul."

"So what about it?"

"Rules to live by: Never share your deepest, darkest thoughts with strangers of any stripe. Avoid rabbis wherever possible."

Letting out a shriek, Lucy beats him over the head with her pillow. "You *are* a self-indulgent slacker!" she tells him. "And my guess is you don't want any help. You just want to lie here numb and anxious, which by the way strikes me as utterly impossible, unless you mean you're numb fifty percent of the time and anxious the rest. *Is that what you mean?*"

"I don't know, maybe," Buddy says, wresting the pillow away from her. "You're quite a powerful screamer," he says admiringly. "It must take an awful lot of energy."

"My heart is racing so fast it might explode," says Lucy, and puts Buddy's hand over her chest as she flops down on her back.

"You can't get excited like this," Buddy says. "It's not good for you."

"If you're worried about my well-being, you'll get yourself out of bed and back to work."

"Getting out of bed is one thing," Buddy says. "Going to work is another."

"First things first, then," Lucy tells him. "How about some breakfast? I've got a bag of dangerously unhealthy croissants for you downstairs."

"Are they laced with arsenic?"

"Just fat and cholesterol."

"Oh," Buddy says. "I thought you might be planning on poisoning me."

"If I were, would I warn you first?"

"Probably not, but you never know."

"You have my word, Buddy, I have no intention of doing you in with arsenic or anything else. Come downstairs and have breakfast with me, and then we'll go get your shoes."

"*You'll* go get my shoes. I'm staying here."

"Excuse me, what am I, your personal shopper?"

"I'm not leaving the house," Buddy says. "Maybe next week or the week after that. Today is out of the question."

"Too busy to go shopping? What are your plans for the day, let's hear them."

"I have no plans," Buddy says flatly. "Plans require a certain expenditure of energy, and I'm all out of that too. I'm all used up, I have nothing left. I'm fading out, like light at the end of the day." Pulling the thin, satin-edged summer blanket up to his eyes, he stares at her helplessly. "I didn't want this," he says. "It's just something that gradually closed itself over me, a web that's got me caught and won't give me up."

Lucy is pacing vigorously alongside the bed, unable to look at Buddy, thinking, *How did you become so fragile? How?* She can't accept what she's just heard; it's unacceptable, yet she believes every word of it. Under the blanket the outline of Buddy's long, thin limbs is visible. She knows them so well, and also those wrists and ankles, almost feminine in their delicacy, the prominent collarbone and hips. His beloved leanness now seems to suggest a lack of substance and strength, a weakness that she suddenly finds intolerable.

"Stop pacing," Buddy says. "You're making me dizzy."

"I'll pace all I want," Lucy tells him, but she slows to a stop and draws the bedspread all the way over Buddy's head, waiting for him to utter a word of resistance. Arranging a half dozen decorative pillows at the headboard, adjusting the spread so that it's touching the floor evenly all the way around, she steps back to assess her work.

"Hey," Buddy protests finally, a large, awkward lump in the middle of the otherwise perfectly made bed. "What are you doing to me?"

"I hate leaving the house with the beds unmade," Lucy says, and watches with satisfaction as he undoes her work and leaps from the bed in a surprising display of energy.

"Wait," he says, running after her as she walks toward the doorway. "There's something I have to give you." From underneath the bed he pulls two pieces of cardboard, nearly twelve inches long and shaped like human feet. "I made these for you."

"A gift?"

"Take them to the shoe store and show them to the salesman. They're a pretty perfect outline of my feet — I traced them and cut them out while you were gone," Buddy says proudly.

Lucy holds them gingerly by the heels, one in each hand, as if they were filthy and evil-smelling. "And what exactly do I say to this hypothetical salesman?"

"Tell him your husband's an invalid." Buddy lowers his eyes. "Or a lunatic. Or a lunatic invalid. In any case, size ten-B." Raising his head to look at her imploringly, he says, "Will you do this for me?"

"I'm not making any promises," Lucy says, but she shoves the cardboard feet under her arm and trails gloomily down the hallway, leaving Buddy behind, ignoring his barely audible "thank you" and the sound of his slow footfalls retreating to bed.

Roz, the rabbi's sixty-six-year-old secretary, is eating slices of hard-boiled egg at her desk and paging through *Newsweek* with her glamorously diamond-tipped nails. Her hair is a puff of pinkish gold; when she smiles at Lucy, there's a bright bit of egg yolk between her front teeth. "You must be here to sign up for our interfaith couples club, am I right, darling?" she asks Lucy. "Have a seat and I'll find the forms for you."

"I'm not, actually. It's my son's bar mitzvah lessons I need to check about," Lucy says, amazed at the smooth flow of words from her mouth, the perfectly acceptable lie that she has seemingly drawn from thin air. She cannot say how she happened to arrive here or why she parked in a space marked "Clergy" when the lot was almost empty of cars. She knows she was on her way to the shoe store not more than five minutes ago; that she drove herself here is indisputable as, perhaps, is the simple, terrifying fact that her memory is shot.

"Lovely," Roz says, and takes a dainty sip from a tiny glass bottle of seltzer, washing away the egg caught between her teeth. "Ugh," she says. "These diet lunches are killing me. But the doctor says I've got to drop twenty-five pounds or better, and when the doctor speaks, I listen, which is more than I can say for my boyfriend, whose blood pressure is not to be believed and yet at the dinner table that salt shaker never leaves his hand. And I mean never." She shakes her head, perplexed. "A stubborn mule, stubborn as only a man can be, do you know what I'm saying?"

"Absolutely," Lucy says. "Is the rabbi in?"

"He's finishing up a slice of pizza, I believe. Let me check for you, darling." Roz disappears, returning two minutes later with the rabbi in tow. He's younger than Lucy, a small, trim man with wire-rimmed glasses and an Albert Einstein hairdo.

"I'm Rabbi Wagner," he says, extending his hand for a firm shake. "Do you like pepperoni?"

"I don't, but is that a trick question?" Lucy asks.

"Not at all. It's just that I've got two slices left, and since Roz here is on Weight Watchers, I thought I'd offer them both to you. And, truth to tell, I don't think pepperoni agrees with me."

"It's garbage," says Roz. "Maybe next time you'll listen to me when I tell you to order the mushroom and peppers instead."

"I doubt it," the rabbi says. He motions for Lucy to follow him into his study. "What's up?" he asks as he perches on a corner of his desk and offers her a wooden folding chair with a red velvet cushion. "What's the story with the bar mitzvah boy?"

"He'll be starting his lessons in the fall," Lucy says. "Max Silverman — he's in his fourth year of Hebrew school."

"Good for him," the rabbi says. "But is it good for you?"

"I'm not a convert, and I don't expect I ever will be, but I have no problem with the bar mitzvah or the Hebrew school or any of the rest of it," Lucy says. She senses that the rabbi is thoroughly engaged in listening to her, that he is studying her eagerly, hoping to discover exactly who she is. This unnerves her, and she contemplates heading straight for the door.

"I like your braids," the rabbi tells her. "I understand it takes hours to get them like that."

"That's true," Lucy says, remembering Buddy striding through the burning sand in search of an umbrella for her to settle under as the woman in St. Martin began to work her fingers through her hair. Their vacation together had been a kind of paradise, the two of them taking an intense, heightened pleasure in each other's company, stripping off their bathing suits in a hurry to make love, lingering in the shower afterward, holding fast to each other as the steamy water poured down endlessly upon them. And here she is a half year later, blinking tears from her eyes in the presence of a near-stranger who no doubt assumes her life is going swiftly down the tubes, along with her dignity and self-control.

"Have a tissue," the rabbi says sweetly. "Here, take a handful."

"I was raised a Baptist, but I have only positive feelings about the bar mitzvah," Lucy sniffles. "Really."

"We don't have to talk about the bar mitzvah at all," the rabbi says. "We can talk about something else, or we can sit quietly for a while. It's up to you, Mrs. Silverman — you think about what you'd like to do, and let me know when you decide."

Lucy rises halfway out of her chair to hand over Buddy's cardboard feet. "These are my husband's," she explains. "He needs a new pair of loafers, but he can't bear the thought of leaving the house to go to the shoe store. Or anywhere else, apparently. We've had this problem before, but this is the first time I've felt truly frightened."

The rabbi walks the cardboard feet across a row of thick books at the edge of his desk. "You're afraid he's showing signs of agoraphobia, is that it?"

"He's a dentist," Lucy says. "He commutes to the city five days a week. We can't afford for him to be agoraphobic — we'll end up in bankruptcy court."

"Does he know you're here?"

"He probably thinks I'm busy showing his cardboard feet to a shoe salesman at this very moment."

"I don't think he's going to be a shut-in for too much longer," the rabbi says, smiling. "If he wants new shoes, he must be planning to take a walk in them sometime soon."

"I wouldn't count on it," Lucy says. "I don't see much cause for optimism." She envisions Buddy's silhouette under the thin blanket on their bed, imagines his flesh disappearing day by day until he's nothing more than a skeleton, a figure made only of parched bones and empty sockets.

"He's all used up," she tells the rabbi. "There's nothing left of him. He's no one," she says in a whisper.

The rabbi scrambles off the desk and pulls Lucy rudely from her seat. "Where's that kind of talk going to get you? Where do you think? Tell me."

"Nowhere?"

"Bingo," the rabbi says. "Now let me give you the names of a couple of very good therapists, all right?"

"Do they make house calls?"

"Not in this lifetime," the rabbi says, and he goes through his Rolodex with a pencil tucked sideways in his mouth. "Our congregation is loaded with shrinks of all kinds — we've got M.D.'s, Ph.D.'s, M.S.W.'s, whatever you'd like."

"Forget it. He'd never confide in a stranger anyway."

"What about me?" the rabbi says, spitting out the pencil. "Even though I'm a virtual stranger, I've been known to make a house call or two, a definite plus as far as your husband is concerned."

Lucy sighs. "I don't mean to be insulting, but you're not exactly his favorite people."

"And *I* don't mean to sound arrogant, but I seem to be the rabbi of choice for people who're turned off by rabbis. So let me get my car keys, and we're off."

"Now?" Lucy says. "He's probably still in his pajamas."

Linking his arm in hers, the rabbi says, "You think I haven't seen people in their pajamas before?"

On the phone with Lucy, Katha says incredulously, "Cardboard *feet*? What did the shoe salesman say?"

"He said, 'As a matter of fact, we get quite a few customers coming in here with these cardboard things. There's actually a lot of this agoraphobia stuff going around these days.'"

"Get out of here — he did not!"

"That's right, he didn't. He looked at me like I was some kind of wacko and said, 'I don't get it. Why can't your husband come in in person?'"

"Not an illogical question, under the circumstances," says Katha.

"So I said, 'He's out of town, that's why.' And then he said —"

"'Well, tell him to come on over when he gets back,'" Katha says with a giggle.

"You think this is amusing?" Lucy says. "It was awful, knowing this guy thought he was dealing with someone who was probably off her rocker."

"You're not off your rocker, sweetie."

"You think Buddy is?"

"Put it this way," says Katha tactfully, "it just doesn't sound like the Buddy we know and love."

"We could lose everything!" Lucy cries. "What if Buddy never goes back to work? What if he never gets further than down the stairs to the kitchen? If he were physically ill, that's one thing. As hard as that might be, I could deal with it. But this is different — I'm totally at a loss here. I'm terrified of pushing too hard, of saying all the wrong things, of saying all the right things but in the wrong way."

At a loss herself, Katha says, "I guess what you're telling me is that the power of positive thinking has eluded you."

"We could lose *everything*," Lucy repeats. She imagines the bank foreclosing on their house, and then the yard sale where her microwave, Cuisinart, and collection of high-tech pots and pans are the first things to go. A swarm of curious neighbors crowds her front lawn, greedily inspecting the sterling silver serving pieces, the Baccarat vases and candlesticks, her carrot scraper, cheese grater, and garlic press. The man who lives in the house directly opposite theirs, an accountant who's come with his wife and infant daughter, looks about furtively and pockets a set of gleaming demitasse spoons engraved with Lucy and Buddy's initials intertwined. Buddy observes the theft impassively, seated in a lawn chair in his pajamas, his hands folded grimly in his lap, his mirrored sunglasses reflecting images of the feverish activity all around him.

Sighing into the phone now, Lucy says, "Feel my hands, they're like ice."

"You've got to warm them," says Katha softly, but she doesn't tell her how.

Lucy dreams the same dream several nights in a row: *she and the boys have been forced to move in with her mother and grandmother, who have, uncomplainingly, turned their bedroom and half their dresser drawers over to them and installed themselves in the living room. Buddy is out of the picture, apparently forgotten by everyone except Lucy.*

Mention the man's name in my home and out you go, her mother warns when Lucy wonders where he is.

She knows where she is: back where she started, in a four-story walk-up whose windows overlook the dismal streets of her childhood.

You know who to blame, Florine says gleefully, her eyes luminous, their irises glowing embers that Lucy turns away from in horror.

Who? she says.

Oh please, don't make me laugh, her mother answers.

When she awakens, the base of Lucy's spine is damp with sweat, and she sees that her fingernails have dug crescents into her palms. She weeps at the sight of Buddy's long limbs drawn up in a fetal position, his head bowed toward his chest. As the sun ascends beyond her window, she gently unfolds his legs; at least, she thinks, she can do this much.

13

KNOWING BETTER THAN TO INTERRUPT Victor while he's in consultation with a client, Katha waits on his front steps, sketching the Russian Orthodox church across the street. Two priests in ankle-length black gowns disappear inside, licking frozen yogurt cones held carefully above their lush beards.

A ladybug makes it slow journey along Katha's bare knee; she nearly brushes it aside, remembering just in time that it might be a good luck charm. Which, God knows, she can surely use. "What did you think, I'd throw you out on the street?" Parker had asked her last week, magnanimously allowing her to stay on in the loft while she searches for an affordable apartment. Now that he's taken off, she finds herself tiptoeing warily through his home, as if he might return at any moment to scowl at the collection of dishes in the sink, the tangled tassels of his Persian rug, the thumbprint of Vaseline on the bathroom mirror. Most of his things, including his bed, have already been shipped to Los Angeles, but at least she has a couch to sleep on and the linens and dishes left over from her marriage.

She has more worries than she cares to count, most of them

financial, and it occurs to her that she has only herself to blame for relying first on her husband and then on Parker to provide her with almost everything with which she's filled her life. If only she could transform herself into something other than an artist, someone who could dress in a business suit, ride the subway with *The Wall Street Journal* tucked under her arm, an initialed attaché case propped on her lap. Occasionally traveling on the subway at rush hour, she has imagined opening a stranger's gleaming leather case only to see a dark swarm of numbers and mathematical symbols, flying out in a rush as if from Pandora's box. Symbols that have no meaning for her, that will never hold any meaning for her. She lives in another world entirely, where brilliant light and dark shadow and nuances of color are everything and a minor talent like hers may just be a curse.

When, at last, Victor's front door swings open, a slender teenage girl with her hair in her eyes stumbles down the steps, inadvertently dumping the violin case she is carrying into Katha's lap. "Whoops!" she says, and seems hesitant to take back the violin, cradled in Katha's arms now like an infant.

"Lucky thing I caught it," Katha says, and she waits for a word of thanks.

"Well, I had to sell the bow to pay for my visit with this psychic dude," the girl says. "If my mother finds out, she'll go ballistic."

"How could you do something so stupid?" Katha cries, as if the girl were hers and she had every right to berate her. "Are you crazy?"

"No way. First of all I'm eighteen, old enough to drive, old enough to vote, old enough to sell my own personal property if I want to. And second of all, I just had the thrill of a lifetime in there."

Katha wedges the violin under the girl's arm. "So you sold your bow for the thrill of a lifetime," she says. Inexplicably, she's close to tears.

"Not my soul, just my bow," the girl says, apparently trying to be of some comfort. "Don't take it so hard." The dainty gold ring through her nostril glitters in the sunlight. "If I were you, I'd go in there and let the psychic have a look at your palm. Maybe he's got good news for you."

Victor ambles out the door as the girl, positioning herself in the middle of the street, jams two fingers in her mouth and whistles for a cab. "*This* is a surprise," he says warmly, standing behind Katha with his hands on her shoulders. "I wasn't expecting to see you until tonight."

"You've got to give that girl her money back. She sold her violin bow to pay for her appointment with you."

Kneading her shoulders now, Victor says, "You're awfully tense, sweetie. Take a deep, deep breath, why don't you."

"If you don't return that money . . . I don't know, Victor. The thought of what she did is driving me crazy."

"Oh, that?" Victor says. "That's the same story she tells every time she shows up here. The big sacrifice. I've heard it from her before, believe me. You don't need to worry about it."

"Are you sure?"

"You'd be amazed at all the people who don't want to foot the bill. Especially if what I've told them isn't to their liking." Victor sits beside her on the steps, placing her hand on his knee. "Listen," he says, "I know I promised never to tell you more than you wanted to hear, but your ex has gotten himself into some kind of trouble. I'm not sure what he wants from you, but —"

"Parker?" Katha says. "Parker's history, and he knows it."

"Not Parker — the guy with the big hair, your husband."

Withdrawing her hand, Katha says, "You don't even know his name, you've never seen a picture of him. I know you couldn't pick him out in a lineup."

"Even so," Victor says, "this dream of mine was very vivid. Your ex had rubber thongs on his feet and no place to go. He looked pretty mangy and truly distraught."

"You're giving me a stomachache, you and your dark visions," Katha says. "I've got more than enough trouble of my own — now I have to worry about Tom? Well, I can't. My savings account is about emptied out, and I don't know how much longer I'll have a roof over my head. Actually, that's an exaggeration, but I can't take advantage of Parker's generosity indefinitely. He's only been gone a week, and I'm already feeling as if I'm trespassing. And, in a way, of course, it's true I'm somewhere I don't belong."

"Stay here with me, then."

"Never!" Katha says, sounding as outraged as if he'd suggested she indulge in armed robbery to replenish her bank account. And then, seeing how hurt he looks, she explains, "I can't take advantage of your generosity either." She smiles at him. "It's just that I can't have my child living in a house with ghosts, real or imagined."

"Oh, they're real all right. One of them is so chatty he'll keep you up half the night."

Katha gives him a playful shove. "Can't you at least pretend to be normal?"

"Why? You don't believe a word I just said anyway."

"As a matter of fact, I've reached a point in my life where I don't know *what* to believe anymore."

"Sounds like progress to me."

"Progress? I don't think so — it seems more a reflection of a general state of confusion than anything else."

"There's nothing to be confused about," Victor says. "I only tell the truth. Plain and simple."

"Well, the guy with the big hair, otherwise known as Tom, borrowed fifteen hundred dollars from Parker, of all people. What do you think that's all about?"

Victor says ruefully, "Just when one guy in your life clears out and leaves some room for me, there's another one waiting in the wings, it seems."

"I don't know what he's hoping for from me, unless it's money, in which case he's doomed to disappointment."

"Am I?" Victor says.

"Let me see your palm."

"It's a little sweaty," Victor warns, "but go ahead and take a look."

Nestling the back of his hand in her palm, Katha says, "I see a life line so deeply drawn, you're going to live forever. And a heart line that shows you're the most unselfish of lovers. And even though I see here that you don't have any children, that doesn't necessarily mean there won't be a child in your life. In fact, there *is* a child in your life — look, there she is, at the end of your pinkie. She's what, eight or so?"

"Nine," Victor says with a half-smile.

"Well, I was off by a year, a minor detail, anyway. How am I doing, by the way?"

"Not bad for a quack. Excuse me, I mean novice."

"Notice I don't even need a magnifying glass," Katha says. "Oh boy, I'm on a roll here, I see a blond in her thirties, I believe she's the mother of the aforementioned nine-year-old, and, please stop me if I'm wrong, but I'm guessing that this is someone you have real affection for."

"The simple truth," Victor says, and clears his throat, "is that I'm in love with her."

Still looking downward into his palm, Katha, her voice a little wobbly, says, "She's an old soul, this blond. She's been here before, as a porcupine, I believe, but that's of no consequence to you. In fact, it appears that she may be falling in love with you as well."

"I've heard appearances can be deceiving."

"A simple truth, but one that doesn't apply in this case." Katha is twisting Victor's wrist so she can read his watch, then looks up and says, "I'm afraid our time today has run out. Feel free to come back in six months for an update. And stop smiling at me like that, it's very distracting."

"Sorry," Victor says. "Do you take Visa or MasterCard?"

"This isn't Bloomingdale's, buster. No credit cards, no

personal checks. Cold cash or certified check only. And by the way," Katha says, casting her arms around him, "I find you utterly irresistible."

"Oh," Victor says," I bet you tell that to every good-looking palm that comes your way."

"You're the first. The one and only."

"Well, that's good news."

"It's the only kind I offer here. The rest I leave to the pros, the ones who really have what it takes, the ones who are so knowing they cause the hair to rise at the back of your neck and your skin to turn to gooseflesh."

"Is that how it is?" Victor says softly. "Is that what I do to you?"

"If I could stay away, I would," Katha says, though almost immediately she finds herself wondering if there is any truth to this. "In any case, I've given up trying," she says with a sigh.

Victor lifts her pale, heavy braid, blows at the fine hairs at the back of her neck. "You're spellbound," he says. "Just like Parker. And if you've got any doubts about that, consider that I've got you both where I want you."

It takes her an instant or two to realize that he is teasing, that in that brief moment of her confusion, she was as frightened as she has ever been. "Never joke around with me like that, Victor, I'm warning you," she says soberly. "Do that again, and you'll find yourself at a table for one tonight. In fact, I'll go into hiding, and even with your considerable powers, you'll be hard-pressed to find me."

"Come on," Victor says, "you wouldn't."

"In a heartbeat," says Katha. "I am, for your information, nobody's fool."

Only half-listening to Tom explain exactly why he can't take Julia for the weekend, as planned, Katha manages to miss most of what he tells her. *I'm sick of people, I don't care about dying, I'm fed up with the whole fucking world.* This is all she hears, the echo of a onetime confession of his that plays itself over and over in her mind now like song lyrics, as he talks to her from just beyond the threshold of the doorway. *Mangy,* she remembers Victor saying; the word seems a bit harsh, a bit cruel, more suited to describing an animal, she thinks. *Shabby* would have been kinder. Even his beloved Jimi Hendrix T-shirt looks as if it's not long for this world, as if it might shred into pieces the next time he pulls it over his head.

"You *said,*" Julia insists, her lower lip already beginning to quiver. "You said we'd go to the botanic garden and to FAO Schwarz and to the movies." Pulling him by the hem of his shirt into the loft, she adds, "And bowling."

"I did?" Tom says. "I doubt I said *all* those things, sweets." He slides his large, bulging backpack from his shoulders and looks around uncertainly. "Where's the rest of the furniture?"

"Parker's moved out to California," Katha says.

"You guys split up or what?"

Katha nods. "Do you mind sitting on the floor? It's all I've got except for my bed over there."

"That's a couch you're pointing to."

"We made a list," Julia says. "We wrote down all the things we were going to do this weekend, and we put it up on the refrigerator. Your refrigerator. You were supposed to bring it with you when you came."

"Oh, baby, I'm sorry," Tom says. "I've been preoccupied, you know?"

"Don't call me 'baby,'" Julia tells him. "And if preoccupied means busy, that's a stupid excuse."

"Your shoelace is untied," Tom calls after her as she rushes up the stairs to her room, pausing at the balcony to shriek, *"I don't care!"*

On the floor, her back resting against the couch, Katha says, "I don't understand."

"Do you think I should go up there and offer her some kind

of consolation prize?" Tom asks. "The least I can do is take her out to dinner at Burger King."

"Let her simmer down first," says Katha. "Now explain to me again why you're living at your mother's."

"You mean why I'm not living at my mother's. She kicked me out, that's why." He stares at her quizzically. "Didn't I explain this already?"

"Maybe you did."

"One of us has attention deficit disorder, and it ain't me, babe," Tom says. "Is it you?"

"What? I'm sorry, were you talking to me?"

"Pay attention," Tom says. "Living on Park Avenue with my mother and my stepfather was no bed of roses, let me tell you. My mother's still in mourning over Richard Nixon. Every day I had to hear about how misunderstood he was. And my stepfather bound and gagged me and took me over to Brooks Brothers. He bought me three navy blue blazers and a half dozen blue-and-red-striped ties."

"Sounds awful," Katha says. "What were you doing there in the first place?"

"Well, my lease was up in Brooklyn, and the landlord wouldn't renew it. He claimed I never paid the rent on time and, anyway, he needed the apartment for his niece. So I paid fifteen hundred in cash to an exterminator who promised to get me a rent-controlled two-bedroom in the city for seven hundred a month. He took me to see the apartment, which was terrific, by the way. I handed over the money, and then he disappeared. He told me not to contact the management company that ran the building, that I had to do everything through him. He even gave me the phone numbers of people he'd gotten apartments for. They all said he was on the up and up, that I could trust him."

"With fifteen hundred dollars of Parker's money."

"Oh, yeah, and don't think I don't feel terrible about it."

"So you and Parker got screwed."

"I'm going to pay him back eventually, don't worry."

"I'm not worried," Katha says. "It's strictly between the two of you — I'm out of it. If Parker calls, that's exactly what I'll tell him."

"Funny thing," says Tom, "after he lent me the money, I developed a real fondness for the guy. Why'd you two break up, anyway?"

"Irreconcilable differences. He believes in scrubbing the soles of his shoes with bleach every night, and I don't."

"No kidding. I had no idea you were living with a mysophobic."

"Neither did I."

"It's a fear of dirt," says Tom. "I myself have no such phobia."

"You do, however, have a fear of new clothes."

"I do, don't I? You think I'll ever get over it?"

"You got over me, didn't you? I think there's hope that someday you'll actually put on one of those blazers Sam bought for you."

"I didn't actually get over you," Tom admits. "Remember at the end of our marriage I told you I could have stayed with you forever?"

"Mmm."

"Well, looking at you now, I'm still harboring a small, persistent hope that someday we might . . ."

Katha smiles. "That's sweet," she says. And then, going farther, "*You're* sweet."

"I'm a romantic old fool," Tom says gloomily. "And ever since I gave up my career as a pot smoker, I've been deeply depressed. It's like giving up the last vestige of my long-lost youth, you know?"

"When did *this* happen?"

"Oh, ages ago."

"Weeks? Months?"

"It seems like years."

"Congratulations," Katha says, giving him a kiss on his unshaven cheek. "I hope you're proud of yourself. *I* am."

"What are you proud of yourself for?"

"Proud of *you*," Katha tells him.

Tom stretches out flat on the floor. He slaps his rubber thongs against his heels a few times, winds a tassel from Parker's rug around two fingers. "I lost one of my teaching jobs," he confesses. "A couple of students reported that I'd occasionally show up for class stoned, that I could barely keep my balance standing at the lectern even when I wasn't stoned, that I spent too much class time playing Bob Dylan albums to illustrate certain points . . . They're so fucking straight, these kids."

"I get the picture," Katha says. Seesawing between anger and empathy, enormously grateful that they are no longer married, she exhales a sigh that comes out sounding more like a hiss of exasperation.

"I'm going to be a little short on cash for a while," Tom says. "Those child-support checks are going to be a problem."

Although she should have known it was coming, hearing this disastrous news reported so baldly, so casually, Katha feels faint. "Can't your mother help out?" she asks plaintively, hating the sound of her own voice.

"She's already taking care of Julia's private school tuition. I can't ask her for much more than that."

The solution, for her, at least, is obvious, Katha realizes — she will simply have to go out into the world and find herself a job that offers a weekly paycheck. She is certified as an art teacher, but with all the cutbacks in the schools lately, it does seem unlikely that anyone would hire her.

Where were you last year when we were collecting résumés, the powers that be will want to know.

Hard at work painting, and organizing expensive birthday parties for rich kids, she will have to say.

Not exactly a résumé that will wow them in the marketplace.

"What a pair we are," she tells Tom. "Precariously close to

the big four-oh and still worrying about how to pay the rent."

"Speaking of which," Tom says, "do you think I could crash here for a while? Not forever, of course, just until I find a second job and I'm back on my feet again."

"Did you say 'crash'?"

Tom sits up straight, runs both hands through his graying cloud of hair, as if trying to spruce up his image in front of the co-op board. "I believe so."

"This is the nineties, my dear. I believe the whole notion of a crash pad died out about twenty years ago."

"Really?" Tom says in surprise. "Well, then, let me rephrase that," he says, and strokes his chin forlornly. "Would it be possible for me to sleep on your floor for a couple of weeks until I can find other accommodations?"

"It's not even my floor," says Katha. "It's Parker's. I've only got a temporary visa myself. He's going to sell this place out from under me as soon as he can."

"So we're in the same boat, is that what you're telling me?"

"We're both up shit creek without a paddle, that's what I'm telling you."

"This downward mobility thing has got to go," says Tom. "I say we take Julia and move back in with my mother and Sam on Park Avenue. She's got a rotten disposition, but she's also got four bathrooms, an eat-in kitchen, and a beautiful view of the Central Park Reservoir."

"She *is* kind of a sourpuss," Katha says. "I'm not surprised she threw you out."

"She described my brief stay with them as 'an unhealthy situation,' which was a pretty fair assessment, actually." Pitching his voice squeaky high, Tom mimics his mother: "'I'm killing you with kindness, darling, and it's not getting either of us anywhere.'"

Katha laughs, and swiftly considers her options: sending her ex-husband off in search of someone with a more generous heart and an extra mattress, or offering him a temporary haven on Parker's floor. Neither seems wise; living with either will bring her a certain amount of discomfort, of that she is certain.

"Could that possibly be a sleeping bag in that backpack of yours?" she asks.

"Who wants to know?"

"Act now," Katha says. "This offer is for a limited time only."

"That's a smile of gratitude and relief you see lighting my face," Tom says.

"I'm glad," Katha says truthfully. "Remember, this is a temporary arrangement. And there are no fringe benefits, you got that?"

"Hope and desire spring eternal," Tom says, and winks at her. "I can't help that."

"Don't wink at me, OK? And don't make me regret this."

"You'll have no regrets, I promise."

"I'd like to take your word for it, but just in case, I think it's only fair to inform you that the guy I'm seeing is seven feet tall, three hundred pounds of pure muscle, and kind of a loose cannon. He gets the signal from me and he'll break you in two."

"Whoa, wait a minute," Tom says. "Parker's body isn't even cold yet and you've already replaced him?"

"I don't want to get into this, especially not with you," Katha tells him. "Why don't you take Julia to Burger King and go rent a movie for the two of you. The fact is, I'm going out tonight, and my guess is you'll be baby-sitting. That's a pretty fair deal all around, isn't it?"

"Who's the lucky guy? And what does he have that I don't — a roof over his head? A successful career? A VCR and cable TV?"

"All of the above," Katha says.

"I knew it," says Tom, and smashes his fist into his open palm. "How am I ever going to compete with someone like that? What is he, another one of those guys with a Rolex on his wrist and a BMW in his garage?"

"He's a clairvoyant," Katha mumbles. She waits for the shocked silence interrupted by a peal of mean-spirited laughter.

"Cool," Tom says, raising his eyebrows only slightly. "Do you think he'll do a reading for me?"

"You disappoint me," says Katha. "I was expecting some heavy-duty sarcasm from you."

"He's one of those high-priced hotshots, am I right?"

"He's expensive," Katha admits. "But people seem to think he's worth every penny."

"Do you?" Tom says. "You let him read your palm and all that, didn't you?"

"Once, and once only. It was months ago."

"And?"

"Never mind about me — there were things he knew about you. And just the other day, he told me you'd come to me for help. He seemed kind of worried about you, actually."

"Shit!" Tom says. Agitated, he circles the nearly empty room, his thongs snapping angrily. He stops at the staircase and sits down on the bottom step. "I don't want anyone worrying about me, especially someone who doesn't even know me."

"He knows you well enough, apparently."

"He's got to help me, then."

"What do you want him to do, find you a job and a rent-controlled apartment?"

"Wouldn't that be something?" Tom muses. "The major crises of my life solved by a psychic."

"Forget it," Katha says. "He's not a headhunter and he's not a real estate agent, he's just someone who knows more than anyone could possibly know."

"I understand that."

"You're on your own, pal, and so am I," Katha says mournfully. "That's the way it goes in this world."

"I understand that, too," Tom says, sounding equally pained.

Katha threads her fingers together, stretches them upward. "Now that I've explained to you the way the world works, what else can I do for you?"

"Lend me a few bucks for dinner at Burger King, OK?"

*   *   *

Unable to sleep, Katha rises from the couch and immediately trips over Tom in his musty sleeping bag. She listens to his faint, incoherent mumbling, watches in the moonlight as his mouth forms an innocent smile that disappears a moment later. She wonders where his dream has taken him, how far from Parker's hard floor he has been transported. Far enough, she guesses, and picks herself up, treading lightly on the tips of her bare toes across the loft. She climbs the stairs to Julia's room, where her daughter lies flat on her back in her captain's bed, her face partially concealed by the damp coils of hair that have fallen across her cheeks. Gently sweeping back the soft, moist strands, revealing the sweet planes of her daughter's face, Katha feels a rush of love and fear that sets her rocking at the edge of Julia's bed. "You," she admits out loud in a whisper, "are something of a failure." The words sting like a needle full of Novocain heading straight for her jaw as she sits in a dentist's chair, preparing for the worst. Poverty beckons; occasionally she can see its miserable face in her dreams, the ones from which she emerges with her heart racing, her face on fire. She remembers the puzzled look her father had given her, when, years ago, she'd explained that all she wanted was to be a painter. An artist. Refusing to finance the fine arts degree she claimed to need after college, he'd said wearily, "What kind of nonsense is this? What is it you're counting on — selling a painting every month when the rent is due?" A civil servant living on his pension in Florida now, his tiny den ornamented with her paintings, he seems unable to communicate anything other than nervous concern for her — in his brief, nicely typed notes and even briefer phone calls, scheduled for Sunday nights, when the rates are low. Now, finally, her worrying matches his own, though on Sunday nights she pretends otherwise.

In her daydreams, she wants everything for her daughter, and something for herself too; no longer young (though in her own mind she is perpetually eighteen), she has to face the fact that the possibilities are no longer limitless. Yet why can't they be, she sometimes thinks — why can't she still hope for a breakthrough in her work, a way to see past her bleakest images to something more appealing, something that will get her a little attention and back into a gallery again? In the meantime, there is the urgency, so deeply felt, to provide for her daughter the barest necessities and more. Her responsibilities seem overwhelming; she feels ill-prepared to meet them, seeing herself, as she does, as someone without the skills or instincts for self-reliance. She will simply have to reinvent herself, create a scrappy, aggressive woman who can talk her way into whatever she needs to get by. Kneading her hands fiercely into the flesh of her thighs now, she thinks, Who am I kidding? She is close to forty, not much of a wage earner, a single mother divorced from a troubled, unreliable man, in love with someone who makes his living peeking into other people's futures.

"What's wrong with this picture?" she asks aloud, waking her daughter, who sits bolt upright, her arms held straight out in front of her like a sleepwalker's.

Julia blinks at her. "Is nine times six fifty-four?" she asks.

"Always."

"That's good," says Julia, and falls back against her bed. And then as an afterthought she adds, "Love you."

"You're my angel," Katha says as her daughter's eyes close.

But soon Julia is tossing her head from side to side, groaning, "What are you doing here? You woke me up in the middle of the night and now I'll be cranky tomorrow."

"You won't," says Katha.

"I will."

"Well, we can be cranky together," Katha promises. "Just you and me. We can be mean and cranky and miserable together, all day long."

"All right," says Julia.

* * *

What she will do, Katha decides, is seek out the kind of job she's never held before, one with health benefits and paid vacations and possibly even a dress code of sorts; a job that will require her to impersonate a solid citizen, someone who can take orders willingly and learn how to satisfy whoever happens to be in charge.

"I've convinced myself this was inevitable," she tells Tom, showing him the list she's compiled of friends and acquaintances who might be helpful in her search. "After all these years, I'm going to have to try to turn myself into a respectable person."

"Wake up," Tom says, and without apology he crumples her list and pitches it to the floor. "You need people who can pull strings for you, people who are owed favors out there in the real world."

"Like who, for instance?"

"Like my stepfather."

"You're crazy," says Katha. "What's my connection to him? Your own mother barely speaks to me. She calls here wanting to talk to Julia and I can almost scrape the frost off the windows. Why would Sam lift even a finger to help me?"

"Because I'm going to ask him to, that's why. Leave it to me."

"You?" says Katha, and begins to laugh.

Tom regards her with a sly smile. "Sure. Who better than me to help you turn yourself into a respectable person?"

This strikes them both as so hilarious that they are soon wheezing with laughter, though not for long. "I'll never pull it off, will I?" Katha says, when she is sober again. "I'll end up as a sullen waitress in some coffee shop, my feet aching and my heart sinking."

"Or your heart aching and your feet sinking."

"Whatever," says Katha, but she doesn't stop him when he goes to the phone to call Sam.

14

IN THE BRIGHT NEW BOWLING ALLEY above the Port
Authority Bus Terminal, Victor crouches beside Julia with
last-minute instructions, just before she sweeps her arm
back and releases the ball. "Let's see," he says hopefully, and
together they watch as the ball takes its sweet time down the
alley. It soon becomes apparent that it's destined for the gut-
ter; burying her face against Victor's shoulder, Julia moans.

"Look!" says Victor, rising to his feet. "Look at what's hap-
pening!" Miraculously, the ball has changed its course and is
meandering toward the center of the lane, where it knocks
down a single pin and comes to a standstill. But the fallen
pin has brushed against the one behind it, triggering a slow-
motion domino effect that eventually leaves only one pin
standing.

Julia leaps upward, clamping her legs around Victor's waist.
"Thank you so, so much," she says gleefully. "Thank you for doing that for me."

"I didn't do anything."

"Yes you did. You wanted me to get a strike, and I almost did.
I know you put a spell on the ball, Victor. It's kind of like cheat-
ing, but I don't care."

"You're mistaken, cutie," Victor says, and lowers her to the floor. "You're being ridiculous, in fact."

"You put a spell on Parker so he'd move away to California, and you put a spell on the bowling ball," Julia insists. "And I'm thanking you for both of those. Now you have to help me get this spare."

"I'm afraid there's been a misunderstanding," Victor tells her. "You're as wrong as you can be, kiddo." Abandoning her at the scene of her triumph, he strides toward Katha in his big clownish bowling shoes.

"A miracle," she says, and unwraps the foil from a chocolate kiss as she studies the scorecard projected overhead on a computer screen. "I've never in my life seen such a slow-moving ball knock down so many pins."

"Your daughter thinks I put a spell on the ball."

"Did you?" Katha reaches forward and pushes the chocolate kiss past his lips and into his mouth. "I mean, could you?"

"Now why would you say such an idiotic thing?" Victor asks with annoyance. "And don't put candy or anything else in my mouth before asking me first, all right?" Slumping into the molded plastic bench behind her, he tries to ignore her injured look.

"Maybe Julia and I ought to finish up here ourselves," Katha says. "You look like you need a few hours alone in front of your fish tank."

Tracing his brows with one finger from each hand, Victor says, "My nerves are shot, if you want to know the truth. I went to a funeral this morning, and I guess I haven't quite recovered. Maybe that's why I'm so —"

"Was it someone you were close to?" Katha interrupts. She scoots over next to him and crosses her bare leg over his, letting him know she has, in an instant, forgiven him.

"No, not really," Victor says. "She came to me only once, not long ago."

"Oh no!" Sliding her leg off his, Katha says, "It's the woman you told me about, isn't it?" Tears spring to her eyes; she turns away from him and gazes out at Julia, who's flat on the floor on her stomach, watching her ball crawl down the alley.

"Everything in her short, sad life had gone so cruelly wrong, you know, and even her funeral was a disaster of sorts, at least from my end," says Victor. "I got into a fight with her ex-husband just before the service started, and then they threw me out in the middle of things. But I did keep my promise to her."

Katha's tears flow unchecked; when he tries to comfort her, she sobs, "This isn't about Elizabeth, not really. It's the bad news I read in the *Times* today."

"Something worse than usual?"

"In one-point-one billion years," she reports bitterly, "the earth will be purged of all life. The planet is doomed to melt when the sun explodes, which it will in all certainty."

"What?" says Victor. He uses the hem of his T-shirt to wipe her face. "This is why you're crying?"

"You don't find it a chilling thought?"

Victor has to laugh. "What could be more irrelevant, really? I wouldn't waste too much time worrying about it."

"You should have seen me," Katha says. "There I was sipping my Instant Breakfast from my favorite mug and reading the paper, and all of a sudden I'm in tears, horribly depressed because a billion years from now the earth will be nothing more than a blob of matter."

"Just the reason for a little carpe diem in one's life," he says, kissing her. He knows she is lying, that these fresh tears are for Elizabeth, and he loves her all the more for it. And observing Julia's gloomy retreat from the alley now, the mournful curve of her tiny shoulders, the downward cast of her mouth, he wants only to see her face lit again with pleasure. He hopes to love her someday as well, to have his affection for her deepen into something he can treasure. He doesn't know how to get there from here, but oh how he envies Katha's love for her child, that pure, instinctive bond they share. *Let me in,* he wants to say to them both. *Make room for me.*

"I didn't get the spare," Julia announces. "That's because *you* didn't help me."

"It's not the kind of thing I can help you with, I told you that," Victor says. "I can't make things happen like magic."

"But you put a spell on Parker — you made him wreck his car and then you got him to leave."

"Says who?"

"Parker told my mom."

"Do you think Parker's always right about everything?"

"We all know the answer to that one," says Katha. She pats her lap, summoning Julia, who climbs into it but doesn't look content there. "All right," Katha says, "I want you to look at Victor and tell me what you see."

"Stand up, Victor," Julia commands.

"Do I have to?" he complains good-naturedly, and gets out of his seat.

Julia studies him silently. "I don't know what you want me to say," she offers at last. "I mean, I could say good things and bad things. I don't want to hurt your feelings."

"Don't worry," Victor says. "I can take it."

"All right," Julia says. "The good things are you're cute. And I like your earrings, especially the silver star. But your hair's too long, and there's too much gray in it. If you want to look as young as my mom, you probably should dye it so it's all blond. And also, your eyes kind of scare me."

"What?" Victor and Katha say.

"What's wrong with my eyes?" Victor asks.

"Well," says Julia, "they're a very pretty color blue, so that's not what I mean. What I mean is, they scare me even though they're pretty."

"But why?"

Shifting around in Katha's lap uneasily, she says, "You see things that no one else can see, and that's spooky for everyone else, like me and my mom, isn't it?"

"Probably," Victor says. "But some of what I see is wonderful, you know, so wonderful that I feel lucky to be able to see it."

"Like what?"

"Well," he says, and hesitates, uncertain whether it's wise to share whatever's in his line of vision, or wiser simply to keep it to himself. And then he thinks, Why not? Why not let them know what's out there for them? "I see your grandmother, Claudia, the one who died not so long ago," he tells Julia. "She's wearing lots of necklaces, they all have hearts hanging from them — lockets and also just the outlines of hearts. There's a big thick bangle bracelet around her wrist, and a thin chain with two linked hearts around her ankle."

"Please don't do this," Katha says faintly. She tightens her arms around Julia; from wrist to shoulder her skin has turned to gooseflesh, and a field of blond hairs stands perfectly straight. And now, abruptly, she is laughing, saying, "My mother wouldn't dream of setting foot in a bowling alley. Too much noise, too many beer drinkers, too many sweaty guys passing judgment on every woman who walks by. A golf course is more her speed, believe me."

"Oh, I believe you," Victor says. "But that's all immaterial now. She's watching over you wherever you happen to be. And if it means slumming it in a bowling alley, well, it's all part of the job."

"Does she get paid?" Julia asks. Brushing the hairs back and forth across Katha's arm, she seems merely curious, entirely without fear.

"Nope. She's here because she loves you, not because she's on salary."

"If she loves me that much, maybe she can get my mom to take me out of day camp for the rest of the summer. I hate it,"

Julia says, glaring at Katha. "All the activities suck, especially swimming. And my counselor's crazy, she has multiple personalities. You know, one day she's mean, one day she's nice, one day she thinks she's a German shepherd."

Katha smiles. "I wouldn't count on your grandmother being too sympathetic," she says. "She sent me to camp every summer, whether I wanted to go or not."

Feeling wilted all of a sudden, as if a series of sleepless nights has just caught up with him, Victor sits back down. "There's a message for you," he says wearily. "Actually, it's for Donald?"

"My father," Katha says. She won't look at Victor, out of fear, amazement, or disgust, he doesn't know which.

"Beverly's favorite perfume is Shalimar?" he says. "Well, whoever she is, that's what she wants for her birthday."

Katha pales. "She's his girlfriend — she and my mother were friends since childhood, as thick as thieves, really."

"I don't care," Victor says. "I just want you to understand that this is how it is for me. I've got this hotline to some unearthly Western Union, and some days it's busier than others. And sometimes, not very often, I'm so tired that I need to shut down for a while and recharge my powers."

"You do look exhausted." Katha's hand moves gently down the length of his jaw. "And I *am* trying to understand. But it seems like the hardest thing in the world for me to comprehend — it might as well be nuclear fission or fusion, or whatever it is, as far as I'm concerned. You could explain it to me a thousand times and I'm just not going to get it."

"It's no big deal," Julia says blithely. "Grandpa's supposed to buy Shalimar for Beverly's birthday. Call him up and tell him."

"You tell him," says Katha.

"What's the matter with her?" Julia asks Victor. "What doesn't she understand?"

"She'll be all right," Victor says. "I'm going to explain it a thousand and one times, and one day it's finally going to hit her."

"Like a ton of bricks, I bet," says Katha. "I'll look forward to it."

She trudges up to the alley, cradling a fourteen-pound ball in her arms. Letting go with all her strength, she knocks them dead.

15

APPEARING ABOVE THE TELEVISION SET in Victor's bedroom, floating lazily on his stomach, Murray says softly, "Hey there, buddy."

Victor slaps his hand to his chest. "Jesus Christ! What are you trying to do, give me a heart attack?" Waiting for his heart to slow, he says, "Can't you see I'm watching a movie? It's three o'clock in the morning, by the way, and I hate to break it to you, but I have no desire whatsoever to carry on a meaningful conversation of any kind at this hour."

Murray hangs his head down for a look at what's playing. "Is that Burt Lancaster and Deborah Kerr?" he says. "Must be *From Here to Eternity*. One of the top ten movies of nineteen fifty-three, for sure."

"Go away, Murray."

"I wouldn't mind watching the movie for a while."

"Watch on somebody else's TV. I just decided I'm going to sleep." Clicking off the television with the remote, Victor pulls the blankets completely over his head and tries to get comfortable.

"You're not a very good host, you know," Murray complains.

"If you're not going to talk to me, the least you could do is put the movie back on."

"Did I invite you here? Did I phone and ask you to drop by for a chat in the middle of the goddamn night? I don't think so."

"I come when I'm called," Murray says. "And sometimes when I'm not."

Emerging from under the covers with a howl, Victor flings a pillow across the room. "What does it take to get you to shut up?"

"I know you were at that funeral yesterday, Victor. I saw the way you grabbed that husband by the throat and put your face right up to his so he'd get the message loud and clear."

Victor can't help smiling. "Yeah, I was pretty tough," he says. "I scared the shit out of that weasel. He's going to take exceptionally good care of that poor damaged child of his, whether he likes it or not. It's too bad that usher, or whatever he was, had to throw me out. I would have liked to have stayed for the service."

"It was a heartbreaker," Murray says quietly. "When they let the little boy have a look inside his mother's coffin, I thought, this is as bad as it gets. If I were still capable of shedding a tear or two, I would have, honestly."

"Actually, it's kind of comforting to know you were there," Victor says. "Thanks for showing up."

"You're welcome. Now how about turning the movie back on out of gratitude to me?"

"You don't give up, do you?" Victor says, surrendering with a sigh. "Keep it low, OK?"

"All right," Murray agrees. "Whatever you say."

The next thing Victor hears is Murray raving, "What a movie! Did I already mention it was in the top ten for nineteen fifty-three?"

"You're still here?" Victor groans. He seizes his clock radio from the night table with both hands, saying, "It's four fucking thirty in the morning!"

"Time means nothing to me," Murray says. "I'm surprised you haven't figured that out by now." Floating near the cushioned window seat, he shakes a translucent finger at Victor. "Don't be such a complainer. You've had your nap, now sit up and pay attention."

"I'll listen," Victor says, "but I'm keeping my head on my pillow and my eyes closed. So what's up?"

"Frankly, I'm concerned about your girlfriend. That ex-husband of hers is going to become a permanent fixture if you don't hurry up and help find him a place of his own."

"I'm not in the real estate business, Murray."

"Maybe you ought to be. Your girlfriend needs a place too, doesn't she?"

"What, did Parker sell the loft?"

"Who's Parker?"

"Never mind," Victor says, relieved that there are some things Murray knows nothing about.

"You've got more than enough room here for her and her daughter," Murray observes. "Why can't they move in with you?"

"Don't you think I've asked her? She turned me down."

"Ask her again," says Murray. "And again."

"She doesn't like to be pushed."

"Push gently," Murray recommends. "So gently, she doesn't realize you're pushing at all."

"What makes you such an authority on women?"

"Oh, I've had a couple of wives in my time. That's more than I can say for you."

"True," Victor says. "I haven't been so lucky in that department."

"Sometimes," says Murray, "I think the key to a successful marriage is lying through your teeth."

"*What?*"

"It worked for me. Both my wives were terrible cooks, one worse than the next. I can't tell you how many lousy meals I consumed over the course of two marriages. And consumed with a smile, I might add."

"What's your point?"

"My point is it's not always necessary to tell the truth. You want your girlfriend to move in with you? Tell her you have no big plans for the two of you, that you're simply offering her a place to live."

"Who said anything about big plans?"

"Gee, I don't know," Murray says coyly. "Even your mother, who'd like nothing more than to see some grandchildren, thinks you've got to move slowly and discreetly."

"Really. I thought seeing me in medical school was her number-one priority."

"I told her I had to stop bugging you, that I wasn't making any headway at all."

"How'd she take it?"

"She's on to some other project now, trying to get some recently widowed friend of hers out of a deep depression."

"How's she going to do that?"

"Don't know," Murray says. "And frankly, I don't care either. *My* number-one priority is you."

About to doze off, feeling strangely contented, Victor says, "You know, I wish I could . . ."

"What?"

"Get you into a new pair of pajamas. Something more elegant than flannel. Something in silk with a matching foulard, maybe. Think how dapper you'd look."

Murray smiles. "Sweet dreams," he says.

While Katha is off at her new job in the art department of *Forbes* magazine, Victor takes Tom apartment hunting, a gloomy affair at best, as he leads him in and out of one dreary walk-up after another.

"I'd really prefer an eat-in kitchen," Tom says, after inspecting an apartment where the refrigerator is out in the hallway across from the bathroom. "And a stall shower rather than a tub. You think I'm asking for too much?" He'd been thrilled when Victor volunteered to help, shaking his hand energetically as they met for the first time, insisting it was an honor just to be in Victor's presence.

"Let's not get carried away," Victor told him, but he was pleased nevertheless.

"This is New York City," Victor says now. "Anything you want is probably too much." He thinks guiltily of his lovely town house, which he'd been smart enough to grab in the late seventies, just before the real estate market went wild. And it pains him that Tom's pickings are so slim — surely he deserves better than what he will inevitably have to settle for.

"A doorman would be nice," says Tom. "My mother's building has six of them."

"Let's not kid ourselves — we know you can't afford a building like that."

"If I can't live in a doorman building, I'll kill myself," Tom teases. "Actually, that would solve any number of problems. And my mother would be sure to have me laid out in the classiest of funeral homes. Ironic, isn't it, she won't lend me rent money for a decent apartment, but I guarantee you she'd spring for a top-of-the-line funeral."

"Hold it right there," Victor orders, and he stops in the middle of a narrow, tree-lined street, not far from where a homeless man is snoozing in the sun behind a row of aluminum garbage pails chained to an iron railing. "Let me see your palm." Squinting in the brilliant sunlight, he says, "See this line right here?"

"This one?" asks Tom, and points to his heart line with a trembly, blunt-tipped finger.

"*This* one," Victor says. "That's your life line," he reports, and then, exaggerating only slightly, he says, "I've never seen a longer one. You could live to be ninety-nine, but only if you want to."

"Oh goody," says Tom, and claps his hands together.

"Do you want to?"

"Yeah, sure, who wouldn't?"

"So I don't want to hear any more talk about funerals, expensive or otherwise, is that clear?"

"Nothing's clear," says Tom. "Since I stopped smoking dope, nothing's been clear to me at all."

Losing patience fast, Victor says, "I just had a vision of you in your new apartment. You're cooking fettucini in a red sauce, and there's a satisfied smile at your lips."

"I *do* like fettucini," Tom says. "But I only like it in a white clam sauce. Maybe it's some other dude you're envisioning."

"No, it's you all right. Now let's go up and take a look at this next apartment."

Using one of the keys the rental agent had given them, they let themselves into a limestone tenement marked with faded graffiti and climb two flights of carpeted stairs coated with dog hair. Victor unlocks the door to the apartment and announces, "Well, here's your eat-in kitchen." There are exposed heating pipes in two corners and blistered paint on the ceiling, but the appliances are brand new, a dazzling white that impresses Tom, who runs his hands over the refrigerator approvingly. The bottoms of his rubber thongs stick to the speckled-print linoleum as he and Victor walk through to the bathroom.

"There's no sink!" Tom wails. "I like the kitchen, but how can I live in a place where the bathroom doesn't come with a sink?"

"Here's the sink, right here," Victor says soothingly, pointing to an alcove just outside the bathroom. "And look at this huge medicine cabinet above it."

"It's not *that* inconvenient, actually," Tom concedes, and Victor's heart soars.

"The rent's four-forty," he says, holding his breath. "Let's go check out the bedroom."

"Four-forty! I don't care if the bedroom's the size of a utility closet — I'll take it. This is great!" Tom says, jubilant, pumping Victor's arm for the second time today. "It's a miracle," he says.

"It's rent-controlled," Victor says. "The previous tenant must have been here for thirty years. And the landlord's going to be looking for any excuse at all to throw you out so he can raise the rent again. You've got to be an ideal tenant." He looks at Tom gravely. "Do you think you're up to the task at hand?"

"In addition to paying my rent on time, I'll even recycle my glass bottles and tuna cans, how's that?"

Entering the long and narrow bedroom, where the walls are painted forest green and the window overlooks a bleak air shaft, Tom says, "It's way bigger than a utility closet, isn't it?"

"Absolutely," says Victor. "And once it's painted white, it'll seem even bigger." But Tom's sudden pensive look worries him. "Second thoughts?" he asks.

"The house I grew up in," says Tom dreamily, "had a library, a room filled with nothing but books. Nobody ever spent much time in there except me; I even loved the smell of that room, the smell of furniture polish and old books that could fall apart in your hands if you weren't careful. You could spend months locked in there and never feel anything close to boredom. Or at least *I* could." Looking past Victor now, he says, "I'm a long way from there, do you know what I mean?"

"I do," Victor says.

Tom gives his head a vigorous shake, as if to clear it of all disappointment. He fluffs out his hair and laughs. "I'm not as much of a loser as I appear to be," he says cheerfully. "There's very little I regret deeply, except the loss of my marriage. That was entirely preventable — I could kick myself every time I think of my own dumb stupidity. But at least my former wife's still fond of me, and our daughter's a real prize. And now I've got this . . . not bad apartment to call my own."

"Remember the eat-in kitchen," says Victor.

"One of these days I'll invite you and Katha over for fettucini in clam sauce."

"Sure," Victor says. "And you'll be entertaining women in your new kitchen before you know it. Someone named Pamela? Oh," he says, and sighs. "And also her three kids."

"That's my sister," says Tom. "Her three boys are so well behaved it's frightening. She keeps them in crew cuts all year round, maybe that's part of the problem. They're a depressing bunch, that's for sure."

Victor studies his watch. "If we hurry and get over to the rental agent to sign the lease, maybe we can still have time for a drink afterward to celebrate."

"Yeah, thanks," says Tom. "Thanks for everything."

"Don't thank me. It was a guardian angel who led us here. In a manner of speaking, that is."

"You're *my* guardian angel," Tom says. "Anyone who can find a rent-controlled apartment in this city has to have heavenly connections."

"His name is Murray Weinbaum."

"Do you think I should send him a thank-you note?"

"That won't be necessary," Victor says.

"A bottle of wine, then?"

"He hasn't had a drink in thirty-three years."

"Well, give him my thanks when you see him."

"Will do," says Victor.

Three weeks later, he is stir-frying scallops in black bean sauce, keeping watch over six dumplings in a frying pan, and steaming rice in a pot that's about to explode, all to impress Katha, who doesn't look particularly impressed. Throughout the day, from the very moment he awoke, he's felt restless and uneasy; trying to pinpoint the source of his misgiving, he's gotten nowhere at all.

"I'm lowering the flame over the rice," Katha says, then returns to her seat at the kitchen table, which is cluttered with broken-backed Chinese cookbooks, their pages spotted with a variety of sauces. "We should have gone out," she says. "I hate to see you working so hard."

"In case you haven't noticed, I'm good at this," Victor says. "I know exactly what I'm doing."

"The dumplings are burning, by the way," Katha points out. After she rescues them, arranging their scorched skins on a china plate edged with turquoise dragons, she sidles up to Victor. She tweaks his ponytail, which has grown, over the months, a good distance past his shoulders. "Hey," she says. "Ask me what's new."

"I give up."

"I," she says dramatically, "sold one of the tunnel paintings today for two thousand bucks. To a friend of Tom's stepfather, actually. I never expected Sam to be the least bit interested in helping me, but first he manages to get me a job, and now this. I guess Tom put in more than a few good words for me."

"That's terrific." Victor slips a scallop into her mouth. "Are you on top of the world, or what?"

"Feeling good about the painting, anyway," Katha says. "And the job's not too terrible, though really I'm little more than an assistant to people who've yet to celebrate their thirtieth birthdays. If I think too much about what it is I'm doing there, I start to feel queasy, so the trick, of course, is not giving it much thought at all. Oh, and by the way," she reports, "the scallop's a little rubbery."

"I must have overcooked them, damn it." Lifting the wok from the stove, Victor carries it to the table, trailed by three interested dogs. "How's Tom doing?"

"Getting by, I guess. And I have to admit, it's a relief having him in a place of his own again. It was getting to be a bit much, coming home to him after work every day — you know, too many shared dinners, too much of his laundry mixed in with my own."

"Come home to *me* every day," Victor hears himself say. And then, "You can even have your own bedroom and bath up on the third floor. And there's that guest room next to it for Julia. The two of you could have your own suite up there."

"What's the rent on this suite?"

"Well, it's not free," Victor says. "A dollar a month ought to cover it, though."

Katha considers this for what seems to be a long while. "I'm crazy about you," she says at last. "You know that."

"But you don't have much faith in our future together as a couple. As a family," he amends.

"I'd like to," Katha says. "I'd love to. It's just that you're still a mystery I can't seem to crack. It kills me that I can't know you inside out, that I'll never fully understand what you are. Not in the way you understand me, anyway. There's an imbalance there — you'll always have the advantage. And I'm the one who'll always be trailing behind. That's not where I want to be in this life, trailing behind with no hope of catching up. Ever."

"Understand this," Victor says, and he summons her over to the table with a wave of a fake ivory chopstick. He pulls her onto his lap, tilts the back of her head against his shoulder. "You're too smart to be so fearful. In your own way, you're as much a mystery to me as I am to you. That's the beauty of it, isn't it, that there's always something that remains unknowable in the person you love. We're not meant to know everything — both of us have to keep something of ourselves secret. It's something that can change from one day to the next, or it's something unalterable. But we can't live inside each other's skins — it's just not possible."

"Not even for you?"

"Well," Victor says, "it's true that I'm privileged to see and hear more than most, to be attuned to the signals that are always out there." It occurs to him that he's been pontificating, rather arrogantly tooting his own horn. He begins to speak, to formulate an apology, and then he stiffens. He shuts his eyes, sees something that makes his skin prickle, his heart beat fiercely. "Goddamnit," he says, and shoves Katha away so he can get to the phone.

"What?" she asks, following so closely behind that she scuffs his heels. "Don't ever push me like that again, you got that? I don't like it."

"It's Tom," he says. He passes her the phone, saying, "Dial his number for me."

"It's ringing," she soon says. "He's not answering."

"Count out fifteen or twenty rings, and then hang up and dial nine one one."

"And say what? What's going on, Victor?"

"Just hand me the phone," he says, and when he speaks into it, giving Tom's address to the 911 operator, his voice is cool and flinty, as if he were someone in uniform simply doing his job.

Katha is already weeping. "What did he do? What's going to happen to him?" Socking Victor in the chest with one fist and then the other, she waits for him to acknowledge that she's hurting him.

"He's in bed," he says finally, still holding on to the receiver, ignoring the relentless buzz of the dial tone. "And there are half-empty bottles of Valium and sleeping pills on the night table. And in an ashtray the butts of a couple of joints he smoked. Roaches." He sighs.

Katha freezes, her fists against his chest. "Impossible," she says. "Out of the question. He quit smoking the stuff ages ago."

"Listen to me," Victor says. "I don't think he meant for this to happen, but God almighty, he really fucked up royally this time. And *I* told him he was going to live to ninety-nine." He lets out a furious, strangled cry and drops the phone. "Me," he says. "I personally delivered the good news. You'd think I would have been more patient, willing to listen more attentively. Well, I wasn't, and now he's gone and done himself in."

"He's dead?" Katha says in a whisper.

"It was only a few weeks ago," Victor says. "He actually mentioned that his mother would spring for a classy funeral if he killed himself."

"Is he dead?" Katha howls. "Why do I have to keep asking you the same simple question over and over again?"

The dogs are nosing around the telephone on the floor, pricking up their ears as the dial tone gives way to an eerie, high-pitched whine. "Get away from there," Victor says listlessly. "Go help yourself to some Chinese food."

"It's a yes or no question. How hard could it be to answer?" Katha shrieks.

"The day you and I met," Victor says, "I told you his future was very uncertain. He was a man on his way down, I saw that at least."

Katha nods. "And what do you see now?"

"You know what I see, goddamnit," Victor says. "And it's best not to look too closely."

Katha covers her face with her hands. "Damn him," she weeps. "What a stupid, stupid waste. How dare he throw away his life like that! How dare he!"

"Why didn't I see this coming?" Victor says. "I should have, and I didn't."

"You didn't fail him," Katha offers generously, and even in his haze of pain and self-doubt, Victor feels a rich mixture of love and gratitude that he will never forget. "He failed himself," Katha says. "Are you listening to me, Victor?"

"Yes," he says. He wants more from her, a lingering embrace, a cool hand at the nape of his neck, but all she does is hang the phone back where it belongs, so carefully it's as if she's handling something as fragile as love itself.

In the weeks following Tom's death, Victor reads nearly fifty palms, magnifying glass clenched tightly in his fingers. Sometimes his hand begins to tremble and he has to put down the glass and take a series of deep, slow breaths. When this happens, the client in the hot seat usually worries aloud about what Victor has seen that has caused his hand to shake so. No, no, no, he reassures the client, it's just something muscular, or maybe neurological, he really should see a doctor one of these days. *It's only my self-confidence,* he wants to say, *coming and going, waxing and waning, always without warning.* And sometimes he sees Tom's life line etched in that big thick hand, and hears his own voice saying, *You could live to be ninety-nine, but only if you want to.*

He hardly knew the man, yet he continues to mourn him, a life discarded, foolishly thrown away in two generous handfuls of all-too-easy-to-swallow capsules. He hasn't seen Katha since the funeral, where she sat up in the front row with Julia, and Tom's mother and stepfather and sister, the five of them seated in size order, their hair illuminated in the stream of sunlight that seeped through the stained-glass windows of the chapel. Tom's coffin was a rich, burnished mahogany, top of the line, just as he'd predicted. Several colleagues stepped up to the lectern and spoke briefly of his innovative classes in the sociology department, how he loved to play Bob Dylan albums for his students, who sometimes didn't get the point. "He was so patient with them," one of the speakers said ruefully, "so absolutely certain he had something of value to impart to them."

Tom's sister, a youngish-looking middle-aged woman in a gray business suit, spoke sweetly of his childhood and the astonishing number of books he'd devoured. "He won a contest, for having read two or three times as many books as anyone else in his fifth-grade class," she told her listeners, and smiled tentatively. "The prize was a hamster, and of course it got out of its cage and bit him almost as soon as he'd gotten it home from school. He had to go to the emergency room for a tetanus shot, and the doctor on duty, an Indian or a Pakistani, I think, kept saying, 'I do not understand what this is that you call a hamster — a small rat, a mouse, what?' And Tom thought this was the funniest thing. 'Oh no,' he told the doctor, 'much bigger, more like a big fat rat, but with wings.' He laughed so hard at the poor doctor's horrified face, and then, of course, he felt so bad he just had to apologize." Looking out expectantly at her uneasy audience, she said, "That was Tom, wasn't it?"

Embracing her former sister-in-law as she took her place at the lectern, Katha spoke in a wobbly voice into the microphone. "He wasn't a terrific husband," she said, "which I think he'd be the first to admit. But he was a loving father and an affectionate ex-husband, and you'd better believe he'll be missed." Moving back from the microphone, she seemed about to walk away and, in fact, took two steps down before changing her mind and returning to the lectern. "None of us could have saved him," she said, "no matter what we might think. None of us," she repeated and nodded slightly, as if in agreement with herself. "It's finished," she murmured.

Afterward, when Victor approached her before she stepped into the limousine headed for the cemetery, she allowed his lips to graze her cool cheek. "Call me," she whispered.

Yet he still cannot face her. She's left several messages on his answering machine, which he's played over too many times, just for the sound of her voice. Eventually he hit the erase button, wishing, only an instant later, that he hadn't.

If he ever gets his hands on Murray, that ne'er-do-well of a guardian angel, he will let him have it but good.

16

BUDDY HAS BEEN on the phone nearly all morning, finalizing the sale of his dental practice to the rabbi's cousin, who's just gotten out of school and can't wait to get his feet wet. Sitting on a chaise longue beside the pool, wrapped in a smoking jacket, cordless phone in hand, Buddy looks like some kind of West Coast mogul, Lucy thinks, and almost laughs. She hasn't had a good laugh in ages, though things, at long last, seem to be looking up, at least in Buddy's view. Her own view is more than a bit jaundiced; now that Buddy has kissed his practice good-bye (without her approval or even her tacit consent), the shape of their future together seems as hazy as their bathroom mirror clouded with steam.

Hoisting herself over the rim of the trampoline, she leaps higher than she ought to, propelled by nothing more than the strength of her frustration. She can see beyond the top of the tall fence surrounding the yard, and into her neighbor's tennis court, where a solitary fluorescent yellow ball is wedged into the net. Above, against a pearl gray sky, the sun is a disappointing white; staring straight up and into it, Lucy's eyes fill with tears. Tiring, she begins to pant and finally collapses on her knees in the center of the trampoline. Buddy is still on the phone, gesturing with one hand toward the pool, throwing it in as part of the deal perhaps, along with the house, and the wife and kids. *Go ahead,* Lucy dares him. *Sell us all down the river while you're at it.*

"Can't you get off that damn thing?" her mother calls from the middle of the lawn, edging closer now, dragging along the afghan she's been crocheting for years, it seems. "One of these days," she predicts, "you'll fall and break an ankle or a wrist, and then you'll be sorry. Don't you know any better than to jump around on there like some crazy fool?"

"It relaxes me," Lucy says.

"Pooh," says Florine. "You're a grown woman. Find some other way to relax." Turning to squint over her shoulder at Buddy, she says, "I'm sorry for your troubles, baby."

"I'm looking at the back of your head," Lucy says. "Can't you look straight at me when you're saying something nice?"

"Truly sorry," Florine offers, and turns back to face the trampoline. "I can't even call him 'the Jewish dentist' anymore, can I?"

"He's still a dentist, Mom, he's just not in practice."

"He did a real nice job capping those two front teeth of mine after I wore them down to nothing."

"You might tell him that sometime."

"What for? It's going on seven years now. The time to thank him came and went a long time ago, I'd say."

"It's never too late to do the right thing," Lucy reflects.

Groaning, Florine climbs up beside her. "These old, old bones of mine aren't getting any younger," she complains.

In response, Lucy stretches herself out into an almost-perfect split and clasps one ankle, then the other. She would like to believe that the worst months of her life are over, that Buddy will be spending the rest of his days fully clothed and gainfully employed instead of lounging around in his pajamas,

a fine dusting of crumbs caught in the curly mat of hair cover-
ing his chest. She would do just about anything, she thinks, to
see shoes and socks on his feet, his rear end planted behind
the steering wheel of their station wagon, one hand grasping
the wheel itself as he shifts into reverse with the other and
backs out of the driveway, heading nowhere in particular or
even to the nearest 7-Eleven for a six-pack of anything at all.

Not that he had been entirely idle all summer. He'd painted
the boys' rooms, stripped and refinished the piano, installed
track lighting in the living room and hallways. Twice a week
the rabbi came by to play chess with him; afterward, whether
he'd won or not, Buddy appeared invigorated and optimistic,
as if the rabbi's company had been a jolt of some potent drug
that brought him tantalizingly close to his old self. Several
times he'd even talked of taking a weekend trip to his
brother's house in East Hampton, but nothing ever came of it;
he simply could not get past his mystifying reluctance to leave
home, and Lucy decided, after encouraging him gently to go
forward with his plans, not to press it. His appetite for food, at
least, had improved — he was eating two good meals a day by
the summer's end, an achievement for which Lucy took full
credit. She fixed, with unusual effort and care, only the things
he liked best and did not argue when he asked for the same
dinner three or four days in a row. His sexual appetite, however, had been dulled by whatever demons still had him in
their grasp. Their most recent experience, initiated by Lucy in
the middle of a rainy afternoon, had begun sweetly enough
and ended miserably, with both of them near tears, humiliated
beyond words. The thought of this now, as she sits up beside
her mother on the trampoline, makes her wince, as if recoiling
from the light touch of her mother's hand at the crook of her
arm.

"What are *you* so touchy about?" Florine asks, and pulls her
hand away. "Can't I even pat my baby's arm if I want to? Next
time maybe I'll be smart and ask for special permission first."

"My mind was someplace else," Lucy apologizes. "Someplace private."

"Well, you better get it back where it belongs."

"It's Buddy."

"It's always Buddy," her mother says. "You pamper him too much, that's your problem right there. You let me get ahold of him and give him a good talking-to, and that would be the end of all this foolishness. I could set him straight in no time. Or you could do it yourself: you grab him by those scrawny shoulders of his and say, 'Stop all this bellyaching and be a man, Mr. Robert M. Silverman!'"

"Dr. Robert M. Silverman," Lucy says, smiling.

"Whatever. You get my point."

"That's right out of the Tough Love school of family management, you know."

"Uhmm," says Florine. "Never heard of it, but I do like the sound of it."

"Well, I don't," Lucy says, then reconsiders. "I mean, I do, actually, but I'm afraid to push him like that right now, given the progress he seems to have made on his own lately."

"You call that progress?" Florine hisses. "An able-bodied man in his bathrobe at two in the afternoon? That's bullshit, baby, and you know it."

"We've got to be patient," Lucy says. "You can't rush the healing process — it could be dangerous."

"Don't give me that," says Florine. "The man's had a whole summer to pull himself together. I say it's high time you gave him a hard push in the right direction. And what about the boys — you think it's healthy for them to come home from school and see their father hanging around the house like some lowlife when he should be out earning a living like the rest of the world?"

In the month since Max and Jonah had returned from camp, they'd been surprisingly solicitous of Buddy, far more generous in their assessment of the situation than Lucy had

hoped. She could learn a thing or two from them both, she reflected, proud of the earnestness with which they listened to
her explain the way things were, the way they'd gone all summer, the way they might turn in the future if all four of them
were exceptionally lucky and if the three of them were as loving as they could be to the one who needed everything from
them. They'd nodded gravely, their suntanned faces strikingly
beautiful as they took in the puzzling news, digested it, and
then went off to see Buddy, who hugged them both fiercely
and offered to shoot some hoops with them in his bathrobe
and sneakers. The boys soon lost their soberness, but almost
every night at bedtime they asked Lucy for an appraisal, wanting reassurance, she knew, that everywhere there were signs of
Buddy's improvement.

"He seems pretty OK to *me*," Max told her his first night
home, his eyes on David Letterman, his hand on the remote
control as he curled on his side and kicked away the blanket
with his shockingly big feet, which had grown a size and a half
over the summer. "Don't you think so?"

"I do," Lucy said cautiously. "But he's still kind of fragile.
We've got to treat him carefully for a while."

"Like he's made of glass?" Max said, and then giggled as Letterman reported that Barbara Bush would be replacing the
man on the Quaker Oats box.

"Like he's made of crystal."

"But he's not."

"Well, we have to think of him as if he were."

"Is he in therapy?" asked Max. "Two kids in my bunk were,
and they were both pretty normal. One of them plays basketball with his therapist twice a week and doesn't have to talk at
all or answer any questions unless he wants to. Maybe I could
get his phone number for Dad."

Pulling him up into an awkward embrace, Lucy said, "You're
a mensch, baby, you know that?"

"Yeah yeah yeah," Max said over his shoulder and switched the channel to MTV. "And guess what — I'm not a vegetarian anymore. The food at camp wasn't exactly awesome, and the only things I could stand were the tuna fish sandwiches and the stuff they had at the barbecues every week. So it looks like I'm a carnivore again."

"Whatever you'd like," said Lucy.

"What I'd like," said Max, "is for Dad to get a job so we won't have to starve."

"We're not going to starve," Lucy said, sounding more confident than she felt. For as long as she could stand it, she listened to the poor dead singer from Nirvana crooning "Rape me," and then she shut off the television.

"He's not a lowlife," she tells her mother now. "He's obviously struggling with something that's very painful to him. Why can't you acknowledge that and give him a goddamn break for once?"

Florine shakes her head, making a disapproving click with her tongue against her teeth. "Why do *you* have to be the strong one through all this?" she says. "Why?"

"I hate it," Lucy confesses in a whisper. "It's selfish of me, but I hate it. My life has been so good for so long, and now it's not. I still can't get over it, the surprise of it, of things going wrong. The psychic warned me, and I laughed at him. I was so arrogant," she says. "You wouldn't believe how sure I was that he was wrong."

"You go to a psychic, you're asking for trouble," Florine says. "They tell you things you don't want to hear, things that keep you up half the night."

"You've been to one?" Lucy says, truly surprised. "You?" She has always thought of her mother as remarkably strong and self-reliant, someone who would never seek help from even the most likely and obvious sources, even her own family. "You?" she says again.

"It was years ago," Florine says, flicking her wrist in dismissal. "Right after your father died. I was sinking deeper and deeper into some kind of hopelessness that just about did me in. Your grandma took me to this old woman in a dark apartment that smelled like too many cats. She looked at some tea leaves and saw the shape of something that made her smile. She wouldn't tell me what it was, only that I would soon recover. Which of course I did. She also told me I would never marry again, but that there was a man close by who loved me."

"Marcus?" Lucy says.

"I knew who she meant, all right — my very own brother-in-law. Good thing my sister died never knowing a thing. It would have killed her, for sure."

"The psychic told you that?"

"Common sense told me that," Florine snaps. "And common sense told me never to go back to that crazy old woman. What did I need her for, anyway? You think I didn't know Marcus had a thing for me? Even while my sister was still alive he would call me up late at night and want to come over and talk. 'We're talking right now, Marcus,' I'd tell him. 'No need to come over when we've both got a telephone.' One time he brings himself over anyway. Your grandmother's asleep, and of course you're away at school. He pushes me up against the edge of the kitchen sink and kisses me like I've never been kissed before," Florine says, sighing. "I enjoyed that kiss and then some, but there were other things to consider besides my own pleasure, unfortunately. 'Go home, Marcus,' I told him. 'Go home right now or I'll have to slap some sense into you.' And he went, dragging his heels all the way."

Lucy smiles. "How many times has he asked you to marry him?"

"Let's see," her mother says. "Every year on my birthday, every New Year's Eve, every Valentine's Day. You'd think I'd break down and give in after all these years, wouldn't you? But really, what for? I get everything I want from him, plus I get to keep my independence. And I don't have to do his laundry or pick up after him or cook his meals every day of the week. No sir, I've got him right where I want him, which is more than you can say for you and *your* man, baby."

Remembering, suddenly, the card she'd drawn at Victor's table that afternoon last winter, the card representing strength, Lucy tells her mother, "Don't forget how tough I am — almost as tough as you, I bet."

"Let's hope so," her mother says. "Because somebody's got to set this family of yours straight."

They both look up as Buddy ambles toward them in his satiny robe. "I'll see you ladies later," he says when he reaches the trampoline. "I'm going out to the mall for a while," he continues casually, gazing over the tops of their heads, surveying his well-groomed acre with a half-smile.

"What's this all about?" Lucy says, not quite able to believe she's heard correctly.

"Don't worry, I won't be gone long."

Lucy tugs at the sleeve of his robe. "Buddy, wait," she says. Her mouth is so dried out and dusty that she can barely speak. "Don't you want someone to come with you?"

"Believe it or not, I'm perfectly capable of going for a spin alone."

"Of course you are," she says uncertainly.

"Then what's the problem?"

"No problem."

"You going to let go of my sleeve?"

Sheepishly, she scoots back from him. "Buddy?"

"*What?*"

"Enjoy yourself," she says, and watches as he marches across the lawn, his shoulders squared in the long scarlet robe he's lived in, it seems, for the whole interminable summer.

It occurs to her that there is probable cause for celebration, yet she's as nervous as if her husband were heading not to the mall but on a solo mission to the moon.

Too apprehensive to sit at home while Buddy roams the mall on his own, Lucy leaves her mother behind, telling herself there must be *something* she can't live without — a new set of sheets, a bathing suit for next year, or maybe a manicure. She parks in the mall's underground lot, then heads upstairs, pretending she's on the lookout not for Buddy but for an end-of-summer sale or two. Cruising the first level, she passes a three-horse carousel, on which a single tiny customer revolves tearfully, calling for his father to rescue him.

"What's so terrible?" the father says. "Can't I even finish my cigarette in peace?"

"Apparently not," Lucy murmurs, and saunters in and out of CD Heaven, Nutrition World, and the 99¢ Store, where she almost buys a bag of sponges and a package of ballpoint pens but then decides against it; on close inspection, the sponges look dusty beneath their plastic wrapper, the pens cheaply made and filled with ink that is already drying out. The truth is, there is nothing she needs or wants here, except a glimpse of her husband keeping step with everyone else, putting one big flat foot in front of the other, shopping bags in hand, perhaps an ice cream cone at his lips. There are countless shoppers strolling through the mall: why shouldn't Buddy be one of them, just an ordinary man with not much on his mind except thoughts of dinner or renting a video for the evening or stopping for a haircut on his way home?

She is obsessed with finding him now, needing to see for herself how naturally he blends in with the crowd. When she spots him, nearly twenty minutes later, exiting the food court with a large doughy pretzel jammed halfway into his mouth, she understands instantly that she has asked for too much too soon, and that the pain of this realization will linger like an ache in her bones. For there is Buddy, in his vividly red robe and dirty sneakers, unaware of the stares he is drawing from all sides, the looks that say, *What the hell's with the guy in the bathrobe?*

Approaching him warily, not wanting to scare him off, she waves at Buddy, then reaches toward him to pull the pretzel from his mouth. "Hey," she says, "how'd it go?"

"I *knew* you'd come after me," Buddy says, and smiles vaguely. "You know, there are so many people, so many goddamn stores. All that money changing hands everywhere you look."

"True," says Lucy. She looks around for a place to sit and finds a bench arranged against a narrow planter filled with plastic ivy. "Let's take a breather," she suggests.

Buddy crosses his bare legs, nibbles at his pretzel. "I'm thinking of buying a business right here in the mall, of going into business for myself. What do you think?"

"I think," Lucy says mildly, "that you forgot to get dressed when you left the house."

Looking down into the V of his robe, thrusting a hand inside to massage his chest, Buddy says, "Whoops."

"This is not a good thing, Buddy," she tells him, reducing everything to its simplest terms, as if she were talking to a child. "You can see how a lapse like this might make me very anxious. Incredibly anxious, in fact."

"Take it easy," he says. "I was preoccupied, OK? I had an urge to get the hell out of the house, and it seemed like such a good, positive impulse that I had to run with it. You'll have to excuse me if I didn't stop to change into a socially acceptable outfit first, OK?"

Lucy seizes the lapels of his robe. She puts her face in his. "Am I going to spend the rest of my life worried sick about you?" she cries. "Is that the way it's going to be? Is it?"

"How the hell would I know?" Buddy says, and plucks her hands off him. "How the hell would I know anything?"

17

IN A SINGLE WEEK, Victor has made appointments for himself with three different clairvoyants and canceled each of them at the last minute. His cancellations are met with rueful laughter, and much sympathy.

"Join the club," number three tells him. "And if I'm ever desperate enough for a peek into my own future, you'll be the first one I'll call."

The fourth time he tries to bail out, his excuses are rejected as fast as he can offer them up.

"No dice, Victor," a psychic named Lorraine tells him over the phone. "You show up at the door at the appointed hour, or you'll find yourself in the deepest shit imaginable. And don't forget that my great-grandmother was the original witch of the family. She passed down everything she knew to yours truly before she died."

"Thanks for the warning," says Victor. "See you at seven."

"Be on time," Lorraine says. "I'm extremely impatient with people who make me wait."

Dressed in jeans and a V-necked sweater that reveals a wide triangle of freckled white skin, she greets him with a kiss, a lighted cigarette between her fingers. She's a sturdy-looking woman, pretty, with surprising, bright green eyes and a big puff of dark bangs rising over her forehead. Hopping onto one of the two wooden folding chairs set up at a card table, she immediately arranges herself in the lotus position. Her feet are bare, Victor notices, the nails painted bronze, the same color as her long fingernails.

"Come on over here, you scaredy-cat," she says fondly.

They've known each other for years, having met when they were guests together on a radio talk show, but they haven't been in touch in ages. It seems to Victor that she'd invited him to a New Year's Eve party a while ago, but he can't recall why he'd turned down the invitation. For some reason he regrets it now, as if he'd foolishly passed up an opportunity he should have welcomed.

Lorraine's living room is small and tidy, with a pair of floral-patterned armchairs facing each other across a fuzzy Berber rug. The drapes are drawn against the dwindling light; across the mantel of a brick fireplace, a row of stubby candles flickers, casting trembling shadows along the wall.

The instant Victor sits down at the table, an obese black cat settles itself in his lap and begins to purr furiously. Within reach is a vase of fragrant roses, pink and yellow, a glass of water, an ordinary deck of playing cards, and an ashtray jammed with cigarette butts.

"It's nice and cozy in here," Victor comments, as he rubs the underside of the cat's chin nervously. "Maybe that's why I'm feeling so relaxed."

"You," says Lorraine, "are about as relaxed as a sky diver poised to jump for the first time in his life."

"When was the last time *you* went for a reading, big shot?" Victor says.

"Let's see," says Lorraine. "I had my teeth cleaned in June, my annual mammogram in August . . . so I'd have to say we're talking the spring of — seventy-five, give or take a year or two in either direction."

"I rest my case," Victor says, and dumps the cat on the floor.

"Not all of us are as brave as thee, my dear. Want to shuffle the cards?"

"Not yet," says Victor. Dipping his head forward to sniff the roses, he says, "How's business?"

"Business is booming, thank you very much. I actually had to hire someone to handle my appointment book."

"Great," Victor says, as two more cats streak through the room, leaping into one of the flowery chairs, where they lock arms and begin biting each other, playfully at first, and then in earnest.

"Boys!" Lorraine says, and she claps her hands together briskly. "Behave yourselves or both of you are going to spend some time in solitary."

"You still dating the guy with the pointed beard and the wire-rimmed glasses? The Yale psychologist?" Victor asks, trying to ignore the squeals of protest coming from the armchair.

"Simon?" Separating the cats, Lorraine disappears from the room, an animal hanging limply from under each arm. "Simon?" she repeats on her return. "Sorry to say we're no longer on speaking terms."

"What happened?"

"He freaked when one too many of my predictions came true, exactly on schedule. If only I'd kept my big mouth shut."

"We all make mistakes," Victor says. He picks up the pack of cards from the table and shuffles them absently, over and over again, until he hears Lorraine cry, "Enough already!"

"Quit stalling, Victor," she says. "I'm going to make this as painless as possible, I promise. And if you have an anxiety attack in the middle, I'll pack you up and send you straight to the psych ward at Bellevue, where they'll take excellent care of you."

"Ha ha," Victor says dryly. "What a comedienne."

"Count out twenty-one cards and give them to me facedown, you big baby."

He counts them out twice, just to be sure, and listens to the satisfying snap of cards against the table as Lorraine turns them over one by one. She lights a cigarette and exhales a plume of bluish smoke toward the ceiling. Speaking rapidly, in a kind of uninflected stream of consciousness, she reports what she sees. "There's a child, first initial J, J-A-, nope, that's J-U, Julie, Julia, whatever, who you've disappointed . . . she doesn't understand where you've gone . . . her father's left her too, but you're the one who owes her an explanation . . . And here's the anger card . . . you and a friend, an old, old friend, you're so angry at this guy you want to shut him out of your life forever . . . you can't find him . . . you need to speak to him to let him know about some mistake he's made . . . initial M, that's all I get here . . . he cares for you deeply . . . There's the blockage card . . . there's been a delay in another situation . . . I'm talking about the love of your life . . . Katharine, Kathleen, Kathy . . . damn, what kind of a name is this? — I can't get it."

"Katha," he says.

"Never heard of it," Lorraine says impatiently. "Well, she's out there, wondering if you're lost to each other forever . . . she's in a minor depression, going about her business, just waiting . . . Now here's a weirdo prediction . . . I see the two of you at a party . . . something like a wedding, only there's no bride and groom . . . this is a new experience for you . . . you're dancing like a madman, someone who doesn't know when to quit." Stopping for a sip from her water glass, Lorraine says, "Jesus, I'm exhausted."

"I thought I was the one who was doing all the dancing," says Victor.

"It's hard work — I've got to rest a minute."

"You're doing fine," Victor offers.

"Sue me if I'm wrong, but I'm going to go with a favorable prediction regarding you and this Katha. What's the story on this chick? Who is she?"

"She was a client," Victor mumbles.

"Huge mistake," says Lorraine, as she lights a fresh cigarette. "You cross that line and you're asking for trouble. The first time Simon and I made love, the whole right side of my body broke out in a rash. If that's not a sign that somebody's headed in the wrong direction, I don't know what is."

"Well, nobody broke out in hives, but she never did get comfortable with the idea of settling in for the long haul with someone like me."

Lorraine unfolds her legs and lifts them under her chin. She smiles sympathetically out over her knees. "I was married once," she confesses, "a long time ago. He was a songwriter, he played electric guitar with a pretty good band. I was working as a waitress — we were living in Key West then — and I started making extra money doing readings for the tourists who came in, and some of the locals too. I never did tell Billy where the money was coming from, but he found out through a couple of friends of his, and, let me tell you, he went crazy. He'd known about my power, of course, but I'd downplayed it during the years we were together, because I knew he thought it was kind of creepy and maybe even a little sinister. And then one day he came into the restaurant and dragged me out in the middle of a reading. 'How dare you take money from these people,' he hollered at me, 'telling them things they're only going to find out for themselves anyway?' He told me I was exploiting them, that I ought to be ashamed of myself."

"If you'd loved him enough, maybe you would have listened," Victor says.

"Possibly. But it helped to ruin everything between us, hearing that from him. And I knew what I wanted then, and it struck me that it wasn't going to be easy, given the person I was."

"A life of ordinary happiness," Victor says in a whispery voice. "That would do it for me."

"Most of the time, it seems light-years away, doesn't it?"

"But not always," says Victor wistfully.

"So I'll stick with my prediction, then."

"I won't sue you," he promises.

Gathering up the cards with three sweeps of her hand, Lorraine says, "Shuffle these again, and I'll go deeper into the future for you."

"I think not," says Victor, because he has enough to get by and will quit while he's ahead.

Lorraine shrugs. "It's your nickel, honey, but I don't think you've gotten your money's worth. There's so much more I could tell you, if only you'd let me."

"But I won't. And don't you know the customer is always right?"

"Now that," says Lorraine, "is the silliest thing I've heard all day."

Preparing for a leisurely soak in the bath, Victor first has to empty the tub of several bowls of neon-bright gravel he's been meaning to add to his aquarium, the net he uses to remove the occasional dead or dying fish from the tank, and a ceramic castle with a broken turret he's long intended to glue back together. He can't recall having dumped any of this into the tub, and it is with considerable annoyance that he clears it all away. The last time he was actually in the tub was on a summer evening, when, after a day with Katha at a friend's weekend farm in Poughkeepsie, he'd returned home with the obvious markings of poison ivy across his back. It was Katha who'd drawn the bath for him after the long drive back to the city and then sat on a tiny stool outside the tub, her nose red with sunburn, her hair smelling of barbecue smoke and their day in the country. She'd dried him off tenderly and applied the calamine lotion to his prickly skin, dropping a line of kisses along his shoulder blades before leading him off to bed. How He's missed her, he thinks. In all the weeks that have passed since Tom's funeral, he has, more than once, found himself on the street outside her studio, hoping she might look from her window at just the right moment and catch sight of him there, penitent and filled with longing but not yet able to forgive himself.

Before he slips into the steamy tub now, he turns off the light over the mirror, leaving only the night-light on. He sets the radio on the toilet tank to a classical music station and positions the bath mat just so.

Underwater, his hands look puffy, as if belonging to a fat man, someone who's indulged himself too often. He brings them up, crosses them over his heart. He closes his eyes, and then, feeling dizzy, opens them again. Unaccountably, there's a draft in the room; his nipples harden into pebbles, and he sinks deeper beneath the water, his arms wrapped around each other.

"Don't say a word," Murray orders. He's floating limply between the sink and the toilet, his shoulders rounded, his head hung low in shame, or so Victor would like to think. "I know in your eyes I screwed up royally," says Murray, "but the fact is, your friend Tom *liked* that apartment. He liked it so much, he wanted to write me a thank-you note."

"I hope whoever's in charge on the other side tries to get you demoted," says Victor. "And you know what, you deserve to fry as far as I'm concerned."

Murray winces. "That's a little harsh, isn't it? It's not as if I had any idea what he was up to. He was a stranger, someone who was standing in your way. I was trying to be helpful, to both of you actually, and I was. Look," says Murray, "if I could have kept him away from that bottle of Valium, don't you think I would have? Unfortunately, he wasn't under divine guardianship, not mine or anyone else's."

"Speaking of which, you're fired," Victor says. "I don't want you hanging around me anymore."

Murray looks amused. "The fact is, you're stuck with me. In sickness and in health, blah blah blah."

"I want to file a complaint with the grievance committee, then."

"I'm innocent, old friend, and so are you. Give it up, Victor. Get back on track. Move along." Waiting for some response, he hums along with the music. "These solo violins are glorious. It's Handel, isn't it? Did you know he's been dead since seventeen fifty-nine? And here we are listening to his music. Amazing."

Victor focuses on a water stain on the ceiling, which at first looks like a teacup, then the silhouette of an elephant, then nothing at all. "What's even more amazing is that I'm talking to a ghost," he says. "That I took advice from a ghost. A ghost who's been wearing the same pair of pajamas for thirty-three years. Maybe I do belong in the psych ward at Bellevue."

"The first time I came to you," Murray reminisces, "you looked up at me so patiently, trying so hard to fathom what this visitor who was disturbing your sleep was all about. And then, finally, you said just the right thing."

"'I'll miss you,'" Victor says softly.

Nodding, Murray says, "And I thought to myself, Now there's a kid I'd like to keep tabs on."

"I liked you best behind the counter of the candy store," Victor tells him. "I looked forward to seeing you every day, presiding over all the treasures of your little kingdom."

"Some kingdom. I had to moonlight as a bartender to keep up my mortgage payments. It wasn't an easy life. And then, too soon, it was over. I wasn't much older than you. Forty-three and a couple of months. That was all I had coming to me."

"What!" Leaning over the side of the tub for a closer look, Victor sees Murray's face as he always does, something drawn in pale grays, his eyes and hair, the sweep of his brows, all white, as in the negative of a photograph. Light shines through his eyes and ears and through the curve of his nostrils. It's a face Victor could put his hand through, if he dared.

Murray laughs and laughs. "What do you think you're looking at, an old man?"

"You were an old man when I was a kid," Victor says defensively. "At least it seemed that way."

"It didn't seem that way to me. And I was robbed of half a lifetime — those years were stolen from me."

Victor feels a wave of heat surging through him and remembers something he hasn't thought of since childhood. Offering up a long-overdue confession, he says, "Listen, the worst thing I ever did as a child, something I wanted to undo almost as soon as I did it, happened in your store, of all places."

"Let me guess," Murray says. "Does it fall under the category of petty larceny?"

"You saw me?"

"Not that I recall, but every kid in the neighborhood stole from me at least once, I'm sure. It must have been some rite of passage for all of you. What did you take? A box of Good & Plenty? A Tootsie Roll Pop? A handful of Dubble Bubble you stuck in your back pocket?"

"That's nickel and dime stuff," says Victor. "This was much worse. It was my friend Wayne who dared me to do it. He was so obnoxious, pestering me all day long, and finally I caved in. Actually, it was a special *Mad* magazine I stole, twice as thick as a regular issue, and twice as expensive. Fifty cents. I zipped it up inside my jacket and sauntered out, cool as could be."

"Fifty cents!" Murray says, impressed. "I guess that was grand larceny in those days."

"You could buy two quarts of milk with that money, or a slice of pizza and a Coke. I threw up at the foot of a tree on the way home that day, thinking about what that fifty cents was worth."

"So justice was served. And I forgive you, if that's what you're looking for at this late date."

"Maybe so."

"See how well I know you?" says Murray. "I don't miss a trick."

"So you've told me," Victor says. "How come you haven't figured out how much I'd value some privacy right now? Don't you know I hate having guys hanging around me when I'm naked?"

"I get the hint," says Murray, who looks insulted. "There's one more thing, though: remember your mother's still hoping for a grandchild or two."

"Jesus Christ!" Slamming his heel against the wall of the tub, Victor kicks soapy water into his face. "Why do you have to say things like that to me?" he asks, and tries to rub the sting from his eyes.

"It's what they pay me for," says Murray. He flaps his hand in a halfhearted wave. "Hasta la vista, buddy." Suddenly and beautifully incandescent, he lights up the room, then leaves it in near-darkness, leaves Victor shivering in a tub of lukewarm water, his eyes burning so fiercely he cries out in pain.

18

Buddy's new business, The Complete Runner, is well situated in the mall, sandwiched between a store that sells nothing but gourmet-flavored jelly beans and the Earring Pagoda, where ears are pierced absolutely free with every twenty-dollar purchase. Against her will, Lucy has been recruited as Buddy's salesperson; as he has already pointed out to her several times, she does seem to have a flair for sales work, selling, in the span of three days, numerous High Performance Body Suits, light-weight backpacks, plastic bottles for carrying water, T-shirts decorated with the words "Everyone Is Beatable" and "Run Like Hell." It isn't the work itself she finds objectionable — it's pleasant enough, really — but the fact that she has to witness Buddy dressed in a warm-up suit with stars and stripes running up his legs, managing a business with such ease it's as if he were born to it.

He loves chatting with customers, skillfully steering the indecisive ones to just the right arch cushions and knee supports, loves gazing at shelf upon neatly arranged shelf of what Lucy simply calls "sneakers," though Buddy, of course, prefers the term "running shoes." Sweeping the varnished, gymlike

floor at the beginning and end of each day, lining up sweatpants and nylon jackets on their hangers, ticketing merchandise, counting sales slips and closing out the register, there is
often, it seems, a look of pure contentment across his face, ac-
companied by the expert whistling of whole Beatles albums
and an array of television theme songs.

This cannot be, Lucy tells herself, the man she married four-
teen years ago, the student willingly sunk up to his ears in
chemistry, biology, calculus, physics. And yet somehow it is.
She aches to tell him that this work is beneath him, that the
sight of him bent over a customer's foot tying laces is almost
too much for her to bear. That she herself might be nothing
more than an insufferable snob troubles her, though the fact
is, while she'd once enjoyed telling people her husband's profession, she takes no pleasure at all in revealing the truth as it
is now. Sometimes she consoles herself by imagining that the
rabbi's cousin has only taken over Buddy's practice temporar-
ily, that any time Buddy wishes, he can saunter back, slip into
his lab coat and a pair of surgical gloves, and return to his real
work.

"It ain't gonna happen," she hears him say, when, on an un-
usually slow morning, she makes the mistake of fantasizing
aloud that maybe he'd like to go back to dentistry part-time,
just to keep a foot in the door. "Why would you even make a
suggestion like that?" he asks in bewilderment. "Can't you see
how well things are going? Sales are up from last month, and
next month is going to be even better."

"Why?" Lucy asks. Taping up a poster advertising a local
marathon, she leaves it hanging by one corner.

"Why? Because before we know it, Christmas will be coming
up, that's why."

"No, I mean, what are we doing here, coming to work in a
mall every day?"

"Ah," says Buddy, "a larger, grander 'why.'"

"Do you have an answer for me?"

"I do, as a matter of fact. It gives me pleasure to be here, to know that this place is mine, ours . . . that people come to me here and find what they're looking for and leave contented."

"It's that simple."

"Well, it's as honest and direct an answer as you're going to get from me."

"I don't understand," Lucy says, as the poster falls to the floor and Buddy, seeing that she intends to ignore it, comes out from behind the register to pick it up.

"I was miserable," says Buddy, "and now I'm not. Remember I once told you I felt as if I were fading away, as if I were losing my self? Well, I don't expect to feel that way again, to ever feel so insubstantial, so absolutely lost. Don't expect me to go exploring in someone's mouth anytime soon. That's how I got lost to begin with."

You're a shopkeeper, Lucy wants to say. *A shopkeeper!* Instead she murmurs, "You went to Harvard. All those nights you were burrowed away in your study carrel in the library, is *this* what you were dreaming of?"

"'This?'" says Buddy, seizing a sample hundred-and-fifty-dollar Nike in each hand.

"Or this," Lucy says, and scales a small package labeled "Le Jacque Strap" across the store and into one of the dressing rooms, an almost perfect replica of a tiled stall shower, complete with a red vinyl shower curtain draped along a metal rod. And then, one by one, she pitches an entire display of jogging bras to the floor. Her hands are on her hips now, and her breathing is labored. "I'm going to wreck this joint," she warns Buddy, but she seems frozen in place. She imagines the floor littered with damaged merchandise, sees her fingers tearing the sleeves off shirts, the heels of her shoes grinding away at the thinnest of nylon shorts. As Buddy grabs her by the shoulders now, shaking her furiously, she struggles to remember what she has done to inflame him. "Let go of me!" she says. His fingers are digging into the fleshy part of her arms; his face is so close to her own, all she can see is a blur of pale skin.

"I know you think I've taken a wrong turn," says Buddy, and he drops his arms to his sides. "But the fact is, I'm not at all disappointed in myself. Far from it."

Pulling one arm out of her shirtsleeve, Lucy is surprised to see there's not a mark on her.

"I've never been that angry before," Buddy confesses. He rests his mouth against the soft, bare flesh of her arm. "Never."

"There was actually steam coming out of your ears," Lucy tells him. "And the sound of a steam whistle."

"You must be confusing me with one of those cartoon characters on TV."

Lucy shakes her head.

"I'm sorry — I couldn't let you trash the place, that's all."

"And I'm sorry for reminding you that you went to Harvard."

Buddy laughs. "That's what I call hitting below the belt."

"I was trying to make you feel like a failure," she acknowledges. "As if you couldn't have guessed."

"Well, it's my tough luck that you see me that way," Buddy says, "but you're going to have to try to get over it."

The challenge of a lifetime, Lucy thinks bleakly. "You've got customers," she says, gesturing with a thrust of her chin toward a pair of women in sweatsuits and frosted hair who've wandered in.

"Ooh," one of them says, "those are the cutest dressing rooms I've ever seen. Aren't they, Lil?"

"Adorable," says Lil. "Do the showerheads really work?"

"I'm afraid not," Lucy says. "They're just for show."

"You really ought to have a bar of Irish Spring or whatever, in the soap dish. Wouldn't that be a nice touch?"

"Interesting," says Lucy. "Why don't you write it up and put it in the suggestion box by the register and we'll think about it."

"Lucy!" Buddy says sharply, worried, she guesses, that she's gone too far, that this stranger alongside her will recognize her sarcasm for exactly what it is.

"Well, if we don't have a suggestion box, we should," Lucy says. "I happen to have a few suggestions of my own."

"I'll bet you do," says Buddy.

Shirley Schacter-Wagner, the rabbi's beautiful and energetic ex-wife, is full of ideas. "Take my advice and go with the silver and white balloons tied with magenta and silver ribbons," she tells Lucy, who's recently hired her as a party planner for Max's bar mitzvah. The two women are standing in the center of the synagogue's reception room, their necks tilted toward the ceiling, where, in a few months, the two hundred balloons in question will float, their streamers hanging above a sea of dancing guests. Buddy is nowhere in sight, having chosen instead to hide out at home, balancing the checkbook and paying bills, his usual preference whenever Lucy and Shirley schedule one of their meetings. From the beginning, he'd let Lucy know that she was to proceed without him, that the countless details of the bar mitzvah itself and the party immediately following were of little interest to him.

"Do what you have to do and leave me out of it," he'd told her weeks ago. "Send me an invitation and I'll be there."

"Aren't you his father?" Lucy said. "His *Jewish* father? I'm not even a convert, and I'm the one in charge of the whole deal?"

"More power to you."

"Maybe," she mused, "we'll have a Christmas tree this year. My mother's got a box full of ornaments she'd be happy to lend us."

"Over my dead body."

"I knew I'd get a rise out of you," Lucy said with satisfaction.

"You know what I think? I think you're just too lazy to give me a hand here."

Buddy stretched his arm across the kitchen table and offered his hand, which she ignored. "It just doesn't mean much to me, this whole bar mitzvah business," he said. "If the kid wants it, he can have it — far be it from me to deny him his heritage and the party of his dreams. But I'm having a hard time forcing myself to summon up some spiritual or emotional attachment I don't feel."

She hated it that he barely felt even the most tenuous connection to any of it and worried that Max would, in some way, feel cheated. So she sat on the floor of her son's room night after night, listening intently as he learned his portion of the Torah reading, the odd, brooding quality of his chanting a comfort to her. Max's voice had deepened pleasantly, and a fine, thin growth of hair was now barely visible above his upper lip. His room often reeked of cologne, and there were phone calls from nameless girls who asked for him in shy, tentative voices. Lucy was filled with a vague sadness as he moved beyond childhood to a more difficult place. That this was the natural flow of things was little consolation; sometimes she imagined herself saying *Stop!* and watching gratefully as everything flowed in reverse, Max's voice rising to a childish pitch, the faint mustache growing fainter and then disappearing, his big hands and feet shrinking to a size that made her want to raise them to her mouth for kissing. At least there was still Jonah, who was eleven now, already long limbed and turning gawky, but who still occasionally called for her in the middle of the night, wanting a sip of water, his blankets smoothed around him, the comfort of her hands at his face.

Her sons were heading swiftly toward manhood, and she knew some of what they would find there. As she and Buddy traveled uncertainly toward the wrong side of forty, she found herself unable to predict with much confidence what would be waiting for them. She preferred to believe in free will, yet Victor Mackenzie's clear-eyed look into her future suggested to her that it had all been laid out as neatly as the slabs of slate that led from the very edge of her lawn to her front door. And there was Buddy, just as Victor had seen him, dressed in one of his many warm-up suits, running every evening after work, jogging through the neighborhood exhilarated, the fluorescent stripes down his sides and at the backs of his heels glowing vividly in the darkness. And, too, Victor had plainly seen that the image he'd had of Buddy in his running clothes was somehow connected to the black cloud he knew was hovering above their marriage, long before she'd had any reason to suspect what was just overhead.

So where was she to look for her own happiness now except in compromise? She would have to cast aside her disappointment and embrace, or pretend to embrace, the newly reinvented Buddy and whatever he was offering. It seemed the only solution, and it sometimes seemed intolerable.

"The balloon guy I'm recommending," Shirley is saying, "will do a terrific job for you. When you and your family walk in here on the big day, you'll be blown away by what you see, I guarantee it. As balloon people go, he's top-notch, a real artist."

"You ever wonder," Lucy says, "how a person happens to find himself in the balloon business?"

"Actually, I haven't. And you know what, it's one of the things you and I don't have time to be contemplating right now."

Fingering the man's business card, Lucy reads aloud, "'Balloonacy, Inc., Designs in Balloons, Stephen Brock, Founder and President.' What do you think, that from the day our friend Stephen here was born, it was determined by the Fates that balloons were it for him?"

"Would you like a cold drink or something?" Shirley asks anxiously. "I'm sure I can get you one somewhere."

"By the Fates, of course, I mean the three goddesses from Greek mythology who were said to determine the path of a person's life."

"Lucy," Shirley says, patting her arm kindly, "he's going to do a wonderful job for you. Stop worrying."

"You don't understand," Lucy says.

"Oh, but I do. You're starting to feel overwhelmed by the thousand and one details we've got to deal with here, and you're telling yourself none of it will ever get done in time. I'm here to tell you that it will. But listen, you still haven't told me what the theme of the bar mitzvah is going to be."

"The bar mitzvah has to have a theme?"

Shirley looks at her in disbelief. "This is the nineties," she says. "Of course it has to have a theme. You might want to think about a sports theme, with cardboard and Styrofoam figures of famous sports personalities for centerpieces, and then, let's see, your dessert could be a good-sized chocolate football or whatever, filled with raspberry mousse. Or you could have something more exotic, like a jungle theme, for example. We could decorate the whole room with lots of trees filled with colorful ceramic parrots, and bananas and whatnot, and the centerpieces might be clusters of little stuffed animals, monkeys and leopards, you know. And then for party favors, you could hand out T-shirts that say 'Max's Jungle' and the date of the bar mitzvah underneath." Her face flushed pink with excitement, though she must have pitched these ideas to a hundred other clients, Shirley says, "The possibilities are only limited by your imagination, really. Why don't you go home and talk it over with Max and Buddy and make it a family decision?"

"No, no, I've got something right now," says Lucy. "Listen to this — how about an interracial theme? The tablecloths will be black, with white napkins, the centerpieces will be big glass bowls of black and white jelly beans — the flavors would be licorice and vanilla, of course — and every white guest will be seated at his or her table between two black guests. And then for dessert we'll have a bittersweet chocolate likeness of Martin Luther King, Jr.'s profile, filled with white chocolate mousse." She smiles uneasily at Shirley's puzzled look, knowing her joke has fallen flat, ashamed that she's indulged herself in front of the wrong audience.

"I adore it!" Shirley says after a moment's hesitation. "It's terribly creative. I'm worried about the dessert, though. It might be next to impossible to get a candy mold of Martin Luther King's face. We'd probably have to special-order it from God knows where, and it would probably cost a small fortune."

"It was a lousy idea anyway," Lucy says, so mortified she is dangerously close to tears. "And Buddy would hate it."

"But why?" says Shirley. "It's so clever, really. So . . . appropriate."

Lucy shakes her head. "I've turned mean in my old age — like the family dog that can't be trusted anymore in a room full of children. I'm surprised you haven't noticed."

"I don't know *what* you're talking about," Shirley says, and she hands her a purse-sized package of tissues. "But I assure you you're not the first client I've had crying over a bar mitzvah in the planning stages."

"I'm not?"

"Are you kidding? People find themselves weeping over the color scheme for the linens, arguing with their husbands about fresh flowers versus silk ones, buffet versus sit-down dinner, and plenty of other things. And in nearly every case, the husband gives in to the wife he's brought to tears, or even his ex-wife. Why do you think that is?"

"Why?" Lucy sobs.

"I have no idea," Shirley says jauntily. "But it seems that the more tears shed, the more beautiful the bar mitzvah turns out to be. And judging by the sorry looks of you now, I'd guess that yours will be a smashing success."

*   *   *

"You can stop laughing now," Lucy tells Katha. "Stop it, will you."

"Oh to have been a fly on the wall when Ms. Party Planner falls for it hook, line, and sinker. What's wrong with the woman, anyway? How dumb could she be, thinking you'd hand out chocolate Martin Luther Kings with white chocolate mousse filling? Anyone would know the white chocolate filling is *so* politically incorrect."

"True." Lucy laughs. "I was so into my interracial theme, I missed that one."

"Tom would have gotten such a kick out of it," says Katha wistfully. "He really was incredibly irreverent." She pauses for a moment before confessing, "You know, I'm sort of surprised at how often I find myself thinking of him. And how much I've cried over him. It feels like more of a loss than it should, somehow." The truth is, she still can't quite believe he's gone from this earth, that she will never again need to worry about whether he's taking proper care of himself. Perhaps, she thinks, if she'd worried more, phoned more often, listened to the subtext of his end of their conversations . . . then what? Would he be alive today? How would she ever know the answer to this? She awakens at five in the morning struggling to get past this, past the shock and the sorrow and the entirely unreasonable feeling that tomorrow or next week she just might hear the sharp slap of his rubber thongs as he moves beyond her to scoop up Julia and lead her in the direction of a large fries and a Coke and maybe even a movie in the bargain. That he slipped away from life with such ease, so carelessly, angers her still. What could he have been thinking, stoned out of his mind, no doubt, as he reached across the night table for something to make him sleep, something to bring him peace? It no longer matters anymore; what is done is done, no matter how much she would like to pretend otherwise.

Cleaning out his apartment, a task she'd foolishly volunteered for, had rekindled her grief like nothing else. Oddly, instead of the sight of his familiar threadbare jeans or his ancient Rolling Stones T-shirt, it was the new set of dishes he'd bought, patterned with hand-painted swirls of primary colors, that she found most painful of all. It was clear to her they'd been purchased on a day when he'd been feeling breezy and hopeful, anticipating, she'd guessed, a new, improved life for himself. *Wrong wrong wrong,* she'd said out loud in the silent apartment, and flung three salad plates against the refrigerator door, each more violently than the last. Down the compactor they went, in a plastic bag stamped with the command "Have a nice day!" And then she had to laugh, because it came to her that those insipid, utterly vapid words were the lesson (if there was one) that she was meant to have gleaned from Tom's death. If life was so precarious, she'd damn well better seize the day, was that it?

"You're entitled," Lucy is saying now. "Obviously there were ties between you that were never undone. And what happened was ghastly. You'd have to be awfully coldhearted not to cry over him."

"And then there's Julia," Katha says. "God only knows what she's feeling these days. She talks about Tom easily enough — it's almost as if she hasn't begun to miss him yet. Or else she's more resilient than you'd think possible. I just don't know."

"Well, maybe Victor could tell you what's on her mind."

Katha sighs into the phone. "He hasn't returned my calls. I'd love to know what's on *his* mind, believe me. I've missed him terribly these past few weeks, actually. I guess I feel as if I've been deserted."

"Not to be unduly pessimistic," says Lucy, "but maybe you have been."

"Or maybe it's some kind of crucible, a test of my patience, while he keeps to himself and sorts things through."

"What things?" Lucy sounds skeptical.

"Don't ask *me*. I'm making excuses for him, can't you tell?"

"I can tell that you don't want to believe you've lost him."

"It doesn't take a genius to figure that one out," Katha snaps.

"Listen, baby," Lucy says, with no effort to conceal her exasperation, "I've got my own problems. This bar mitzvah may just drive me over the edge. Max has decided he's a vegetarian again and doesn't want any meat served at the reception. He won't wear leather shoes or a leather belt with his suit, and he's threatening to distribute some very nasty leaflets to any guest who shows up in a mink coat."

"There's your theme right there," Katha says. "Animal rights."

"Perfect!" says Lucy. "For party favors, we can give each guest a miniature steel trap with a bloodied stuffed animal caught in its jaws."

"You've gone over the edge, all right," Katha says gleefully. "And if word gets out about you and your party favors, I doubt they'll be nominating you for the Jewish Mother Hall of Fame this year."

"I guess not."

"Cheer up, sweetie. There's always next year."

"I should live so long," says Lucy.

19

"W ATER," says Julia pitifully, as if she were in the desert, crawling on all fours through miles of sand under a fiercely burning sun. "Water!" she calls from her bed. "Please!"

"I heard you the first time," Katha says. She climbs the steps to her daughter's room resentfully, calculating the trips she has made upstairs since Julia went off to bed tonight. Five? Six? Possibly even seven. In the bathroom she fills a plastic tumbler with cold water and catches sight of herself in the mirror; there are bruise-colored circles under her eyes, and her hair is in tangles from twisting it through her fingers all night as she stared indifferently at the eleven o'clock news, and then *Nightline, Late Night,* and *Later.* Looking into the mirror now, she sees the face of an ageless woman who'd passed her on the street today, an electrical cord wound tightly around her neck. In the woman's mouth was the plug, which she'd been sucking on like a pacifier. She'd given Katha an unaccountably scathing look and descended the steps into the subway, where, presumably, like any other traveler, she passed through the turnstile and waited for the next available train.

"Not to be believed," Katha says out loud. She blinks, and the woman's face is gone, replaced by her own, which looks careworn, and older than she could ever have imagined.

She brings the water to Julia's darkened room and does not turn the light on.

"This has got to stop," she says. "I can't keep coming up here every ten minutes. It's two o'clock in the morning, and I have to go to work tomorrow. And, more important, *you* have to go to school."

"I can't fall asleep," Julia complains. "I keep telling you that, why can't you help me?"

"Read a book. You've got a roomful of books here."

"I'm too tired to read."

"Then go to sleep."

"I counted backwards from five thousand like you told me to, and then when I got to zero I did some negative numbers too. It was really boring," Julia reports.

"Sometimes people fall asleep when they're bored," Katha says hopefully. "Try counting forward this time."

"Oh my God, I think I'm nauseous!" Julia cries. She shoves Katha's hand under her nightgown and over her heart. "Feel how fast it's beating," she says. "You know I have a phobia about throwing up!"

"You're not going to throw up, baby doll." She rubs Julia's chest for her in the dark, waits for her wildly pulsing heart to calm. "You're too tired to do anything but sleep."

"If Daddy had thrown up all that medicine he took, he wouldn't have died."

"That's right," Katha says.

"Well, maybe he wanted to die. Some people do, you know. Like that boy in camp last year whose mother hung herself. Josh and his father went to the movies, and when they came back, there she was —"

"That was different," Katha interrupts, close to tears. "That was someone who'd given up, who couldn't bear to live any-more. Daddy's dying was an accident, a mistake, that's all. He was confused, and in his confusion he did something very stupid. I wish more than anything that we could have been there to help him, but it didn't turn out that way."

"I keep thinking I'm going to see him again, like he might just stop by sometime and take me to Burger King for French fries."

"It's the saddest thing in the world for you," Katha says, as gently as she can. Under her hand, Julia's heart slows.

"But not for you."

Startled, Katha says, "That's true, it's different for me. But still terribly sad."

"Well, maybe Victor will see him sometime and there'll be a message for us. Like, 'Julia should have a makeup mirror for her birthday. And her own telephone. And also her own TV set and VCR.'" Sighing, Julia says, "That's the kind of message I'd love to hear."

"Don't count on it, sweetie." Katha is horrified, really; that this beloved child of hers could be hopeful of ever hearing from her dead father strikes her as nearly as pathetic as the death itself. Not that she can blame her; after witnessing Victor's performance in the bowling alley, who wouldn't fall for his song and dance? Only Katha herself, forever a skeptic, taking the proof Victor offers her and holding it up to the light, turning it this way and that, looking for holes, shoddy craftsmanship, evidence of deception.

"Why not? You don't think Victor will find him if I ask him to?" Julia says.

"Victor can't do everything we want him to, you know." He can't even return calls left on his fucking answering machine, she wants to say. "And you know what else? I think that when people die we don't need to hear from them again. We can miss them and cry over them, but we don't need them sticking their noses in our business. We don't take advice from ghosts, not in this family. Maybe some people do, but we don't. So if you want your own phone for your birthday, you talk to *me* about it. *I'm* the one who earns the money to buy you things, not some ghost your friend Victor may claim to have seen in a bowling alley or Burger King or the Museum of Natural History."

Julia is leaning back on her elbows now, staring at Katha, bewildered. "Do you have PMS or something?"

"Go to sleep, Julia."

"I don't like you very much right now," Julia acknowledges. "Not at all."

"I'm sorry you feel that way," says Katha. "And if you're not asleep in the next three minutes, I'm going to . . ." Her voice fades; she looks at her hands, as if instructions were written there in ink, like crib notes.

"Going to what?"

"I have no idea," Katha says in surprise. "Not a clue."

As clearly as if he were standing in the blaze of daylight, Victor reads the words etched in the granite tombstone.

> DEAR FRIENDS WHO LIVE TO MOURN AND WEEP
> BEHOLD THE GRAVE WHEREIN I SLEEP
> PREPARE FOR DEATH FOR YOU MUST DIE
> AND BE ENTOMBED AS WELL AS I

He sees, too, the girl sitting in a pile of brittle leaves not far from the stone. Her face is sweet and rosy; her hair blows across her eyes in the breeze that stirs now, lifting her pinafore away from her knees. She begins walking along the rim of a large cement-edged pond, waves to the swans gliding leisurely by. Behind her, mausoleums perched here and there on rises in the land are outnumbered by more modest grave plots, some adorned with statues bent in grief, most ornamented with nothing more than names and dates.

He knows the child in the pinafore, seated on a bench now,

her floral-patterned hairband off her head and slung around her neck like a collar.

Waking abruptly, he sees that he has overslept, though not by much. The air in his bedroom is pleasantly cool; the past few days of Indian summer have, overnight, given way to something crisper, the sort of morning that would normally fill him with pleasure and a sense of well-being. But his underarms are gluey with fear-induced sweat, and his stomach feels unsettled, as if he had eaten an uncommonly rich meal the night before.

"Behold the grave wherein I sleep," he murmurs, and a shudder goes through him, a frisson of dread. Then loneliness overtakes him — why isn't Katha in bed beside him, listening to his creepy graveyard dream, calming him with a soft word, the feel of her warm lips against his? Without her these past weeks, his life seems stark, devoid of warmth and hope. Perhaps her life feels the same. (Didn't Lorraine, the clairvoyant, tell him as much?)

Calling her feels like a big deal. He has to prepare himself first. He showers and shaves, blow-dries his hair. He puts on his good-luck underwear — Disneyland boxer shorts decorated with images of Goofy, a gift from his friend Dan — and his favorite denim shirt, soft and thinned out from so many washings over the years. He adds a narrow red cotton tie for extra flair.

He will call her from the kitchen while he prepares his breakfast, something to keep his hands busy as he talks. But his stomach still doesn't feel quite right, and he sips at a can of Pepsi instead.

"Art department," she says smartly.

"Hey," he says into the phone. "It's me."

"I have two questions for you," Katha says. "First, are you still alive, and second, if so, what the hell is your problem?"

He has to smile at the determined way she immediately

gets down to business. "I'm alive," he says, "and thrilled at the sound of your voice."

"Great. And while we're on the subject, how dare you ignore the messages I left on your answering machine, you bastard!" she says cheerfully. "Who the hell do you think you are!"

"I'm not sure, but ask me how many times I stood outside your studio like some lovesick fool, waiting for you to come to the window and get a good look at me in all my misery."

"A lovesick fool, huh," says Katha. "So have you come to your senses?"

"All six of them," Victor says. "And please allow me to fall all over myself in apology. The truth is, I couldn't get my act together," he says lamely. "I felt drained of all my confidence. I couldn't face you."

Katha considers this for a while, making him wait. "Apology accepted," she says finally.

"Really?"

"Yes, really."

"Terrific," he says. And then the vision of Julia at the cemetery returns, vivid as an image on a movie screen. He really should tell Katha, he thinks, yet he knows what her response will be: exasperation skirting anger. He doesn't want to risk alienating her, not now, just when he has said all the right things. *Don't start this crap with me again,* he can hear her say. *Please.* And so all he says is, "Julia in school today?"

"She's crazy about her new teacher this year, in fact. He's a guy, of all things. Twenty-four years old and cute as can be."

"Good," Victor says. "I'm glad everything's cool." He tries to tell himself this is all he needs to know about Julia, that she's happily in school, lucky enough to have a teacher she likes. "OK," he says.

"Victor? Now that I know you're alive, will you come with me to a bar mitzvah I'm invited to? It's next month, or maybe the month after, I have to check."

"I'll go anywhere with you," he says. "Except to a funeral. I'm done with those for the rest of my life."

"Victor?"

"Hmm?"

"Want to meet me at the loft at lunchtime?"

"For what?" he says stupidly.

Katha softens her voice to a whisper. "Well, we could have lunch, or we could have something better."

"Oh," says Victor. "Of course. Absolutely."

"I'm going to tear your clothes off with such abandon, there'll be buttons flying everywhere."

"With abandon?" Victor says, and laughs.

"You heard me."

"Are your colleagues standing around listening to your every word?"

"Each and every one of them. How does one o'clock sound?"

"Like the very distant future," Victor says longingly.

He arrives at the front of Parker's building early, a bouquet of daisies dyed an assortment of pastel colors in one hand, a dozen peach-colored roses in the other. While he stands around, a trio of Chinese waiters on their break sit at the back door of Wu's Bamboo Garden, silently feasting on enormous slices of pizza.

Two women in their thirties, both dressed entirely in beige, stand on the corner, conversing in voices too loud to be ignored.

"I don't know, I used to love sex," one of them says. "Or at least I used to love kissing."

The other woman nods. "It must have been the kissing."

"And now it's like I sort of close my eyes and let it happen. And then when it's over, Larry always says, '"Wow, that was intense.'"

Her friend rolls her eyes. "Men are pathetic."

"Clueless," says the one who sleeps with Larry.

Unnerved by what he's overheard, Victor watches as the roses drip water from their waxy green wrapper onto the toe of his shoe. He probably shouldn't have bought both bunches of flowers; the roses would have been enough. Actually, he'd been tempted to buy out the whole store, an absurdly extravagant impulse that made him smile self-consciously at the shopkeeper. He thinks of poor Larry, loudly mocked by his girlfriend on a street corner. Victor wonders if any of the women *he's* slept with could ever have been so indiscreet, and instantly imagines Sarah informing the entire Philharmonic of his occasional failure to arouse her.

When Katha finally steps out of a cab, her short black skirt riding almost to her hips, her lovely pale hair caught in sunlight, he approaches her shyly, worrying that the flowers are too much, too overwhelming, that he looks like someone who is trying too hard.

"The daisies are for Julia," he says, handing her the roses.

Kissing her on the street, he tastes and smells cotton candy. "You were at the circus today?"

"What? Oh," she says, and pulls a piece of bubble gum from the side of her mouth. "I bought it for Julia, but I kept smelling it through the wrapper, and I couldn't —"

"Don't talk so much," he says and goes back to kissing her, which he continues to do in the elevator riding up to Parker's nearly empty loft.

"Ready for lunch?" Katha says as he follows her in. "I can make you a lovely bologna and cheese sandwich."

"Not hungry," he says. "At least not *that* kind of hungry."

She yanks down three sets of blinds, one after the other, turning her back to him. Her thin legs look shapely in the black tights she's wearing; her hair swings back and forth across her waist as she works the blinds.

"That ought to keep your ghostly pals from spying on us," she teases. "And, of course, the living, breathing neighbors from across the street."

"This place is absolutely ghost-free," he assures her and feels himself blush, remembering Murray's visit to her studio in the spring, the first time they'd slept together.

"Well, then, come on over here, cutie," says Katha and, true to her word, tears open his favorite shirt, popping a handful of buttons that skid across the floor in all directions.

His heart ticks madly as he helps her out of her clothes.

The love seat has striped sheets tucked around its cushions, and a pillow at one end in a matching case. "Oops, forgot to unmake the bed this morning," Katha says, breathing hard.

They take their time with each other, until they can wait no longer, and then he is inside her, where he decides he will stay forever.

"I've missed you like crazy," he murmurs. "I've been miserable without you."

"Tell me again," says Katha. "And then you can tell me again after that."

Later, she reminds him gently that she has to get back to work.

"Work." He sighs. "Right. I've got a woman, her daughter, and her granddaughter all coming in together this afternoon."

He finds most of his buttons while Katha is in the shower and shoves them into his pockets, smiling. As Katha is dressing the phone rings, but she isn't about to answer it. "Probably someone offering a credit card at a new, lower-than-ever interest rate," she says. "Who else would be calling now?"

"Answer it," he says.

"What for?"

"Just answer it," he says evenly.

She is threading a suede belt through the loops of her skirt. "OK, no big deal."

"This is she," he hears her say, and he is at her side when she reaches out to grab his hand. "What do you mean?" she says. "What are you telling me?" Her face is ashen. She sinks onto the floor, letting go of Victor. She is curled into herself, her face against her raised knees. "What do you suggest I do? I'm not blaming you," she says, in a tone that suggests she most certainly is. And then, "But who else can I blame?" She holds the receiver over her head; Victor takes it from her and hangs it up in the kitchen.

"They don't know where she is," she says in a monotone. "Fifteen thousand dollars a year for her tuition, and *they lose my kid?*" she shrieks.

He nods, knowing all the terrifying, morbid thoughts filling her head; Julia's tiny, broken body in a satin-lined casket, the funeral crowded with the mothers of her classmates, every one of them weeping, Katha herself crazed with grief.

"Stop it," he says.

"Stop what? They have a bus that takes them from school to the gym three days a week, and after the gym class today, Julia apparently didn't get on the bus. One of her friends saw her getting into a cab but didn't think to mention it until they got back to school. Where would she go?" Katha says, as if to herself. "She doesn't even have any money. The cabdriver probably strangled her when he realized he wasn't going to get paid. And now I have to comb through every inch of the city to find her?"

"Listen to me," Victor says, pulling her up from the floor. "She's at the cemetery."

"What cemetery? How do you know? She told you she was going to a cemetery?" Katha asks frantically. "When did you speak to her?"

"A cemetery with a pond," he says. "There were a couple of spouting fountains in the center, and swans, I remember."

"You *remember*? What do you mean, you've been there, but you don't remember where it is?"

"Stop yelling," Victor says patiently.

"Why should I stop yelling? Will it make me feel any better?"

"Stop and think for a minute," Victor says. "What about the cemetery where Tom's buried — is it possible you saw a pond there?"

"Maybe, I'm not sure. But how do you know she's there?"

"I saw her there." Victor hesitates. "In a dream, that is."

"Oh, Victor," she says, and, at last, bursts into tears. "Why do you have to do this to me?"

Why do you have to do this to me? he wants to ask her. *Where's your faith in me?*

"Go check your dresser drawer where you keep all those twenty-dollar bills," he says.

"What for?"

"We're wasting time," he says. "Do it."

He calls the parking garage where he keeps his car and tells the attendant to have it ready for him. "Number three seventy-nine G, a silver Acura," he says.

"Three four five E," the attendant says flatly. "Okeydokey."

"Don't you okeydokey *me,*" says Victor and repeats the number before the man hangs up on him. "Moron," he says.

Katha returns, smiling faintly. "I've been robbed," she reports. "By a nine-year-old."

"I guess this trip of hers was well planned," he says.

"Can you believe that kid? She cleaned me out. There was over two hundred dollars in that drawer."

"Let me drive you there," Victor offers. "Where is this place, anyway?"

"Off the Taconic Parkway. What, you didn't drive there in your dream?"

"You may be surprised to learn this, but you hurt me when you say things like that."

"I can't help myself," Katha says. "I'm sorry."

"You should be," says Victor. "And then some."

*   *   *

In the front seat beside him, Katha ignores his efforts at small talk. She puts on a pair of sunglasses and dozes off, looking stiff and uncomfortable even in sleep. Turning on the CD player, Victor listens to the overture from *The Marriage of Figaro*. The music is lively and playful, boosting his spirits as he and Katha leave the city behind. The traffic has thinned to almost nothing; he taps the steering wheel, keeping time with the music.

Awakening, Katha slides her sunglasses over her head. She rubs her eyes. "Mozart, right?"

"Did you know he was an avid pool player? He had a pool table next to his piano."

"I don't think they had pianos in those days."

"Harpsichord, then. Whatever."

Katha puts her hand over his on the steering wheel. "Julia wanted you to find Tom for her. She was hoping for a message from him. About her birthday presents."

"I'm sure you were thrilled," Victor says dryly. Like Katha, he just can't help himself.

"We're driving all the way up here because of a *dream* you had," Katha says, sounding amazed. "Doesn't that tell you something about me?"

"It tells me that you're desperate," he says.

"If we don't find her, it'll be the end of me."

"She's there," Victor says. "Trust me."

"There's nothing I can do except trust you. You're my best hope."

That I am, says Victor, but only to himself.

Driving through the gates of the cemetery, Victor says admiringly, "Wow!" What he sees looks like acres of a beautifully landscaped park, dotted with obelisks rising twenty feet toward the sky, miniature Lincoln Memorials large enough for a child to play in, tiny cottages of pink granite bricks and stained-glass windows.

"Nice mausoleums," says Katha. "If you're into mausoleums, that is."

"I bet there aren't too many peons buried here," Victor observes. "My guess is you have to have quite a bundle to afford this as your final resting place."

"Kind of ironic that Tom ends up in such a chichi neighborhood."

"Any idea where the family plot is?"

Katha shrugs. "There must be an office here that's got a directory or something."

"Never mind," Victor says. "We're just going to look for that pond."

"Julia would never know how to find the grave. It's not marked yet — the stone's going up whenever Tom's mother decides to take care of it."

Victor drives carefully along the narrow, winding road; except for a man bending over a grave with a bright green watering can, there's no one in sight. Eventually the pond comes into view from a distance. He wants to speed up, to floor it, really, but the road is too narrow and serpentine, and he keeps his foot lightly on the accelerator.

"Oh God," says Katha. "I can't stand this."

"We're almost there," Victor says. "Look — there are the swans."

"Julia!" Katha cries. Without waiting for Victor to stop the car, she opens her door and jumps out, racing in her high heels, then stopping for an instant to discard them in the grass.

He gets as close as he can in the car, then shuts off the motor. Grateful for this gift of his that has led them here, he smiles to himself. Like everyone else, he loves to be proven right. And then he has to remind himself that this is only secondary; the real cause for celebration is the discovery that Julia is past danger, completely intact. He considers the perilousness of ordinary life, the dicey, unpredictable, unstoppable flow that carries us from one day to the next, sometimes gently, sometimes cruelly. If he had a child of his own, he'd be sick with fear watching her get on the school bus that might crash or the skis that might propel her headfirst into a tree. How do parents get by, he wonders, sending their children daily into the whirlwind out there — crossing their fingers, praying a little, trusting that they've been born under a lucky star? He has to hand it to Katha, who seems, most of the time, to be blessed with a composure that, frankly, baffles him. Even this afternoon, no doubt one of the worst of her life, she has managed to keep herself whole.

He opens his door, closes it quietly behind him. Walking toward Katha, he passes chipmunks scampering over graves, a mausoleum guarded by two marble sphinxes, a glossy pink tombstone that reads like a newspaper headline:

THERE IS NO DEATH!
WHAT SEEMS SO IS TRANSITION

He sees Julia and Katha seated on a granite bench, their heads, dark and light, pressed together, Julia's hands cupped in her mother's. He has no need to hear what they are saying to each other; he can imagine it easily enough. And he has no need of Katha's gratitude, only a desire to hear her acknowledge what she should have known all along — that he is for real.

It doesn't seem like much to ask, after all.

20

INSIDE A SYNAGOGUE for the first time in his life, Victor finds himself enjoying the slightly mournful music from an invisible choir, the fragrance of fresh flowers lining the center aisle of the sanctuary, the stained-glass windows marked "In Memory of Sadie Bernstein" and a dozen other departed souls. He stares at the bar mitzvah boy, who looks frozen in the throne they've installed him in up on the bema, next to a man in a black gown sitting solemnly in an identical seat. The choir is silent now as the poor kid is summoned by the rabbi to take his place at the pulpit.

"What's his name?" Victor whispers to Katha, ashamed that he has already forgotten, this despite the fact that the rabbi has mentioned the kid a half dozen times since the service began.

"Max," Katha says into his ear, her mouth grazing against him, her breath lingering warmly at his neck.

Dressing in his best suit this morning, the same one he'd worn to Tom's funeral, Victor had put his hair back in a pony-tail and taken out his silver earrings for polishing. He looked pretty spiffy, he thought, and left early to pick up Katha and

Julia, neither of whom was ready when he got there. He helped himself to a couple of tangerines from a bowl in the refrigerator while Julia and Katha finished dressing upstairs. He read the newspaper that had been left for him and listened to the low murmur of voices overhead, punctuated by the sound of Julia yelling, "You're *hurting* me! Why can't I wear my hair down like I always do?" Listening to them, it all seemed very familiar, as if he had sat waiting for them innumerable times over the years, a husband and father hanging around expectantly, trying to occupy himself while his family struggled to get themselves together, arguing in their customary way, a little cranky with each other, a little impatient, but still, somehow, always affectionate. In fact, he reminded himself, he was neither husband nor father, only a lover with privileges that could be revoked at any time.

When they came down, finally, slightly self-conscious in their dressiest duds, Katha announced that it was too soon to leave. "No way do we want to be the first ones there," she said emphatically, as if there were something horribly wrong with that.

"You look spectacular, Miss J," he told Julia. "And your mother, too."

"Thank you kindly, sir," said Katha. "But it's still too early to leave."

Victor moved over, and the three of them tried to arrange themselves comfortably on the love seat that doubled as Katha's bed. There was a silence, and then Julia sighed. "Look at this place," she told Victor. "Isn't it weird that we don't have any furniture? Except for all the stuff of mine in my room upstairs, we don't have anything nice anymore."

"It *is* weird, but you won't be living this way forever," Victor said. "And I predict that with great confidence."

"Me too," said Katha. "Parker finally found a buyer, and we have to be out by the end of next month."

"No kidding," said Victor. If he were still a smoker, he realized, he would have lit up at this very moment. Instead he flung his arm over the back of the couch nervously. He'd sensed that things had shifted in his favor ever since that afternoon when he had found Julia in the cemetery. Katha hadn't said much except to thank him, letting him know that what he had done was nothing short of miraculous. And in his presence these days, she seemed happy and absolutely at ease, as if, at last, she had considered him from all angles and was content with what she found.

He thought about making a long, impassioned speech inviting her once again to move in with him, but decided against it. "I've been looking for a couple of tenants for so long that I've about given up hope," he said. "You think I'll ever find anyone suitable?"

"You might," said Katha serenely. "Stranger things have been known to happen."

He listens now as Max's surprisingly deep and steady voice sings the story of a prophet and his divinely inspired revelations. Following along with the English translation in his lap, fighting to stay awake, Victor conks out once or twice, his head on Katha's shoulder.

In the front row of the sanctuary, wearing an elegant dress of royal blue wool and a diamond necklace, a gift from Buddy in better times, Lucy weeps noiselessly, proud of this son of theirs who can stand before one hundred and fifty invited guests and belt it out like a pro. She weeps, too, over the surprising epiphany, just revealed to her now, that she feels a true and solid link with the Jewish people — or at least with every mother of every bar mitzvah boy who labored for months over the arduous task assigned him until at last he could perform perfectly, even in his sleep. "Perfect," she sees the rabbi mouth as Max finishes up, singing out the final blessing, elated, knowing he's home free.

She pokes Buddy between the ribs, startling him, wanting to ask, *Don't you feel anything?*

"What?" he says, as she makes a circle with her thumb and index finger, raising her hand in the air so Max can see.

Buddy's seven-year-old niece, dressed like a fairy princess in a puffy white dress and rhinestone-studded ballet slippers, scoots down the aisle carrying a wicker basket filled with hard candy wrapped in cellophane, which she passes out to Max's friends in the first few rows. Immediately, they begin pelting him with the candy, a tradition Buddy swears he knows nothing about.

"What's going on?" he says. Candy whizzes above Max's head; a single piece strikes the bridge of his nose, and he stumbles backward, his hands to his face, pretending to be wounded. "Duck!" Buddy hollers, as candy continues to fly in his son's direction.

"Settle down, please," the rabbi says into the microphone. "And that means you, too, Buddy."

Florine, seated between Lucy and Jonah, leans across her daughter's lap to get Buddy's attention. "Hush up, you," she says. "You don't want to bring shame to your family, do you?"

Eyeing the pearl-topped hat pin in his mother-in-law's pink turban, Buddy thinks fleetingly of seizing it and stabbing her through the heart. "I wouldn't dream of it," he says, and folds his hands in his lap.

"I'm waiting," the rabbi says. A last candy ball is flung into the air; the rabbi catches it one-handed and pockets it. "That," he says, "was one of the more joyful traditions we Jews indulge in, but now it's time to get serious. Max Silverman," he announces, putting his arm around the boy, "son of Dr. and Mrs. Buddy Silverman, has done his parents proud."

Hearing the word *doctor* Buddy flinches and begins whispering furiously to Lucy. "I thought you told him not to refer to me like that in front of all these people. I thought you straightened all that out."

"I did," Lucy insists. "And anyway, I'm sure nobody noticed."

"*I* noticed."

"Don't do this," his wife says, "not now," and he sees that she is in tears again, her shoulders trembling poignantly in the expensive dress he will be paying off at 18 percent interest in the months to come, along with a load of weightier bills that will sink him, no doubt, almost as swiftly as a concrete block tied to his ankles. If he could, he would leave it all behind, and her too, and start over in some distant paradise, where the natives walk the beach in running shoes, in a wide variety of styles and colors. But of course this is bullshit, he tells himself as he stills his wife's quivering shoulders with the gentle pressure of the flat of his hand. Because he has loved her even from one difficult, exasperating moment to the next, and does not know how to stop, even knowing, as he does, that her love for him is tainted with disappointment.

The rabbi is asking the two of them to stand at their seats now, to recite a few lines thanking God for allowing them to reach this joyous day. Buddy rises dreamily to the occasion and listens to the sound of his voice mixing with Lucy's.

"A-men," his mother-in-law says and smacks her lips faintly, savoring the moment.

The sushi chef stands at her station in the reception room, smiling hesitantly, offering a lovely display of California rolls, yellowfin, salmon roe, eel with scallion.

"Yes?" she says as Victor and Katha approach. "Will you try?"

"I certainly will," says Lucy, cutting in front of them and snatching up two of everything, which she loads onto a gilt-edged hors d'oeuvre plate barely large enough to hold her loot.

"Some of us are in danger of making pigs of ourselves," Katha observes lightly.

"Oh, don't mind me — I'm storing up for the cold winter ahead," says Lucy. "Because some of us will be leaving our husbands before too long and may find ourselves with nothing very good to eat for a long, long time."

"Are you drunk?"

"Two whiskey sours later — or maybe it's three — I'm holding my own, thank you very much." She offers a California roll to Victor, who is studying a melting ice sculpture nearby carved in the shape of a Ferrari. "Guess what, baby," Lucy tells him, "you were absolutely right about this marriage of mine."

"Really?" he says, and swallows the sushi in two bites.

"Oh, I'm as sure as I can be about that."

Victor doesn't like the sound of this; swiftly, he changes the subject. "Did you know that's a two-hundred-thousand-dollar car you've got carved in ice over there?" he says. "And that it can accelerate from zero to sixty in less than five seconds?"

Lucy considers this fact in silence. "That is truly an adorable guy you've got there," she says finally, addressing Katha. "He's a veritable prince among men. And the things he could tell you . . . If I were you, I'd listen up, baby. I'd pay close attention to his every word. That's one sweet, spooky guy you've got there."

Nodding, Katha agrees. "He's a sweet mystery, all right."

"What?" says Victor, abruptly distracted by a familiar voice echoing in his head. And there is Murray floating nonchalantly above him, saying, "I never thought I'd show up at a bar mitzvah in my pajamas, but there you have it."

"Take a walk, will you," Victor urges. "Can't you see I'm otherwise engaged?"

"All right, just don't forget to check out the miniature pizzas," advises Murray. "Goat cheese and portabella mushrooms — yum!"

Victor waves to Julia, who's racing toward him now with two girls hurrying along behind her, the three of them panting as they slow to a stop at his feet.

"They want you to read their palms," Julia says breathlessly. "But there's kind of a problem, because they can only pay about five or six dollars." Dressed in black and white velvet, and black patent leather party shoes, her mouth gleaming with pink lipstick, her hair pulled back in a high ponytail, she looks, Victor suddenly realizes, irresistible.

"Here you are wearing makeup, and it seems like only yesterday your mother was pushing you down the street in a stroller," he says.

"You didn't even know me then." Julia takes out a violet-colored plastic compact from her purse and looks at herself in its mirror.

"I've always known you," Victor says.

Julia snaps the compact shut. "Show him your palms, girls," she orders. "You can get the money from your parents later."

Victor shakes his head. "Come back when you're eighteen, girls," he says. "That's the law."

"Yeah, right," Julia says. "There's no law like that."

Sweeping her into his arms, Victor says, "Come dance with me, and I'll explain it to you." He carries her off, lowering her to the dance floor with a flourish. The deejay is playing "Twist and Shout"; Katha looks on in amusement as Victor teaches her daughter to swivel her hips and feet in one direction, her arms in another.

"Well," Lucy says, "if his psychic powers ever fail him, he can always make it as a dance instructor."

Over the dance floor, a dense canopy of silver and white balloons hangs beautifully in midair; Katha imagines herself invisible and stretched luxuriously across it, looking down on the swirling figures below.

"You're not serious about leaving Buddy," she says.

"Oh yes I am," says Lucy. "This marriage of mine has been losing altitude for so long, it's about ready to crash and burn. I've got my parachute all set to go, and a couple more for the bar mitzvah boy and his brother."

"And Buddy?" Katha murmurs, already wishing she hadn't asked.

"I guess he's the guy who's on his own," says Lucy dolefully.

"When are you going to break the news to him?"

"I'm not sure," Lucy says. Unaccountably, her mood shifts and she seems almost exhilarated. "Wait, see the deejay over there? See that microphone he's got set up for himself? After the last dance, I'm marching straight up there and making my announcement."

"Are you out of your mind?" Katha says, appalled. "Of all the times and places to end your marriage, this is what you pick?"

"I just want him to get the message loud and clear, that's all."

"You don't need a microphone for that, kiddo."

Now Lucy is busy talking herself into and out of a whole menu of possibilities, but Katha is only half-listening. She stares at the checkered racing flags suspended from the chandelier overhead, and the huge marquee where the words "Max's Raceway" are proclaimed proudly in blinking lights. "It's *all* a mystery," she says under her breath, and is surprised to find she takes comfort in the thought. Beside her, Lucy has fallen silent; she follows Katha's gaze across the room.

Spellbound, as if they were witnessing something utterly astonishing, they watch Victor and Julia twist themselves joyously down to the floor and then back up again, their ponytails whipping from side to side in perfect, mesmerizing sync.

"I'm going up there," Lucy murmurs. "I can't wait forever."

"You're not," says Katha, and a chill goes through her as Lucy pushes past her and strides between a half dozen pairs of dancers in her way. Furiously Katha calls Victor's name, but it's impossible to be heard over the music, so she begins to run, bumping elbows, stepping on toes, hissing *sorry sorry sorry,* not caring, really, whether anyone hears her apology.

Lucy is already at the microphone, gesturing to the deejay to shut off the music; he shrugs and does as he is told.

"Excuse me," Lucy says, her magnified voice tremulous and uncertain. "Excuse me, everyone?"

Clusters of dancers still on the floor, guests standing around with champagne glasses at their lips or sitting with forkfuls of breast of capon warm in their mouths, all turn to look at her expectantly.

"What's up?" Buddy calls from a nearby table of friends.

And then Katha sees that Victor has flown to Lucy's side, a gray-suited angel incandescent in the light of the enormous chandelier hanging above them. Katha blinks; now it is Victor who is speaking into the microphone, offering to read every palm in the room, every heart that is willing to open itself up to him even a little.

"Even yours," he tells Lucy. "Especially yours."

"Butt out," she says tearfully. "Mind your own business, OK?"

Katha knows Lucy doesn't mean it. And, too, she knows with all certainty that if Victor were to disappear an instant later, she would spend nothing less than the rest of her life looking for him.